## "You don't have enough fun, do you?"

Color bloomed in Nan's cheeks and her eyes sparkled with a feisty light. "I have more than enough hilarity for a woman in my situation."

"You do not." John spoke the words flatly, glaring out at her from under lowered lids.

She pursed her lips together as though she were biting back harsh words. He pressed his advantage. "Come, then. Stand up. Dance with me."

She shook her head, her eyes wide. "No indeed. There's no music, for one thing."

"I shall hum." He stood, holding his hand out to her.

"That would be ridiculous in the extreme."

"But it might be fun."

She shook her head once more. He bent down and took her hand in his.

"You are a graceful dancer, and should indulge in the pastime more often." He began to hum a familiar tune, leading her through the figures of a country dance.

At last, she looked up at him. He must be a little winded from the dance. That was the only way to account for the sudden catch in breath he experienced when she lifted her chin and looked at him squarely.

Growing up in small-town Texas, **Lily George** spent her summers devouring the books in her mother's Christian bookstore. These books, particularly ones by Grace Livingston Hill, inspired her to write her own stories. She sold her first book to Love Inspired in 2011 and enjoys writing clean romances that can be shared across generations. Lily lives in northwest Texas, where she's restoring a 1920s farmhouse with her husband and daughter.

### Books by Lily George

### Love Inspired Historical

*Captain of Her Heart*
*The Temporary Betrothal*
*Healing the Soldier's Heart*
*A Rumored Engagement*
*The Nanny Arrangement*
*A Practical Partnership*

Visit the Author Profile page at Harlequin.com.

# LILY GEORGE

## A Practical Partnership

**HARLEQUIN® LOVE INSPIRED® HISTORICAL**

Recycling programs
for this product may
not exist in your area.

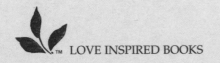 LOVE INSPIRED BOOKS

ISBN-13: 978-0-373-28349-1

A Practical Partnership

www.Harlequin.com

**Printed in U.S.A.**

For God hath not given us the spirit of fear;
but of power, and of love, and of a sound mind.
—*2 Timothy* 1:7

For Zach, with whom I always wanted to elope.

# Chapter One

*Tansley Village, Derbyshire*
*March 1819*

Hannah Siddons, commonly referred to by the practical and prosaic nickname of Nan, entered the village shop and tugged her bonnet lower on her forehead. Through all of her eighteen years, she had blended into the background, eclipsed by her lovely and tempestuous older sisters. Now, more than ever, she needed to become one with the shadows. Her very career depended on it, in fact.

She rounded the corner, neatly stepping past a display of brooms, and halted, drawing breath slowly. Her heart thundered in her ears. She glanced over at the counter, but the shopkeeper was engaged with a customer, rolling out a bolt of cloth. Nan nodded. *That's right. Stay busy, old fellow.* She ducked around a few barrels of flour and paused again, taking in the tableau before her.

Yes, the rumors were true.

A girl, gaily dressed and sporting an elaborate coiffure, sat at a low table. Her nimble fingers flew back and forth as she stitched lace onto the brim of a neat straw bonnet. Her lips were pursed with concentration, creased on either side by a charming dimple. She didn't utter a sound, but if she had, it would probably be marked by a lilting accent.

The general store had engaged a French milliner, and that's why Nan's millinery shop had seen fewer and fewer customers over the past week.

Protectively, Nan touched the rough brim of her own bonnet. That straw the girl was using wouldn't last a week in Tansley Village, subject as they were to sudden winds blowing up from the moor. Nan's bonnets were designed with practicality in mind, for she had long since made a study of Tansley's particular weather patterns. What use was a bonnet if it fell to pieces after the first summer storm, or a capricious breeze blowing across the fields? She had built the family business after her sisters had left it behind, by catering to the women of the village and offering them sturdy bonnets that would last season after season.

That was what the women of Tansley wanted. They wanted to spend their hard-earned money on bonnets and hats that were durable. Or at least that's what Nan assumed. There'd never been a reason to doubt her assertion—until now.

She was staring, and the French girl would surely see her if she continued staring. She shrank back against the wall, bumping the small of her back into the window ledge. She could either brazen her way out by purchasing something, or she could slink away, hoping never to be seen. Judging by the lightness of her purse, thanks in no small part to this upstart milliner, it would be much better to slink out and save her money.

As Nan prepared to make her stealthy flight, two voices coming from the slightly opened window caught her ear.

"Please don't make me go in there, John. I feel such a fool. Surely the bonnets I have are pretty enough."

"Jane, we've discussed this at length. You know as well as I do that you simply must begin dressing yourself as a proper young lady should."

Nan pivoted slowly on one heel and glanced out the window. A tall man, powerfully built, was leaning over a slight young woman, who was dressed in a simple gown. With the expertise born of years of practice, Nan summed up the pair based solely on what they were wearing. The young man was dressed as any gentleman should be in the country, but the cut of his tweed coat was particularly fine and spoke to a London tailor's hand. The young lady, though dressed in a plain black gown and wool shawl, gave the air of one who didn't particularly enjoy dressing up, but did what one had to for one's station. She looked to be about Nan's own age.

The pair stood side by side, not close as a husband and wife should be. Perhaps they were relatives?

Whatever their relationship, they certainly had money, and they were going to spend it here, rather than at *her* shop.

Could she allow one more paying customer to get away?

As swiftly as she dared, Nan made her way around the perimeter of the shop and darted out the door. She sprinted down the steps and around the corner of the building, skidding to a halt before the young man and his reluctant companion.

"Pardon my intrusion, but I couldn't help but overhear your quandary. If I might speak so boldly, I don't think you should go into this shop if you require a really good bonnet," she panted. Oh, if only she hadn't run. Now her breath came in short gasps, making it difficult to speak properly. "If you should come to *my* millinery shop, I can assure you the bonnet will be of the finest quality." She paused as both the young man and woman looked at her curiously. She had never before in her life run after a customer—she had never before run after anything. Her life was ordered, prosaic and, well, dull. But she couldn't very well lose her livelihood—and with it, her independence—to some upstart French milliner. No, if she was to survive, she must be bold.

The man arched an eyebrow as his gaze carefully combed over her in silent judgment. "*You* own a shop, miss? Aren't you a little young for that sort of thing?"

Nan swallowed. "I'm old enough. I own it myself. It's called—"

"But John, I—I don't really care for shopping, or for bonnets," the young lady admitted, cutting Nan off. Her face turned a deep shade of red as though she'd admitted something truly terrible.

Nan's heart sank. The fear of losing this potential

customer was too real. "I understand," Nan replied
swiftly. Part of her job as a milliner was to determine
what her customer wanted, before the customer knew
it herself. "I hate all the fuss of shopping, as well. But
my shop is quite small and cozy. I live above it, as
a matter of fact. If you'd like to come by, we could
have tea. Perhaps, if you would like to tell me exactly
what you are looking for, I could put together a hat
that would do you justice."

A spark lit Jane's blue eyes. "Truly? Would you
listen to my suggestions?"

"Indeed, I would."

The girl nodded slowly. "That could be enjoyable."

Beside her, the young man spoke again. "Why
do you think your bonnets would be better than this
place?" He motioned his hand toward the building.

"You see, sir, the lady inside uses straw that's far
too fine. I fear that in a strong windstorm, the bonnet would break apart easily. My bonnets are much
more suitable for all kinds of weather."

With her frantic heart pounding hard against her
ribs, she waited for the man to reply. He studied her
for a few, earth-trembling moments. It was difficult
indeed to maintain her composure while being scru-
tinized so closely, particularly by a man as good-
looking as he. His dark brown eyes swept over her, as
though committing her to memory. When her panic
began to simmer just below the surface, he squared
his jaw and the critical expression eased from his
handsome face.

"Is it far?" he asked.

Relief washed over her and she tried not to breathe

a noticeable sigh. "Not at all." Nan waved over at the squat little building on the very edge of the string of village shops. "Just a healthy walk."

The young man's eyes widened. "Healthy? Are you certain?"

Before Nan could answer, the man burst into laughter, and Nan's cheeks reddened. Was he mocking her?

"John, enough," Jane rasped, digging her elbow into his side. Then she turned to Nan. "Please ignore my brother. He is a notorious clown."

He shrugged, ducking his head boyishly. "The way she said it—I don't know. It was amusing." He shot Nan an impish look, his brown eyes twinkling with glee. "Can we take our *healthy* walk now? I must say, Jane, I've spent more time trying to convince you to purchase a silly bonnet than I ever spent on a girl I fancied."

Jane rolled her eyes at Nan.

Nan straightened her spine. Was that a gibe toward her?

She'd grown up the youngest in an affectionate and warm family of women, employed in a job that catered to ladies. Men were something completely out of the ordinary to her. She didn't understand them, and more to the point, she had no particular use for them. None of the men in the village found her worth a second glance, and she'd grown secure in the knowledge that her little shop would keep her in comfortable spinsterhood.

It didn't matter if she thought he had a nice smile— now that he finally showed it to her—she had absolutely no retort for this John fellow, and it was better to go along as a meek and mild shopkeeper and gain his sister's business, rather than lose out thanks to a tart reply.

Perhaps the healthy walk would quell him into silence. One could hope, at any rate.

John Reed followed a few steps behind his sister and this extraordinary young woman who'd coerced them both into visiting her shop. She was just as small as Jane, who barely reached his shoulder, but there was something prepossessing about her all the same. She had a straightforward way of looking at a man, and though her words were gentle enough, the fire in her blue eyes spoke of a vivacious spirit.

She wasn't as conventionally pretty as the women he generally escorted about. No, in London he showed a marked preference for willowy blondes. But there was something about this one, something of the spitfire that he rather enjoyed.

She had also managed to convince Jane to at least look at a more fashionable style—although, judging from that rough country bonnet she wore, she was no arbiter of taste and refinement. For Jane's London debut, they would almost certainly need to return to London and order clothes and hats from a proper dressmaker upon their arrival. But first, small steps.

Jane was as reluctant about her debut as he was about his new role as the head of his family. No, reluctant wasn't a strong enough word. He hated his new role, but he was resigned to it. If he refused to accept this mantle, Grant Park would go to wrack and ruin. He must force Jane to accept the reality that she must

find a good match, just as he had to find the strength
to be master of his family's estate. This afternoon ex-
cursion could at least introduce Jane to the possibility of better attire, and for that, he would be forever
grateful to this forthright milliner.

As they neared the shop, John squinted to read
the sign leaning up against the wall. Siddons Sisters
Millinery Shop.

Siddons.

There was surely but one Siddons family in Tansley Village—and he and Jane were visiting one of
them now. After Father died, John had no idea what
he had to do, and frankly, he hated trying to figure
it out alone. There was no one to turn to but Paul
Holmes, an old friend, for advice on getting his affairs in order and for taking over the proper management of a vast estate. Paul had welcomed the Reeds
to Kellridge Hall in Tansley. John and Jane had been
enjoying the hospitality of Paul and his wife, Becky
Holmes née Siddons, for the past two days.

"I say—" he began, but the young woman ignored
him, opening the door to her shop with a flourish.

"Please come in," the woman said, ushering them
both inside. She removed her bonnet, displaying a
coronet of tightly wound chestnut braids. Funny, it
was not a fashionable style in the least, for women
of his acquaintance preferred Grecian styles, or long,
tumbling ringlets. Yet despite its severity, it suited
her rather well.

Jane stepped in hesitantly. "It is rather more like
a home than a shop."

The milliner drew a chair before the hearth and

stirred the fire. "I'll have tea ready in just a moment," she called as she bustled about, retrieving the tea things from a nearby cabinet.

John watched her flying around, and once again, that mischievous urge tugged at him. "I'd rather like a chair, too, if you don't mind."

Jane shot him one of her I-shall-throttle-you-if-you-don't-behave looks, for his mild-mannered sister loathed his jesting nature. He thought he would be able to get away with his outrageous behavior, since Jane had not chided him earlier for goading the milliner, even though he'd been teasing her since she first walked up and started talking to them. He returned her look with his I-shall-force-you-to-a-London-soiree eyebrow raise, for his sister's weak point would always be her hatred of all social events and functions. Jane's cheeks reddened and she shifted her gaze to the fire.

"Oh, of course," the milliner replied. Though she trotted over obediently enough, he caught the sarcastic curl of her lips. She was playing at being polite although he could see it wasn't exactly aimed toward him. That knowledge ignited the spark of jest within him.

"Thank you." He sank into the chair she drew up and crossed his legs with the practiced elegance of a dandy. "I prefer sugar with mine. And a biscuit."

She nodded, biting her lip as though biting back an acerbic insult or two, and he was hard-pressed not to laugh. She was jolly fun, whoever this Siddons girl was. Being in her company could almost make him forget that the weight of the world—or at least, the weight of his family's good name—now rested on his shoulders.

"Pay my brother no mind," Jane spoke softly to the milliner. "As I said before, he loves to tease. And he'll be happy with any kind of tea you have. I know. His tea appetite is simply appalling. Father used to say he would eat us out of house and home."

The milliner shot Jane a grateful look, and her small smile tugged at his conscience. He didn't mean to hurt her feelings. As she swished past him to retrieve the tea things, he tried to give her a wink, but she was looking in the other direction.

"You have the advantage of us, miss," he observed, taking off his gloves and holding his hands to the fire. "You at least have heard my sister and I bickering enough to know our given names. But we know nothing of you, other than that you are a rather direct shop owner. Are you a Siddons, then?"

"I am Nan Siddons," she replied, graciously enough, as she set the tea table before them.

Nan. He'd vaguely heard Nan mentioned in passing around Kellridge. Always her name, it seemed, was coupled with work.

"I am Jane Reed, and this is my brother, John." Jane stepped in gracefully, taking over the flow of conversation as she assisted Nan with serving the tea.

John watched his sister, working with Nan so easily, talking to her as though they were old friends. Jane had never responded this effortlessly to strangers before. Jane was as quiet as a church mouse, bookish and given to playing endlessly on her violin. Her impending debut—once they were out of mourning, of course—was the cause of much consternation in their home. Yet here, in the comfort of the Siddons Sisters Millinery Shop, she was holding her own quite well.

He accepted his teacup from Nan with a nod of thanks. This sudden change in his sister's demeanor gave him pause. Perhaps Nan was the right person for this job after all. Not just for one bonnet, but for every agonizing step in preparing his sister for her London debut. Her calming nature, along with her candid manner, made her quite a good candidate as his partner in this venture thus far.

Much as he turned to his friend Paul Holmes for assistance in wrestling with his father's vast estate, could he turn to Nan Siddons for assistance in transforming his shy, reluctant sister into a diamond of the first water?

He eyed her over the rim of his teacup. The color in her cheeks rose, and she twitched in her chair, moving so that he could only see her in profile.

"Let us discuss the matter of your bonnets," she said to Jane in a brisk tone. "What, do you feel, is lacking in the bonnet you have now?"

"Nothing, really." Jane cast a reproachful look at John. "My brother feels I should be more fashionably dressed. I don't feel it's right, since I am in mourning."

"You dressed plainly before Father died," John scoffed. This was a familiar, and tender, point of contention between them. "When our mourning period ends and you go to London for your debut, you simply must dress as a young lady of your station should. No more unadorned gowns and simple hats. If I have to rise to the occasion, taking over as man of the family, so should you rise to the occasion of being a typical well-bred young lady."

"Whether it's fair or not, people judge a woman by what she wears," Nan put in quietly. "Here, in Tansley, a young lady can dress in basic, practical attire. In fact, my shop caters to the women of the village. My hats and bonnets are sturdy, rather than elegant, because I want them to last a long time. But in London, you will be compared to other young women, and if you look shabby, it could reflect badly on your family."

"It would reflect badly on *me* as head of the family," John added pointedly. Nan understood his position, even if his sister did not, and for that he was ridiculously grateful.

"So the intent of dressing you well, or at least to a certain outside standard, would have two purposes. First, and most important, to make you feel more comfortable in your role as debutante." Nan took a sip of her tea. "Second, to assure your place in society as you try to find a husband."

Jane made a tiny groaning sound. John sighed. This was further than he'd ever been able to get. Normally by now, Jane would've fled. A tiny ray of hope shone into his soul. Nan Siddons could help him. Perhaps, if he could convince her to come, this one aspect of his new role would be a success. He might be a scoundrel, and he flirted with atheism, but all the same, he could do well at one thing in his life. It would be good not to be a bitter disgrace to his parents' memories.

But could Nan produce the kind of fashionable

clothes that a London debut would require? He studied her once more. She was neat and something in her demeanor was attractive enough, but she would never be called stylish. He looked around the room, peering at the bonnets in various stages of creation. These were, as she indicated, sturdy and practical. Not at all suitable for, say, a ride along Rotten Row.

"I don't mean to be impertinent," he began, and both Nan and Jane shot him disbelieving glares. "But how can we be certain that you can create a fashionable bonnet?"

Nan squared her jaw and set her teacup down with a defiant clink. "Let me show you my sketches."

She leaped gracefully from her chair and bustled over to a wicker basket, pulling out sheet after sheet of foolscap. "My sisters and I started our business making bonnets and hats to order for The Honorable Miss Elizabeth Glaspell and her friends." She held out a sheaf of papers, and he accepted them. "These are my sketches. I worked with the gowns Miss Glaspell already owned, creating bespoke bonnets that matched perfectly, as though they had been crafted at the same time."

John nodded slowly, perusing the sketches. As he finished looking at each sheet of paper, he handed it over to his sister. Assessing her work from the male perspective, the hats and bonnets looked stylish enough. The women of his acquaintance would not be ashamed to be seen in them. Judging by Jane's smile, she was satisfied with Miss Siddons's skill, as well.

Jane's smile was the first real sign that his sister was beginning to thaw a trifle when it came to choosing any garment that might show her off on the Marriage Mart. Jane was slow to accept change, however. If he insisted on more than just a single bonnet today, she would likely dig in her heels and vow to stay at their country home as a spinster forever.

"Very well," he began, casting the rest of the sketches aside. "You may make one bonnet for my sister. Something to go with the gown she has on. If that works well, we may have other commissions for you. But I want to see your handiwork first. After all, these are mere sketches. I'd like to see the finished, fashionable result." What he proposed was true, after all, and if he made it sound as if he was unsure of Miss Siddons's talent, Jane might well jump to her defense.

"I'll create a sketch this evening," Miss Siddons replied with a snap, two red spots appearing on her cheeks. "I think Miss Reed's dress is perfectly suited to mourning, and I shall look forward to creating something to bring out her natural beauty."

John grinned. He couldn't resist. Miss Siddons was just walking that line between trying to get a difficult customer's business while maintaining her dignity. She was doing a smashing job of it, too. He touched Jane's arm. "Come, Jane. We'll leave Miss Siddons to it, then."

Jane cast an apologetic look at Miss Siddons and rose. "I am certain it will be more than lovely. Thank you for your time." She shook her head at her brother, pursing her lips.

"We'll come back for the sketch later," John added. "I assume you can have it done in one evening?"

"You assume correctly, Mr. Reed." Miss Siddons gave a defiant lift to her chin.

His admiration for her restraint and her confidence surged, but he gave no outward sign of it. He trusted few people, and admired fewer still. So often, he had seen the reality of human nature—its pettiness and its greed. The people he kept company with in London were perfect examples of this, but they were all good for a laugh. Laughter was his most prized pastime, because it made him forget about Mother. He could forgive a great deal if it took his mind off Mother's death. He shut off his thoughts with a snap. He could not show his admiration. After all, if Jane saw him weaken, then she might, too.

"Glad to hear it." He gave a brief nod and followed his sister out the door.

Why had she promised John Reed that she could come up with a sketch by morning? Nan scrubbed her hand wearily over her forehead. *Because he goaded you, that's why.* She longed to wipe that smug expression off his handsome face. Handsome? She shook her head. Whether he was good-looking or not had nothing to do with her current misery. Since the pair had left her shop just a few hours ago, she'd done nothing but ponder over the lines of Jane Reed's simple gown, trying to come up with an idea that would set Jane's small but regal bearing off to perfection.

The clock on the mantelpiece chimed seven o'clock. She was due to have supper with Paul, Becky, Susannah and Daniel over at Kellridge Hall in less than an hour. In fact, Susannah and Daniel would come by in the carriage sooner than that. As a spinster, Nan had to rely on her wealthy wedded sisters' largesse when it came to transportation. The shop, even at its most profitable, had not allowed Nan the funds to buy her own horse and buggy.

Nan heaved a gusty sigh. What a day it had been, and it wasn't over just yet. Not only was she creatively stymied, but she needed to put her frustration aside and pretend to enjoy yet another interminable family dinner.

Not that she hated her family.

It was just so difficult, watching her lovely older sisters with their doting husbands. Susannah's small son would likely stay behind in the nursery, but her sister Becky would be there, her pregnancy just beginning to show under the high waist of her voluminous skirts. All her life, Nan had followed the path that seemed predestined for her, as the youngest, plainest and most sensible of the trio of Siddons sisters. She would be the one with a practical head for business. When her tempestuous sister Susannah finally surrendered to Daniel Hale's charm, she'd left the shop behind for Nan and Becky. However, Becky was far too impulsive and romantic for such a prosaic occupation, and soon fled the millinery shop to become Paul Holmes's wife.

As the business at the shop settled, it created a pleasant enough rhythm for Nan's life. She thought she could be satisfied with the lot she was handed. Even when Becky told her of her pregnancy, Nan fought back a rising tide of jealousy. She was simply never meant to be a wife or a mother.

Once the village shop engaged the French milliner and her business began its sudden plummet—well, that was another matter entirely. Here she was, alone and with only her business to support her. She was beginning to question whether or not she even liked hats, which was entirely beside the point. Nan Siddons was the practical woman of the family, and managing the millinery shop was her destiny.

What would happen to her if the business failed? She clenched the foolscap and breathed deeply.

*I know we are supposed to trust in You, God. Just please, please, please—don't let the shop crash.*

Nan tossed the sheet of foolscap aside and sprinted upstairs, as though she could outrun the depressing thought of being a spinster aunt, a hanger-on, a charity case in one of her sisters' grand homes. Quick as a wink, she changed into a somber silk evening dress and washed her face.

She must look as pulled-together as possible. No need for her sisters to guess that her world might just tumble down around her ears.

The sound of the carriage crunching on the gravel outside caused her to scurry down the stairs. She grabbed her shawl, winding it tightly about her shoulders as she rushed out the door. Why was she in a hurry? She couldn't very well outrun her own troubling thoughts.

Daniel was standing outside the carriage, ready to help her up. It was a particular trait of his, a brotherly gesture, as he wouldn't let the footmen do the job for him.

Nan smiled wanly at him as he held out his hand.

"I do hope you can manage a happier expression than that, Nan," Susannah scolded as Nan made her way into the carriage. "It's more than just family tonight. Becky and Daniel are entertaining guests. We must make them feel welcome here in Tansley."

"Guests?" Nan arranged her skirts carefully about her as her stomach sank.

"Yes." Daniel clambered inside, tugging the door shut behind him. "An old friend of Paul's, and his sister."

Oh, no. Surely not. Nan breathed carefully in and out. She was barely able to force herself to attend a family dinner tonight, but if the guests were whom she thought they were—

"The Reeds." Susannah tugged on her glove as Daniel rapped on the window of the coach. The carriage started forward with a low rumble. "John Reed, and his sister, Jane."

## Chapter Two

"I daresay you'll enjoy meeting my sister-in-law, even though she can be a little trying," Paul Holmes muttered from his place by the hearth. "She's got a fine head for business, but it's difficult to get her to talk about much else. You won't find her much of a dinner partner."

John shrugged. He didn't really want to spoil the surprise by telling Paul about meeting Miss Siddons earlier in the day. No, it would be much more fun to play dumb until she walked back in the door. "Why won't she talk about much else?" He might as well find out a little more about her while they were waiting for her to arrive. It would, at least, distract them from the real purpose of his visit. Learning how to be a proper master was certainly no stroll down Rotten Row.

"I spent some time with Nan and with my wife, Becky, before even Susannah and Daniel were wed. Picnics, games, that kind of sport. Nan's all right. A bit practical, mind you, but a good girl of a fine

Christian family. Of course, my mind is always taken up with my wife—even before I knew I was in love with Becky, I spent as much time with her as I could."

"Even to the point of hiring her as your niece's nursemaid?" John couldn't suppress a roguish grin.

Paul eyed him sharply over the rim of his teacup. "Watch yourself, man. As I said, the Siddonses are above reproach, particularly where the finer points of morality are concerned."

"I don't intend to imply anything unseemly. Beg pardon." John choked back his gleeful grin. It never failed to amuse him that he'd discovered Paul's feelings for Becky before the man himself knew them to be true.

"As I was saying," Paul continued, with the air of a man being robbed of all patience, "I concentrated my thoughts upon Becky. Susannah was, of course, already spoken for by Daniel. Nan was a bit of a gooseberry, I suppose. She is younger, too, than her sisters. I suppose she maintains her pretense of practicality, and devotes herself to her work, as a way of proving herself worthy."

"Worthy of what?" John desperately wished for a before-dinner sherry, but there was not a drop to be had at Kellridge Hall. Now that Paul had changed his entire life around and found, as he said, the Lord, anything that led to debauchery had been banned from the Hall, including liquor.

"I don't know exactly what. All I can tell you is that Nan is seeking to prove herself just as her sisters did before her. She lacks Susannah's fire and Becky's beauty and grace. But there's a charm about her all the same, for all her plainspokenness. Once, Daniel told me that the Siddons girls work on a man like a tonic. I vow it must be true." Paul broke off as the door opened and his lovely wife, Becky, entered the parlor. Both men rose to greet her.

"Whatever are you two men talking about?" Becky stood on tiptoe to peck her husband's cheek, and the sudden movement revealed the thickening about her middle. Paul would be a father soon, and he would be a good one, too. A rush of inexplicable emotion washed over John, leaving him feeling—of all things—envious. Paul was an excellent master, and a stalwart husband. He had taken in his niece, Juliet, as his ward, and was as good to her as a father would be. In a matter of months, he would become a father again by Becky, and would do credit to those duties, as well.

What of it? John shrugged his shoulders, irritated by these thoughts. Paul never came to the gaming tables any longer, or squired women of ill repute around to dubious locations in London. Surely he missed that sort of fun.

John watched hungrily as Becky patted her husband on the shoulder. What would it feel like, being that beloved by someone? "Jane and I are waiting for both of you. Why don't you come join us in the little parlor off the dining room? Daniel and Susannah will be here in a matter of moments."

It was not lost on John that she failed to mention Nan, too. Nan Siddons was, it seemed, truly a lost member of her own family—forgotten and neglected.

Yet, he was anticipating her arrival much more

keenly than any other person in her party. Would she pretend not to recognize him? Would she join with him in witty repartee? Would her personality be any different than it had been when they met earlier in the day?

He rose and followed his host and hostess out of the room. Kellridge Hall was not as grand a home as his own Grant Park, but it was well run and graciously appointed. Paul ruled the household with a firm hand, that much was certain. Nothing ever seemed out of place at Kellridge. That was why John sought him out. No man could give better advice on the running of a vast estate—something that other fellows seemed born to do. Perhaps, once matters at Grant Park were well in hand, he could leave it behind for months at a time, and continue his roguish ways in London. That was how Paul had managed his life—well, before he met Becky.

As they passed by the front hall, the butler opened the door. A decidedly irritated-looking Nan Siddons marched in, yanking on her bonnet strings.

"Nan!" Becky broke away from her husband and trotted over to embrace her sister. "So good to see you."

Nan patted her sister's back and then said, her voice low and urgent, "I need to talk to you and to Susannah. I've some news about the shop."

"The shop can wait," Becky replied with a little laugh. "We have guests. Mr. John Reed, may I present my sister, Nan Siddons." She waved her arm in John's general direction.

Nan nodded and bobbed the slightest of curtsies.

Her eyes flashed, and her brows drew together. He cast his most charming smile her way, and bowed deeply. There was something about the spark in her eyes that he wanted to investigate further. His initial suspicion was correct. Nan Siddons could be jolly good fun if she'd let herself go a bit.

"Yes, I know Mr. Reed. I met him today, and will be making a bonnet for his sister." Nan turned as Susannah and Daniel came through the doorway.

Any sensation Nan's response might have stirred up was drowned out by her eldest sister's arrival. Susannah commanded the attention of everyone in the hallway, kissing her sisters, curtsying to John, ordering Daniel about and chiding Paul for what she perceived as the lack of proper maintenance on the curving path that led up to the front gates of Kellridge Hall. This, of course, raised Paul's ire, and John watched as Becky, Paul, Daniel and Susannah drifted down the hallway, engrossed in loud conversation.

Nan stood with her bonnet dangling uselessly from one hand. "Now I'll never get the chance," she muttered fiercely.

"I beg your pardon?" John drew closer to her side. She looked both angry and deflated.

Nan turned to him, as though surprised he was still there. "I had rather hoped to speak to my sisters about a pressing matter of business, but it appears I will have no opportunity to do so."

He offered her his elbow. "Perhaps we should join them?"

Nan shook her head and cast her bonnet onto the

polished mahogany table nearby. "You may go in without me. I need a moment to collect myself."

"You really should allow yourself to have more fun, you know," he chided gently. "Why not talk about business matters some other time?"

Nan rounded on him, her blue eyes darkening to black. "Fun? If my business crashes because the village shopkeeper has hired a French milliner, do you know what kind of fun I shall have? I shall be nothing. I'll be reduced to the status of spinster aunt, living in one of my sisters' homes. This has absolutely nothing whatsoever to do with my perceived lack of a personality, and everything to do with my sisters' refusal to help me in my time of need!" She paused, drawing in her breath deeply.

"Oh." He felt like the worst sort of joker. Her anguish was real and profound and he had clumsily teased her at the worst possible time. "Perhaps I can be of assistance?"

"Not unless you know how to keep a business from failing." She offered him a wan smile. Her outburst seemed to have calmed her nerves. Her eyes lost some of their hunted look, and her movements were graceful and fluid once more. "I suppose we should go in," she added with a sigh.

He offered her his arm once again. "I promise I shall give your problem serious thought. Perhaps I can come up with a solution. Stranger things have happened, you know."

She took his arm, her fingers resting lightly on the crook of his elbow. "Forgive me. I shouldn't have said anything. It's not very nice to let a potential client know that your business may be on the verge of collapse," she admitted. Her tone was neutral enough, but a thread of sadness ran through it.

"Not at all," he admitted. "If anything, I appreciate your honesty."

She glanced up at him, the tight lines in her face relaxing. She was a pretty thing in her own right. All these Siddons girls were lovely. Why was she so certain she was destined for spinsterhood? Her sisters had made brilliant matches of their own, even without a fortune or family to back them. Surely some fellow around here would take a second look at her.

Nan listlessly poked at the food on her plate as her dinner companions talked and joked around her. Everyone, even shy Jane, seemed to be enjoying themselves. Every time she took a bite, though, the chicken tasted like sawdust and a lump rose in her throat. If she couldn't get her sisters' attention long enough to discuss the problem of the French milliner, then she would have to go home and give vent to a good, long sob. No one knew about the tears that wet her pillow so often. She'd hidden the fact that she cried at night from her sisters for years, because someone had to be the practical one of the trio. Susannah would throw temper tantrums and Becky would go off on endless walks whenever trouble threatened. Nan would merely stuff her fears deep down inside and, after bedtime, allow the tears to slide down her cheeks unchecked until her pillowcase was damp.

Thus she had gained the reputation of being stolid

and unshakable when really, she just was terribly clever at hiding her hurts.

"I do wish you'd eat more," a smooth voice spoke up beside her. "You've hardly tasted anything all evening."

Nan flicked a glance over at John Reed, giving him a tiny smile. It was difficult to decipher his character. At the shop this morning, he'd been a dreadful tease and seemed to enjoy putting her on edge. On the other hand, his affection for Jane was genuine, and his offer to help when they were standing in the entry hall had an authentic ring to it. He was so handsome that she had to force herself to meet his gaze—something she'd made herself do when she was trying to convince him her shop was worthy of their business. Now, in the intimacy of a family dinner party, being so closely regarded by those brown eyes was well-nigh unendurable.

"I believe it was Byron who said that a woman shouldn't eat anything in public," she rejoined. "I am merely following his dictates."

John laughed. "I find it very doubtful that someone with your strength of character would follow the edicts of any man."

She didn't know whether to be flattered or annoyed. Her head ached and the lump simply wouldn't stop choking her throat.

"I know you are worried about your business, but have faith," he rejoined. "I am certain we can find a solution to the problem if we simply ponder it."

"No one really wishes to ponder it," Nan replied

as lightly as she could manage. "But I do thank you for your offer."

Susannah rose, and with her, Becky and Jane stood. Placing her fork to one side, Nan followed suit. Now, perhaps, she would have a few moments to get her sisters' attention.

But as soon as they entered the parlor, Susannah turned conversation to Becky's pregnancy. Nan sighed as she took her place beside Jane on the settee. As Susannah prattled on about nursemaids and physicians, Nan's patience grew thinner and thinner. Becky had ample time to plan the circumstances of her first child's birth, and more to the point, she had a right to choose how it happened without Susannah's list of instructions.

"Oh, do be quiet, Susannah," Nan finally snapped. If she heard any more from her eldest sister, she'd not even make it home before she began crying in frustration.

Becky and Susannah stared frankly at her, and Jane gave a pained little gasp. Regret tore at Nan's heart. She'd hate for Jane to think ill of her, even if she was highly annoyed with her sisters.

"I beg your pardon?" Susannah leveled her best glare at Nan, the one that had worked so many times before to bring Nan to heel.

"I said, do be quiet," Nan repeated. Now that she was in, she might as well muck on further. "It's ridiculous to prattle on when Becky has loads of time to plan her child's arrival. Let her be."

Becky breathed a little sigh of relief and cast a

grateful glance Nan's way. Perhaps she had grown weary of Susannah's bossiness, as well.

"There is a problem that's more pressing than anything else at the moment, because it threatens the well-being of our business," Nan continued, meeting Susannah's gaze steadily. "The grocer has hired a French milliner and her work is cutting deeply into our profits."

"Is this all?" Susannah rested her back against the seat of the settee, arranging her skirts so they hung in graceful folds to the floor. "Surely one milliner won't hurt the shop. Indeed, some competition could be good for business."

"I've only sold two bonnets in the past week." On the one hand, it was humiliating to admit the truth. On the other, it was a bit of a relief to share how badly things were going. "You know that we usually do at least three times that much, even when things are slow."

"I don't see how the new milliner can really be hurting your shop." Becky's subtle emphasis on *your* was not lost on Nan. If there was ever any doubt that the shop was hers alone to make a success of or not, this conversation was making the matter as clear as could be. "I am sure, as a Frenchwoman, her designs are quite smart. Your designs tend toward the practical, Nan. I am certain there is room for both in this village."

Tears pricked the back of Nan's eyes. Once, the three sisters had braved the difficulties of life in Uncle Arthur's home, as he squandered what was left of their small fortune. Later, their closeness had

endured through Susannah's courtship with Daniel.
Even Becky's courtship with Paul had not left Nan
unaffected. Yet now she was really and truly alone.
Her sisters, so quick to rush to each other's aid in
times past, now had different concerns and priorities.

She was about to say something—anything—to
try once more to get them to understand, when the
parlor door opened and the gentlemen filed in.

Well, there was nothing to do now. She would simply have to take care of this matter on her own. She
found a seat in a quiet corner of the room, her head
throbbing. Jane cast a tight little smile her way and
then turned her attention to her brother. In all likelihood, Jane was telling him that the Siddons shop was
a dismal failure, and that they should take their business elsewhere. Well, Jane would say it more nicely
than that. But her impassioned plea to her sisters probably cost her the one customer she'd gotten in the
past few weeks.

"I daresay there's at least one lady present who
can play the pianoforte," John spoke up, rising from
his seat. "Why don't we have a dance? Just an informal little hop."

Becky rose. "I can't really dance right now, so I
will be happy to play."

Nan stifled a groan as her brothers-in-law moved
chairs and settees back to the sides of the room, and
rolled up one of the rugs. She really wasn't in the right
frame of mind for a dance. Even at her most light-
hearted moments, she had little patience for dancing.
At the moment, her feet felt positively leaden.

Becky struck up a simple little tune, playing variations on the theme as the gentlemen finished preparing the room. Nan rose. Perhaps she could leave early. She cast a quick glance out the window. Dusk had deepened over the moor. There was no way she could walk without possibly tripping and falling or getting lost. She could ask Susannah for the use of her carriage, but that would call attention to herself. The only way it would work is if she was able to slip away unnoticed.

"Don't tell me that you're about to make a jump for it." Nan jerked slightly as John spoke. He must have sidled up to her when she was preoccupied with managing her escape. "The way you are staring out that window, I wouldn't be surprised if you threw up the sash and leaped out onto the moor."

Nan forced a polite smile. "I don't care much for dancing."

John extended his palm with a bow. "I doubt that. I think you would be an excellent partner."

Becky swung into the country dance as John led Nan out to the cleared space in the middle of the room. She pushed aside all thoughts of her business as she concentrated on the steps. They were so intricate and if she wasn't careful, she'd slip and end up on the floor.

"Already you look more at ease," John remarked as they moved through a figure. "Somehow, I knew you were born for dancing."

Nan's heart fluttered the tiniest bit. *Stop being so ridiculous.* That was the sort of compliment young men gave to young women all the time. He meant nothing by it, and she mustn't let a mild pleasantry turn her head. "Why, thank you."

"I think I have a solution to your business problem," John continued, taking her hand as they stepped closer together and then apart. "If your work is pleasing to my sister—and she will need to see a sample of it first, of course—I should like to hire you to do her entire wardrobe for her Season in London. Everything she needs, from gowns to riding habits to, of course, bonnets."

"Everything?" She hesitated for a fraction of a second, and it threw their timing off as they danced. With the skill surely born of years of practice, John smoothed over her missed step and continued as though she'd never stumbled.

"Yes. My sister is beautiful, and I think she will have great success once she makes her debut. But I know she's shy and uncomfortable. If she had clothes made just for her, and if she worked closely with you on the designs, it might make her feel more confident. You can sew, can't you?" he continued after a brief pause, sizing her up as though he was entirely unsure of her abilities at anything.

"Yes, of course I can sew." She cast him an exasperated look, and his eyes danced as though he was hard-pressed not to laugh. "But if you'll forgive me for saying so, you didn't seem very impressed with my skills earlier today. Just a few hours ago, you questioned my ability to turn out one single stylish bonnet. Now you want me to create an entire bespoke wardrobe for your sister. Why this sudden change in attitude?"

He paused a moment, and her heart lurched. Would he say something pretty and flowery, something that would compliment her skill and flatter her? Few men did, although her sisters received compliments all the time. In all likelihood, his hesitation was because he didn't know what to say. She was demanding an explanation, and he must know she wouldn't take less than an honest answer.

"I was being a bit of a joker this afternoon," he began slowly. "I was trying to jest with you. Tease you, I am afraid to say. Jane took me to task for it after we left."

"Do you make a habit of teasing innocent shopkeepers?" She could not suppress the wry smile twisting her mouth, and he grinned back.

"Only when they come and fetch us, demanding our business."

A warm flush suffused Nan's cheeks. "I must admit, that was out of character for me. A move born of desperation, I'm afraid. I know I should trust in the Lord, but it's hard to always remember that."

"I don't know that I would hold with some notion of a god playing with us, like a bunch of chess pieces." John guided her through the closing figure of the dance. "I think boldness in business is a highly admirable skill."

Becky's playing grew softer and ended with a single note. John bowed as Nan curtsied, but the end of the dance wouldn't mark the end of the interrogation. His remarks discomfited her, but at the same time, there was not much she could say in return. At least, not now. The idea of starting a new argument, this one about the existence of God, was too much after an already long day.

"I suppose I should be glad you admire boldness. However, you still haven't answered my question. Did you make your sudden change because you felt badly about your behavior?"

He laughed. "You give me far too much credit. No, I can't really explain why I've changed my mind. I suppose if you were going to tie it to just one thing, it would be because you get along with my sister so well already. Jane allows very few people into her circle. She never warms up to anyone as quickly as she warmed up to you. I think your very presence would have a calming effect on her."

Nan nodded as he guided her over to one of the chairs pushed up against the wall. "I like Jane very much."

For all his teasing ways, John must be feeling some hint of nervousness, for his shoulders relaxed as she spoke the words. "So, you will agree to it, then? I can entrust Jane to you, and no longer worry about the matter?"

"I did not say that." Nan took her seat with a flourish, smoothing out her skirts. Somehow, the knowledge that he'd been nervous, too, made her feel a bit more confident. "I will think about it. I don't know how I would manage both the shop and an entire wardrobe for Miss Reed, but I will give the matter some thought."

"The shop?" He shrugged. "That's an unnecessary complication. No, we must have your undivided attention. You would simply have to close the shop."

"Close it?" Nan shook her head. "I had not even considered that."

"Look." John drew a chair up close to Nan and cast a most persuasive gaze upon her. "You said yourself that the shop was doing poorly. Why not let it go? You'd have to come to London with us anyway. Or at the very least, you'd be spending the next several months with us at Grant Park."

Nan blinked. There was some truth to what he said. "I hadn't thought of that at all."

"Come along, you two." Paul clapped his hands and strode over. "We're about to start a new dance. Whatever are you talking about so intently, all tucked away in this corner?"

"I've just made Miss Siddons an offer that could change her whole life," John replied, giving Paul a boyish grin. "Provided, of course, that she has sense enough to accept it."

## Chapter Three

Nan glanced over at her young helpers, Abigail and Mercy. The two girls had been with the sisters' millinery shop for some time now, and they were both quick and eager workers. Despite their nimble fingers and helpful ways, they never grew any closer to Nan than after they'd started. Nan stifled a sigh. It would be a relief to unburden herself to them—to tell them both about the previous night, and how John's challenge was taken as a proposal of marriage by Susannah and Becky.

Her cheeks burned at the memory of her sisters leaping up, embracing her and telling her how happy she would be. John's excessive apologies afterward cleared up the mess but somehow also made her feel like even more of an old maid than she was. He had just been offering her a job, not asking for her hand in marriage. His tone of voice, echoing in her ears, grated on her last nerve. Nan clenched her teeth and tightened her hold on the bonnet brim she was trimming. The sudden pressure made the brim snap.

Abigail and Mercy gasped in unison, staring over at Nan with round eyes.

She couldn't blame them. She'd never spoiled anything she'd worked on, ever. A mistake cost the shop money, and she would never lose money if she could help it. Nan gave them both a taut smile, but it was hardly a welcoming and calming expression, she was sure. She needed to get out of the shop. If she stayed, she'd start pacing—her pet habit when agitated. If she started pacing, then Abigail and Mercy would know something was wrong.

"Better go out for a while—need to get bread for dinner," she said, but her nerves were so frayed that the words tumbled out in an unintelligible rush. She left the shop in a swirl of skirts, banging the door shut behind her.

Now what should she do?

If she headed farther into the village, she'd be tempted to go spy on the French milliner. If she applied reason and logic to the situation, she would know that there was no good that would come of staring at the poor woman. Yet, she was not the kind of girl who could find comfort by rambling for hours over the moors, as her sister Becky did. So, should she go into the village? Or roam the fields? Neither choice was particularly appealing.

Tansley Village was so awfully small. Funny, she hadn't really noticed the village's closeness until just now. If you had to go somewhere for privacy, where was there to go?

There was no place to go. For once, she craved the anonymity of a city street so that she could lose herself among the bustling crowd. Someplace like London, where she could merely fade into the background and be alone with her thoughts.

*Father, help me. Help me move past all this.* If only God could blot out the memory of her humiliation, and remove the sting. If only it had never happened.

Instead, she directed her feet toward the moors. They offered the only sense of solitude she could find in Tansley, and she needed some time alone to think.

The crisp autumn breeze rustled her skirts, and she tugged her bonnet off, letting it dangle down her back by its ribbons. If she was Becky, she would also loosen her braids and let her hair tumble its full length, just touching the small of her back. But then, it would take forever to coax the tangles back out so she could wind her locks into their coronet of braids.

She might follow in her sister's footsteps as far as walking out on the moor, but she would only take her imitation so far.

John's words echoed through her mind.

*Offer.*

*Change her life.*

*Accept.*

No wonder everyone thought he'd been proposing marriage. She scowled and scuffed at a rock with the toe of her boot. "Handsome men are such fools," she breathed aloud, finally daring to say the hot words that had been bubbling under the surface since the ridiculous scene last night. "What was he thinking? He wasn't thinking at all." Typical. Disheartening and a stark reminder of the characteristics of all handsome men. She'd been allowing herself to soften toward

John until his preposterous turn of phrase humiliated her before her family and brought sharp, painful reminders of her impending spinsterhood into bold relief.

A movement caught the corner of her eye. Someone else was walking out on the moor. Nan paused, anxiety rising in her chest. She really had no wish to socialize with anyone right now. Perhaps it was just a local villager, whom she could pass with a brief nod and hello.

She peered closer. A lithe young woman with dark hair was climbing the steep hillside. It was Jane. Last night she had begun observing Jane's movements and gestures as a way to understand how best to dress her. A woman couldn't be properly attired unless her dressmaker made a thorough study of how she moved. Unfortunately, so few dressmakers took the time for such minute details. This young woman, with the uncertain way she moved and her hesitant steps, could be no one but Jane.

Nan raised her hand in greeting. Even if she thoroughly disliked John, at least she liked his sister.

"Nan! Hello!" Jane's voice carried over the moor. "Wait for me."

Nan nodded and stood still so Jane could come closer. She bore Jane no ill will, despite John's stupidity. She seemed a genuinely sweet person—a little like Becky, if Becky wasn't so dreamy and romantic.

"Oh, I am so glad to find you," Jane panted when she got within speaking distance. "I was hoping to today. I thought for certain you would be in the shop."

"I just came out here for a few moments, on my

way to the bakery." Guilt gave Nan a twinge. She was, after all, supposed to be working on a bonnet—or at the very least, a sketch—for Jane. She was not supposed to be moping about just because some thoughtless young buck hurt her feelings.

"Well, I wanted to stop and ask if you had considered my brother's offer. Not, of course, the offer everyone thought he was making." Jane's cheeks flooded with color and she seized Nan's arm. "I am so very sorry about that," she whispered. "Sometimes I think John has the manners of a pig."

"Oh, I've met some swine who could school your brother in etiquette," Nan replied drily.

Jane's eyes grew sadder and she shook her head. "I can't think of what to say. Let me beg your forgiveness, once more, on his behalf."

Nan gave Jane a halfhearted smile. No need for her to continue apologizing, when it wasn't her fault. John had said he was sorry, and made such an uproar, that she really didn't want to hear any more on the matter. In fact, she would stop brooding about it altogether, starting now. There was no need to be so missish, for it was a simple mistake, after all.

"I was only teasing." Nan shrugged off Jane's hold. "It was nothing, I assure you."

"Oh, good," Jane breathed, her pretty face relaxing. "So, will you consider John's idea? Will you come with us, and act as my personal seamstress? I won't feel half so scared if you are there helping me."

"I hadn't really thought of his proposal in detail." Now that John had offered her more than she'd ever hoped for, she didn't know what to do. It had been far easier to focus on her hurt feelings than on the hope of financial security. "I don't know how I would manage with the shop."

"My brother would, I am certain, help with that," Jane offered. She smiled tentatively. "Of course, I can understand why you wouldn't want to leave. For one thing, with your own store, you have new things to do every day, and new people to talk to. If you were just designing clothes for me, you would be stuck with me, boring as I am." She gave a halfhearted laugh that tugged at Nan's heartstrings.

"Believe me, my career is much less exciting than you imagine." Nan sighed. "Women out here have a tendency to order the same thing over and over. So I have developed ways to make it more interesting. I found a method to weave straw so it's stronger. My bonnets hold up very well against Tansley weather. But that's something I had to come to, not the other way around."

"I can well understand that," Jane agreed. "I suppose there isn't as much call for, say, ostrich plumes and velvet out here."

"Yes. I schooled myself to learn to love and appreciate the most simple and basic of bonnets, because they truly are the backbone of my store," Nan agreed.

Jane slipped her arm through Nan's elbow, and began guiding her back down the hill. Nan allowed herself to be tugged along. It was strange for Jane to lead rather than follow; based on the very little she knew of Jane's personality, she was not strong willed like Susannah—much more likely to go along with things than take the lead. At the foot of the hill, Jane paused, studying the view.

"It's so beautiful here. Rather like home."

Nan nodded, silently. She wasn't as enamored of sweeping vistas as Becky, but anyone could appreciate this view. The sun was gaining its summit in the sky, and a fresh cool breeze rustled the long moor grass.

"I don't ever want to leave the country. I don't understand why my brother insists on it."

Nan turned to look at Jane. Had she really no idea of the role she must play? "I am sure he insists because it's your duty. Just as I have my duty to my store, and he has his duty to your home, you must see that you must at least try to meet an eligible young man and marry well."

Jane's face fell. "Now you sound just like him. I thought you would be on my side." She turned away, her shoulders slumping.

Nan shook her head. For one thing, that stiff black bombazine that Jane wore was simply not made for her movements. She needed softer fabric, something that would move gracefully with her. Small wonder she felt uncomfortable all the time. For another thing, and on a completely different note, she needed a friend. John Reed was insufferable enough as a passing acquaintance. What a horror he must be as a brother.

Of course Jane must make her debut, as any young woman of her station in life should. In fact, if circumstances had been different, and had Uncle Arthur not run through her parents' fortune like water, it was likely Nan would have seen Jane socially in London. However, that was neither here nor there. Her duty was to help Jane feel more comfortable with her debut. If Jane could do so in clothes that suited her, with the help of someone she trusted, she would have a much higher chance of success than if she was to go through it alone, with no one but her brother helping.

Nan laid a careful hand on Jane's shoulder, reminding herself to be patient. She had a tendency to blurt out the hard truths of life at the most inopportune time, and it never went well. Susannah and Becky would agree most heartily to that, if they were standing here right now.

"I daresay a London ballroom won't be half as frightening if you are dressed in a gown that suits you. We all feel much better when we are well dressed. I may have forced myself to love plain hats and bonnets for my business to survive, but that doesn't mean I have shunned the fancier stuff forever."

Jane gasped and whirled around. "Does this mean you will come with me?"

"I still don't know how to make it happen, but I will find a way." Now it was Nan's turn to gasp as Jane threw her arms around her, laughing. She hadn't embraced one of her sisters in ages. Since they married and had families of their own, her sisters simply didn't have the time or feel the need to embrace that much anymore. She missed it. Until now, she had no idea how much she really grieved the loss of her sisters, with a deep-down ache that brought hot tears to her eyes.

Giving in to the desire to cry would serve no purpose now. She must squash her hurt and wait until later tonight, when she could sob silently into her pillow.

"Now, now. That's quite enough." Nan took a step back, assuming the brisk practicality that had served her so well thus far. "I suppose I need to talk to your brother. Where is he this morning?"

*I really am trying to concentrate. Look at me, the very picture of a gentleman of means.* John forced himself to stare at the ledger book as Paul trailed his quill along page after page of spidery handwriting. It was the dullest thing he could think to do on a day with such fine weather, but it would be very rude to tell Paul so. After all, his friend was taking valuable time away from his lovely wife and family to school him in the proper manner of estate management.

"So you see, with just one small change to the way in which we harvested the grain, we ended up saving a large percentage of the crop. Enough, in fact, to net a tidy little profit." Paul grinned and bent closer over the page, as though he could gobble the figures up to make a satisfying meal.

John glanced down at his boots. They were really of an excellent cut. He'd have to order another pair just like them from the boot-maker, for when these needed a rest or a cleaning.

"How do you reap your grain?" Paul glanced up sharply from the ledger book.

"I haven't the foggiest, old man." John stifled a yawn.

"It's your duty to know." Paul slammed the ledger book shut. "Who is your estate manager? Crowell?"

"No, Crowell passed away years ago. Father hired a new man to take his place." John searched his mind for the fellow's name. "Weatherford? Whetstone? Bother me, it starts with a *W*. That's all I know." If Paul would hurry up, they'd have time for a ride this afternoon before dinner. This latest lesson was taking forever to end.

"If you want my advice—and after all, you came all this way here for me to offer it—then you will return to Grant Park and have a meeting with this Mr. W. Talk to him. Get a feeling for how the harvests are managed. If he has any suggestions for improvements or changes, do listen to him and think the matter over. Estate managers can be vastly acute. Just look at the changes Daniel has wrought at Goodwin Hall, now that he is listening to his man."

John nodded. If he continued looking the part of an interested pupil, perhaps Paul would act less like a stern schoolmaster and would just let him go. A quick canter would be just the thing in this fine weather.

"John," Paul began in the tone that usually indicated a lecture was at hand, "this really is yours to care for now. Grant Park is a vast estate, and it's imperative that you run it in a manner that will do your family credit. Had you no sense that it would become your responsibility some day?"

"I thought Father would live forever." A flippant statement, perhaps, but a true one. He had never given any thought to the fact that, one day, Father would die and leave him responsible for managing his family's wealth.

"And now that your father has proven himself mortal, where does that leave you?"

John shrugged. "Prevailing upon my friends with better common sense than I possess."

The door to the study banged open and Nan Siddons whirled in, her cheeks a rosy pink and her eyes bright. John rose, a nervous rush of energy sweeping through him. Nan had proven herself a good sort last night, when he had stumbled into what her family had considered a marriage proposal when it had, in fact, merely been an offer of employment.

It couldn't have been an easy predicament—indeed, he was still a trifle embarrassed when he remembered it himself—but she handled it with grace and aplomb. Her poise had convinced him that she could be an excellent guide for his sister as she made her debut. Surely Jane could weather any ballroom disaster in London with Nan instructing her surreptitiously.

"Pardon the interruption," she managed, looking less like her usual practical self than he could have imagined. Her bonnet was dangling down her back by its ribbons, and several tawny locks of hair had escaped her braided coronet. Her breathless disarray, coupled with her flushed cheeks and starry blue eyes, made Nan Siddons look downright pretty.

"We were just finishing up," he replied, looking over his shoulder at Paul. Paul stood, his expression one of bafflement. John could well hear his friend's thoughts. Should he stay and play chaperone? Or give them both some peace so that they could discuss a business proposition in private?

"I'll go…and leave the door open." Paul nodded at John, the etiquette problem resolved, as he left the room.

John waited until Paul rounded the corner, his tall form passing out of sight. Then he turned to Nan. "You look like someone who's made a momentous decision."

"I suppose I have." She smoothed her hair with hands that trembled visibly. "I don't know how to make it happen, but I think I would like to have a go at being Jane's dressmaker."

A feeling of relief and excitement poured through him. "Good. I was hoping you would." Then he paused. What did she mean about making it happen? It was a simple enough matter, surely. "All we need to do is make arrangements for you to accompany us to Grant Park."

"I also need to make certain my sisters agree that this is the right course of action for me to take." She looked pointedly at the settee. "May I sit down? My feet ache terribly. I ran almost the entire way here."

"Of course." His manners had fled the moment she arrived. Then again, this wasn't really his house, so who was he to offer guests a seat? Would a gentleman offer anyway, even if he was the one visiting, and the lady was related to the head of the house? He would never wrap his head around etiquette. It was a very good thing that Nan was agreeing to help Jane. He was such a dolt, he'd never make heads or tails of any situation.

Nan sat on the settee, arranging her skirts around her, glancing up at him with an expectant look on her face. "Please, sit, sir. I cannot continue with you standing, as though you might bolt from the room at any moment."

"My apologies." He pulled a spindly wooden chair up so that he could sit opposite her. "I know we can convince your sisters. Have no fear."

The corners of her mouth quirked. "You've not spent much time in my sisters' company. They are not as easily persuaded as you seem to think. That's not the only thing that makes me hesitate, however." She waved her hand as though brushing the matter of her stubborn sisters aside. "There is also the matter of my shop. I don't see how I can continue running it efficiently if I am to be staying with Miss Jane in Grant Park."

He smiled with relief. Was that all she was concerned about? That silly little shop of hers? "Oh, I am certain I can pay you more than that tiny place can make in a year."

Nan's posture grew rigid and her expression hardened, making her look more like a spinster than he had ever seen her. "Do you really think so?" Her words, though perfectly polite, were an icy challenge.

He leaned back in his chair, studying Miss Nan Siddons from the top of her braided coronet to the tips of her slippers peeking out beneath her skirts. She was a bit of an enigma. Talented, to be sure, and far too intelligent to stay hidden away in a country hat shop, toiling away for years and years on the same ugly old bonnets. She was spirited beneath the mask of stolid composure she always wore, and she hated being teased.

He knew for a fact she couldn't bear to be made fun of, and that thought attracted him at this moment more than anything. Nan Siddons could be jolly good company if she let herself go just a bit, and the only way he could force her to relinquish some of her prim airs was to tease her quite hard. He glanced over at the doorway. No sisters, either his own or hers, were present to interfere or tell him to stop.

"I do think so," he responded, a slow grin spreading across his face. "In fact, I know so. Why, if I paid you to create one gown for Jane, you'd get a bigger profit than you have these few months, I think. Why else would you have come running after my sister and me, trying to snag us as customers, if you weren't desperate for cash?"

Nan's steady gaze faltered, and as she stared at the floor, her shoulders sagged just a trifle. Why wouldn't she speak up? He wanted a spirited debate with her.

"I don't see why you need to consult with your sisters, either," he continued, leaning closer in toward her. "After all, you had quite a bit of trouble getting them to care about your shop last night. Why do you persist in asking for their permission?" Nan seemed a decisive enough person. Why did she persist in asking her sisters for consent, as though she was a child? It was so strangely out of step with the rest of her straightforward, efficient behavior. Her candor was one of her most appealing characteristics. Why hide it?

"Because…" she trailed off, shaking her head. "I don't know. I suppose I feel I must."

"Aren't you your own woman?" He raised his voice a little in challenge. She needed to let go of this ridiculous notion that she must ask blessings of her sisters. She needed to drop that mask of practicality and deference, and revert to her usual frankness. If she did, then he would see that feisty side of her that he enjoyed so much. "You've run your own business for long enough, I daresay, to determine whether or not you can do as you choose with your life."

"I don't know…" The expression on Nan's face walked a fine line between anger and triumph. She was rising to his bait, and at any moment, she would agree to his challenge.

Life would not be dull at Grant Park if he could spar with Nan Siddons. Why, he might be able to submit to the yoke of being master if he could look forward to a few moments of skirmishing with her a little every day.

He would try a bit of a different tactic. "Of course, if you're scared—"

"I'm not afraid," Nan snapped, and she rose from the settee. She began pacing, her slippered feet making no sound on the rich Oriental carpet. "If I could only make you understand. My sisters and I have always been quite close. The shop was Susannah's and she left it to us. It's been our hope of independence all these years."

"Times change." He rose, too. Why was she holding back? "Your sisters don't need the shop anymore. You won't either, if you have any sense. Do you really want to be chained to a dingy little shop for the rest of your life, making ugly old bonnets for tired old women—"

Nan spun around on one heel and slapped him, hard, across the face. "They aren't ugly!"

As he touched his burning cheek, Nan fell back a step, breathing rapidly. "Oh, forgive me. I am so sorry. I should never have struck you. I just couldn't bear to hear the shop spoken of that way."

He had pushed too far, teasing her more than she deserved. In his haste to help her declare her independence, he had reached Nan's limit. "No, don't apologize. I shouldn't have said that. Jane says I am too harsh." He eyed her carefully, rubbing his sore cheek. "Do you still want to work for me? I should say, for my sister?"

She closed her eyes for a moment, as though gathering strength. Finally, she looked up at him as though really seeing him for the first time.

"Yes."

## Chapter Four

Nan trudged up the pathway that led to Kellridge, her valise banging against her hip with each step. The Reeds had offered to pick her up at the shop in the carriage, but somehow, she could not accept their kind offer. For a journey of this magnitude, she must put one foot in front of the other. Striking out on her own was just the way to start this new phase of her life.

To some, it might seem as though she was merely walking to Kellridge, where she would meet the Reeds and ride off with them to their country home. But this meant so much more. Meeting them and leaving Tansley from the shop would seem too hasty, abrupt even. This walk provided distance. Though she had spent the past fortnight working to put the shop in order, thereby allowing it to hum along smoothly in her absence, there was still a tug at her heart as she closed the shop door behind her.

She would be home to check on things in another fortnight, before returning to the Reeds' home.

She must remind herself of this fact. This was not

the end of her life in Tansley. She would be back soon, but it just wouldn't be the same.

Life would never be the same again.

She inhaled deeply, breathing in the brisk spring air. Winter was leaving for certain, and yet there was still an icy, keen edge to the wind. This was a perfect time of the year for new beginnings, if one believed in poetic comparisons. She was striking out on her own as cautiously and yet as willingly as a sprout pushing its way up from the earth.

Nan stifled an internal groan. She was becoming as ridiculously poetic as Becky.

As she picked her way down a particularly rocky vale, her foot slipped on a rock. She tripped and slid down the last bit of valley, nearly losing her valise along with her footing. She skidded to a stop and tugged at her dress and cloak. She must have looked so ridiculous. What a way to begin her new attempted independence. Falling down was inefficient when one was hoping to land firmly on one's feet.

"Nan! Are you quite all right?" Jane's voice echoed in the valley. Nan glanced around and caught sight of her friend making her way down a steep path, one that led to some of the smaller, nearby farms. "I thought for certain you were going to fall."

"So did I," Nan replied with a smile. She picked her way over to Jane's side, taking care to keep from sliding down atop an avalanche of pebbles. "What are you doing out here? I thought you would be at Kell-ridge, making last-minute preparations and saying your goodbyes."

"No. I—I had a few friends I wanted to say farewell to before we left." The color rose in Jane's cheeks until it reached her hair.

Nan paused in her rush to start her life anew. Why was Jane so embarrassed?

She took a closer, more practiced look at her friend. Why had Jane taken her violin with her on a social call?

"I see," she said softly. "You've only been here a few weeks. I am glad to hear you've made good friends, even in that short of an amount of time. Is it difficult to leave Kellridge?"

"I find it hard to leave." Jane's dark eyes flashed and she pursed her lips. "I haven't met any families as congenial as those here in Tansley. I am sure the questionable delights of London will pale in comparison."

Nan smiled, even as she was heartily confused by Jane's vehemence. What families had Jane visited? Hadn't she been here mere weeks—a very short time to form such a strong connection to someone? There was no one nearby except for a few families who resided on small farms on the outskirts of the village. She had made bonnets for the women of these houses for a while now, but she didn't recall any of them as being particularly pleasant.

"Well, I am glad to see you found friends who share your taste in music," Nan replied, for wont of something more intelligent to say.

Jane threaded her arm through Nan's and began guiding them through the valley path toward Kellridge. She had a remarkably good grasp of the terrain, almost as though this rocky little valley was familiar to her. Nan had lived in Tansley for years, traversing this path often on her way to Kellridge from the shop, and she was far from being as nimble as Jane.

"Hmm." Jane murmured in a distracted fashion.

They fell silent for a few moments as Jane led them over the side of the hill and up to the plateau that stretched toward Kellridge. Nan caught her breath as she looked at the large stone manor house. What a lovely place it was, and how fortunate Becky was to be mistress of all that grandeur. Becky's place in life was now secure, and she could do as she pleased. She had a husband who adored her, a baby on the way, a stepniece who thought of her as a mother and a grand home filled with servants.

It was difficult indeed to swallow the bitterness rising in her throat.

Never mind. Once she was secure in her own right, she could afford to be happy for her sister. For now, and only to herself, she thought it a terrible injustice that she should be so shut out of the loveliness and happiness life had to offer.

As they paused for a moment on the brink of the plateau, Jane snapped out of her reverie. "Nan, do you know the Holdcroft family?"

Nan stuffed her jealousy back down deep inside. "Yes, I believe so. Mrs. Hugh Holdcroft is a customer of mine. I delivered a new spring bonnet to her just recently."

"Remarkable people, the Holdcrofts. Very old English family." Jane turned to her, giving a sweet, and slightly sad, smile. "Of course, they don't have the wealth they used to command. They are farmers now, even though in previous generations they were quite well-to-do."

"Unfortunately, that happens often in families." Nan shrugged. "My sisters and I were wealthy until my uncle Arthur spent all of our money. Well, that's not true. He didn't spend it as much as he lost it at the gaming tables."

Jane gasped. "How horrible! Were you able to save anything?"

"My sister had enough money left to purchase the shop in the village, but since then we have supported ourselves." It was difficult not to sound boastful, but what the Siddonses had accomplished with such limited means was worthy of pride. "Poverty is nothing to be ashamed of. In fact, I think people should be more concerned with how they treat others, especially those they consider beneath themselves, than about the balance on their ledger books."

"That is brilliantly put." Jane clapped her hands. "I must say I agree with you. The Holdcrofts are quite an amazing family. I wish you knew them better."

"I do, too," Nan replied, but her mind was focused more upon leaving Tansley than on getting to know the other villagers better. Funny, though she and Jane walked side by side and even arm in arm, they seemed to be on completely different paths. While she was ready to push forward, toward Kellridge and her new future, Jane was lingering on the past and on the friends she'd made in Tansley. "Come, let us hurry. If we don't arrive at Kellridge on time, I am sure to endure a scolding from Susy. She is quite a stickler for punctuality."

Jane nodded in agreement, and the two of them quickened their steps, arriving at the front portico out of breath and red-faced. The butler showed them in with a bemused glance at their windblown locks and pinkened cheeks.

As Nan entered the drawing room, a tingling feeling shot up her spine. John must be here. She glanced around casually and spotted him in the corner, speaking with Paul and Daniel. She dropped her gaze again. She'd managed to avoid John almost completely since slapping him a few weeks ago. All of her arrangements had been made with Jane, for after all, she was going for Jane's benefit.

"About time you two arrived," Susannah scolded from her place on the settee. "I was beginning to worry about both of you."

Nan kissed her sister's cheek. How nice it would be to be on her own, and once in a while, be late if she had the inclination or the need. "Our apologies. I nearly fell headfirst down a valley. Fortunately, Jane rescued me."

Neither sister seemed particularly concerned with her brush with death. They merely greeted Jane and then turned assessing eyes toward her.

Becky patted the settee cushion beside her. "Come, sit."

Nan obediently sat, while Jane walked across the room to chat with her brother.

Nan fiddled with the banding on her sleeve. She was now imprisoned between her two sisters, one of whom had grown quite large during her pregnancy.

She had to sit with her elbows pinned against her sides to avoid hitting either of them.

"Now, before you leave, we both have some advice for you," Susannah began in the tone of voice that usually indicated a lecture was at hand.

Nan stifled a groan and flicked a glance over at her traveling companions. Jane and John were both laughing, and Paul and Daniel seemed to be caught up in telling a lively story. Everyone seemed to be enjoying each other's company immensely, and none of them made a move to leave.

"Now, when you are employed by someone outside of our family, you must remember to temper your blunt ways," Susannah admonished. "Many's the time that you've hurt our feelings with your plain talk. Remember that another employer—a stranger, to be perfectly frank—might not be so understanding or forgiving."

"I wouldn't say the Reeds are strangers—" Nan began.

"Well, they aren't well-known to us. Not like Paul was, when Becky began working for him." Susannah gave an irritated twitch of her shoulders. "So heed what I say, Nan. Please temper your words."

"I shall." Much of her bluntness over the years had been developed as a shield—a way to deflect the criticism of her elder sisters. In some ways, too, it had been used as a sword. After all, someone had to cut through Becky's romanticism or to pierce Susannah's vanity. The only way the Siddonses had survived—and thrived—was by gathering their strengths together while breaking down one another's weaknesses. So it stood to reason that, deprived of her sisters' annoying habits, she would find little need to be abrupt.

"But even as you work on supporting yourself, on striking out on your own—leave room in your heart for love," Becky added, fanning herself lightly. "I was so certain that love had left me behind that day when Lieutenant Walker jilted me. Now I know that I was made for Paul."

Nan resisted the urge to roll her eyes. After John's supposed proposal had gone so hideously awry, she had felt no desire for romance for quite some time. Leave that to the very young and the very pretty. Of which she never felt a part.

Would they ever leave? She shifted slightly on the settee—not that there was that much room—and fought the desire to give way to nervous pacing. As she moved, she caught John's glance from across the sitting room. The corners of his mouth quirked and he sent her a knowing, bemused grin.

She turned abruptly, knocking Becky's fan to the floor. "Oh dear," she muttered, and bent to retrieve it.

"Allow me," a deep voice answered. How had John managed to cross the room, soundlessly, in less than two seconds? He handed Becky her fan with a flourish and offered Nan his arm.

"I hate to leave Kellridge, as my hosts have been so generous and wonderful," he added, pulling Nan to her feet. "But the horses are restive and we've several miles to go before reaching Grant Park."

Gratitude surged through Nan, and she allowed herself to look him at him fully for the first time in weeks. "Then by all means, let us go."

\* \* \*

In truth, John was in no hurry to return to Grant Park. Life at the Park meant taking on the yoke of responsibility that he had no desire to don. It meant ledger books, meetings, servants and crops. It meant living in Father's shadow. It meant seeing the traces of Mother everywhere, the mother he had disappointed and caused grave danger to all those years ago. These were all matters he had managed to neatly avoid for years, but there was no avoiding them now.

One look at Nan Siddons, miserably squashed between her two sisters, was all he needed to spur him on. Even if he couldn't have fun, Nan should at least have a go at it. She had been avoiding him for weeks, and her absence was something he actually noticed. This was quite an accomplishment, for a young woman. Usually if one young lady shunned him, there were plenty of others standing in line waiting for his attention.

That was in London, though, and not Derbyshire.

"How far are we from Grant Park?" Nan had been peering out the window of the carriage since they left.

"It's only an hour and a quarter from Tansley," he answered, shifting lazily in his seat. If only it was farther.

"Still in Derbyshire?"

"Yes, near Wessington." He should have told her more about the Park, given her some idea of what she was getting into before she took the leap. He gave himself a good, sharp, mental kick. His sister was absolutely no help, for once Kellridge had faded from sight she moped quietly in her corner and then fell asleep. "The house is very nice. I daresay you'll like it there. Jane has her own suite of rooms, and we'll put you in her wing. That way you can be close by for fittings and consultations and whatnot."

"Thank you, sir." Nan nodded respectfully.

He stifled a grin. After slapping him, she must be working doubly hard to stay on strictly professional terms.

"Call me John," he replied easily. "Even if I am forced to be lord of the manor, I hate to be addressed as sir."

"I don't know that I can do that." Nan shrugged, looking stubbornly out the window. "I don't think that's quite proper."

"Nonsense. Call me John, and, of course, you already refer to my sister as Jane."

"I don't think I can. Calling Jane by her given name, well, it's easier because we are friends." She cast a discomfited look his way. "I'm not trying to be rude."

It was on the tip of his tongue to tease her, or at least reference how close they had gotten when she slapped his cheek, but he thought better of it. If she was thawing out a trifle, it would be better not to provoke her now. "Well, if you find it difficult, you could just call me Reed."

Nan tilted her head to one side, as though giving the matter serious thought. "Very well, I think I could call you Reed."

"Excellent. Shall I call you Siddons?"

Nan burst into laughter, a pretty smile lighting her

face. "I daresay that sounds silly enough. But no sillier than Nan."

"What, don't you like your name?" It was so good to hear laughter that he was ready to draw the moment out as long as he could. She had a lovely laugh. Pity she didn't indulge it more often.

"Nan?" She made a face. "No, I never have. I prefer my proper name, but I never had a say in the matter. Once Susannah called me Nan, I was Nan for life."

"Well, Susannah's not here." He leaned forward, as though they were sharing a great secret. "So you can be whomever you want."

"Oh, I am still myself." She was getting into the spirit of the game as well. "I only wish to cast aside certain aspects of my life that were forced upon me, such as a most unattractive nickname."

"What is your given name?" Genuine curiosity got the better of him.

"My name is Hannah." She shrugged, drawing her shawl closer about her shoulders. "Susannah said it sounded too much like her name, you know, too many 'annahs' in the house. So she shortened it to Nan. So I've been, ever since."

"That took some cheek." He sat back, eyeing Nan— no, Hannah—with genuine sympathy. "I was the eldest in my family, but I never saw fit to change Jane's name."

"Susannah has always been rather high-handed," Nan admitted, turning her eyes toward the floor of the carriage. "She is a very good sister, though," she added hastily.

"I am sure she is, but that doesn't solve our problem right now. The problem is, who are you? Nan Siddons? Hannah Siddons? Siddons? The choice is yours."

"In the interest of speed and efficiency, you may call me Siddons. Just as I shall call you Reed." She smiled. Then she added, "I am Hannah Siddons."

# Chapter Five

Hannah Siddons, formerly known as the practical and prosaic Nan, stared up at the ceiling as she drifted awake. The mattress beneath her was soft and deliciously fluffy and the fire in the grate crackled merrily, chasing off the early morning chill. This was as different an awakening as she could imagine.

For as long as she could remember, waking up meant the squeaking protest of mattress ropes and a cold hearth that needed to be stirred to life. Nothing would ever be accomplished unless she and her sisters roused themselves and began their chores. Here at Grant Park, silent servants took care of the minutiae of existence, lighting fires in hearths or making beds. She no longer had to worry about a million little trifles. Instead, her whole life and purpose was to make Jane into a desirable candidate for matrimony.

Hannah sat up, even though it was hard to give up the warmth of her quilt. The change in her circumstances was as dramatic as the change in her name, and she was having a difficult time getting used to being called by her given name. Focusing all of her efforts on one task was, in truth, a bit daunting. Yet focus she must, because failure could mean only one thing—spinsterhood.

With that daunting thought, she jumped from the bed and grabbed her wrapper. Breakfast was surely being served somewhere, and she couldn't simply lie about all morning. She must dress herself and then find Jane. They had arrived just yesterday, but it was time to start working.

A knock sounded on the door.

"Enter?"

Jane opened the door wide enough to just let her peek through. "Oh good, you're awake." She bustled in with a breakfast tray. "I thought we could eat together. Normally I dine in bed, but it's terribly lonely. Dreadful way to start the day."

"That sounds lovely." From a practical perspective, it meant that she could begin working with Jane right away, before the day had even really begun. From a deeper, more private perspective, Jane's presence also pushed aside any lingering loneliness she might begin feeling. Her sisters had gone off and married months ago, and one would think she'd be used to being alone by now.

She wasn't.

Jane pulled two chairs over by a little marble table near the hearth. "There we go. This is nice and cozy, don't you think?"

"Perfect." Hannah waved her over to her seat with a well-practiced flip of her hands, then she began pouring the tea. "In fact, we can get started better this way. I'd like to know how you see your role at Grant Park, and how you want to present yourself to others outside your inner social circle."

Jane accepted the teacup Hannah offered her, her brows drawn together in thought. "I never really thought of myself as playing any kind of role. I suppose, if I had to describe it, I would call myself a simple person. I don't have many wants or needs. I help out as much as I can as mistress of the house, but I don't feel that we are at a social level that requires much showiness. Does that make sense?"

Hannah nodded. Yes, that made perfect sense. "In other words, when one isn't a duchess, one doesn't need to worry about her morning dress."

"Or her afternoon dress...or her riding habit..." Jane set the teacup aside, her spoon rattling against the saucer. "Oh, I am not trying to belittle what you do, in making clothing or hats. It's just that I have always considered myself a country girl. When I marry, I shall marry a simple country farmer. I won't have a need for frills and furbelows."

"True, but to meet your simple country farmer, you will need to attend the kinds of functions in which you are expected to dress well." Hannah selected a scone from a wicker basket, lined with a linen napkin. She broke it into halves. "That is where I can help you."

"Actually, I have already met him." Jane leaned forward, her dark eyes sparkling. "I've wanted to tell you for the past two days."

Hannah shook her head. Had she heard aright? "What do you mean? Are you already engaged?"

"No. I am already in love, though." Jane sighed and leaped gracefully from her chair. "I told you about the Holdcrofts as we were leaving Tansley."

"Yes." She was still holding one half of a scone in each hand, a silly pose if there ever was one. She put one half down and rubbed her hand on her napkin.

"Well, I got to know them well when I was at Tansley, and, oh, I fell in love with Timothy Holdcroft. Hannah, he is everything I could ever love in a man. Wait until I tell you how we met." Jane spun around on one heel, her dark hair flying. "I was playing my violin out on the moor. You don't know how lovely it can sound when the wind begins to rise out there. Anyway, I was playing, and there he was. I stopped as soon as I saw him, because I must have looked so strange out there, playing by myself, but he begged me to continue. After that, we talked, and I walked over to his farm, and I knew this was where I was meant to spend the rest of my life."

Had Jane really said all of this, or was Hannah still dreaming? "You met Timothy Holdcroft out on the moor, and now you want to marry him? If that is so, then why all this bother about gowns and preparing for a London Season?" More to the point, why was she even here at Grant Park? If Jane was already practically engaged, then her efforts were no longer required. Funny how that thought caused her heart to sink.

"John doesn't approve." Jane's shoulders slumped as she threw herself back into her chair. "I tried to tell him about Timothy and about the Holdcroft family, but he is determined that I should have a London Season."

"What were his particular objections?" She had an idea, but hated to put a voice to it. For some reason, it pained her to think that Reed would deny his sister's happiness over material wealth.

"What you would imagine if one's brother were an insufferable snob," Jane said with a sigh. "He told me that it was quite likely that Timothy is after my fortune, and that if he had to rise to the occasion as master of Grant Park, then I had to endure at least one Season. John is determined to do things the correct way, the way he says my father would have done things, even though it could break my heart."

Jane's eyes were now welling with tears, and Hannah would have a weeping, heartbroken, young damsel on her hands if she didn't take action soon. While Jane was much more sensible than Becky, she shared many qualities with Becky. So in dealing with Jane, she must use the same brisk practicality that served her well when dealing with her elder sister.

"I shall talk to Reed," she declared. "Perhaps I can make him see reason. The Holdcrofts have never struck me as the kind of people who would turn fortune hunter. Perhaps they don't have a great deal of money lying about, but they do own quite a bit of land in Tansley. Would marriage to Timothy make you happy, do you think?"

"Oh, yes," Jane breathed. She clasped her hands together. "He is quite the most wonderful, most amazing—"

"I understand," Hannah replied, cutting Jane off

with a wave of her hand. Now was not the time to wax poetic. "Where would I find your brother this morning? I will talk to him when we are done with breakfast."

"He is trying to fit himself into the role of care-taker of Grant Park, so I imagine he will be in his study," Jane replied with a shrug. "He's ill-suited to this life, but I must say he is giving it a go."

"I will talk to him before we do anything else this morning." Her heart sank a little at the prospect of talking her employer out of her job. She had been at Grant Park less than one day, but already it had wrought such changes in her life. Because of Grant Park, or more to the point, because of John Reed, she was no longer Nan Siddons. She was Hannah Siddons, and that transformation could never have happened while she was under the family's thumb back in Tansley.

She had rather anticipated more from her stay. She was looking forward to creating beautiful things and to working with Jane. But if Jane was already happy, then her job here was done. She must trust in God, knowing that His way was right.

This was the first time in quite a while that she hoped God was wrong.

John sat in the room his father had occupied every morning for as long as he could remember. He was at his father's desk, holding his father's favorite quill pen. He was supposed to be writing out figures in the ledger book, as Paul had shown him to do. The pen wouldn't write. He couldn't make it write. This house oppressed him. Everywhere he looked, he saw traces of his mother. The guilt was nigh unbearable. The weight of expectation and tradition had slowed his movements down to the point that he was like a stick stuck in molasses. Why was he here? Why was he pretending that he could do this?

In London, he would be waking up now with a blistering headache and a fierce need for coffee. He would have nothing planned for the day save anything to do with fun and amusement. When he grew tired, he would stretch out for a nap. When he was hungry, someone would feed him. Here, people expected him to provide. It was a terribly uncomfortable way to live.

There was a knock on the door and before he could even compose himself or arrange himself so that he looked as if he was actually working rather than tussling with difficult memories of the past or bemoaning his responsibilities, Hannah Siddons burst into the room.

He rose, casting aside the quill.

"If my sole purpose in life is to prepare your sister for matrimony, why, pray tell, did you tell her she couldn't marry?" She flung herself into a nearby chair, regarding him with an expression that was both fierce and somehow disappointed.

"I beg your pardon?" He sank back into his seat. Arguing with Siddons was better than engaging in nightmarish memories or pretending to be lord of the manor.

"Your sister has fallen in love with a young man, Mr. Timothy Holdcroft. She met him while she was in Tansley. When she told you of her feelings, you denied her your blessing and continued these ridiculous plans for a London Season. May I ask why?" She fixed him with a pointed glare.

"You seem to be intent on talking yourself out of a job," he rejoined. At least that answer gave him some time to find a more considered, measured response. "If Jane has a London Season, you have all the time in the world to create the kind of wardrobe that would have you become one of the most talked-about milliners or seamstresses in London. Why throw that away?"

Siddons's glare wavered and the color rose in her cheeks. "This isn't about my career," she said after a brief pause. "This is about Jane's happiness."

"My sister is of a shy and retiring nature, and would concoct any kind of excuse to stay away from the social whirl of London." He shrugged and sat back in his chair. How many times had Jane feigned illness to get out of even the most trifling of village affairs? She would much rather stay at home and play violin or read than dance at a ball. "I could see her making much more out of a friendship with the Holdcrofts if it meant foregoing a Season."

"She's not faking an engagement," Siddons snapped. "I truly believe she has fallen in love."

"I am still not convinced that she has truly lost her heart, but even if she has, she cannot marry a Holdcroft." How could he say this without sounding like a terrible snob? He rolled the quill back and forth across the desk. "You must understand what I am saying, Siddons. My sister has a role to play, as do I. If it were up to me, I would still be in London and someone else would run Grant Park. If my sister had her way, she would never have to attend another social engagement again. We have no choice in the matter, though."

"Why do you find it so difficult to be the master of Grant Park?" Siddons leaped from her chair and began pacing. "To have such security and wealth at your command—you do realize, don't you, that there are many people in this world who would happily change places with you?"

"I would gladly switch places in a heartbeat. It's no stroll in the park, I can assure you. There are aspects of this endeavor that are brutally painful. More to the point, it's a role that I find stifling."

"Painful? Stifling?" She fixed him with an incredulous stare, her blue eyes widening. "What on earth do you mean?"

"It's just not…fun." He faltered under her gaze. Fun was the only antidote to the pain, but saying the words out loud made his dilemma seem very weak indeed.

"There speaks a man who never had to worry about where his next meal was coming from." She rolled her eyes. "Life isn't always fun, Reed. Surely you know that."

"I do. But I also understand the importance of enjoying life while we can. I've seen wonderful people die without ever having a moment's pleasure." The words poured forth in a torrent and he was powerless to check them. "You don't understand, this isn't merely about frivolity or about doing only what I care to do. For years now, I have made a point to sample life's bounty while I could. Now that my father has died, it is up to me to manage this house and our family in the way he would have wished. My own feelings, my own wishes, no longer matter."

Siddons was staring at him, her head tilted to one side. This was the first time since their meeting that she was giving him her full attention. She was not formulating her response, nor was she distracted by her own cares and woes. Being listened to so fully was a heady experience. He was not used to anyone heeding a word he had to say, much less a woman.

"I do understand what you mean," she replied after a pause. "Duty must always come before pleasure."

"Yes." Yet even as he agreed with her, his mind staged its own revolution. Why should he care about whom Jane married? Why should he devote all his time to Grant Park? This house had asked everything of his family, especially Mother, and all had been given to it in the name of obligation. The strange, heady panic that seized hold of him whenever he thought of Mother and of Father and of the weight of his numerous responsibilities swept over him, crushing any spark lit by Siddons's interest in their conversation. He had no one to turn to for help while he was here. He grasped the quill so strongly that it snapped in his hands.

Siddons gave a pained gasp and her eyes widened, but she said nothing.

Just as well, for he had no reply at the moment. He was so good at social conversation, but if he had to continue now, all of the venom that filled his soul might spill forth. That might be a trifle bewildering, even to someone as staunch in character as Siddons.

"I… I am sorry I intruded, Reed. Please forgive me. I just want the best for Jane. She's a dear, a truly sweet-tempered girl, and I do wish her every happiness." Siddons rose, backing up a couple of feet. "We'll just continue our plans…as planned."

He gave a curt nod. It would still be best not to talk. Somehow, he trusted Siddons to never speak of the matter again. She was serious and perceptive, unlike anyone he had called friend while in London. The crowd he ran with chased pleasure, which was exciting enough, but he would never trust anyone as far as he could throw them.

Siddons bobbed a brief curtsy and bustled out of the room. As the door closed behind her, he allowed himself one long sigh.

Grant Park would either bring him to heel, or cost him his sanity.

## Chapter Six

Hannah was not one to back down from an argument, but the look in John Reed's eyes and the sharp tone of his voice had been enough to end any attempt at intervention on her part. She gathered her skirts and mounted the steps, making her way back to Jane's wing of the house. While she had expected to berate a lazy young buck who thought of no one but himself, or perhaps a snob who found the idea of country in-laws beneath him, she had confronted something else. John Reed was angry, full of a smoldering, white-hot wrath. Who knew that the carefree prankster she'd come to regard as a necessary pest would have a deeper, darker side?

Her knees were still shaking. What had she to fear? After all, even as furious as he was, Reed would never cause her harm. It was just being close to that much raw, passionate anger was a daunting experience— rather like standing on the precipice of one of the cliffs out on the moor, unsure if one slip of her foot could hurl her headlong over the edge.

Jane stood waiting at the top of the stairs. "What did my brother say?" She clasped her hands over Hannah's arm. "Upon my word, you are trembling. Was he that awful?"

"He was just… He was merely…" Hannah could not catch her breath. "Could we go to your room?"

"Of course. Poor dear." Jane led her down the hallway and into her room. "I am so sorry he was mean to you. I can't thank you enough for even trying to talk sense to him." Jane pressed her into a chair and scurried back to close her door. "I suppose, then, the talk didn't go well?"

"He doesn't want you to associate with the Holdcrofts any longer." Nan smoothed her hands over her skirt in an effort to calm their shakiness. "He feels—very strongly, I must say—that he has his duties and you have yours, and that personal feelings must not get in the way of these obligations."

Jane sat in the chair opposite, her long, dark hair swinging around her shoulders. "Yes, I know. He's made that quite clear to me, too."

Hannah glanced at Jane. Had he shown his anger to her as well? Somehow, she needed to relate the past few moments to someone else—to understand and to dissect what had happened—because it was so very far from what she had assumed would happen. "Jane, to own the truth, he seemed quite incensed."

"Yes. I can imagine. John can have quite a temper when he chooses." Jane heaved a great sigh. "He's very upset that he must live here and be master rather than live a debauched bachelor life in London."

"This went beyond mere disappointment." Hannah suppressed a shiver. This was fury in its most basic form. So strange when, really, all he was being asked to do was what every other man of his class was called to do. Such a basic fact of life should have been readily apparent and understood. Why, then, the ferocity of his countenance? His eyes had smoldered like coals in a grate. "This was inexplicable, really."

Jane leaned forward, grasping Hannah's hands in hers. "You must help me, then. You'll be returning to Tansley often. When you go back, would you send word to Timothy? I can even write a letter and you can give it to him."

"What?" Hannah drew back sharply. "You intend to continue, even though your brother has told you no?"

"If John wants me to have a London Season, then I will go along with it. But I shan't marry anyone except Timothy Holdcroft. I want to tell him so. I want to let him know that no matter how many crowded ballrooms I am pressed into—thanks to my brother's pride—I will wed no one but the man I truly love." Jane gave her a tremulous smile and unshed tears sparkled in her eyes.

Hannah sat still for a moment, trying to wrap her mind around the issue at hand while still reeling from her encounter with Reed. She knew nothing of the Holdcrofts, save that Mrs. Hugh bought a few bonnets from her and seemed a nice enough woman. Had Jane fallen head over heels for a man who was merely after her fortune? Or had she stumbled across true love? "I cannot, in all fairness, go against your brother," she began slowly.

Jane released her grasp on Hannah's arms as a single tear trickled down her cheek.

"Please help me, Nan! I mean, Hannah." In her obvious distress, Jane must have forgotten how she should refer to her dressmaker, even though her brother had made it abundantly clear upon their arrival. "I must be with Timothy. Ever since we left Tansley, I can think of nothing but him. I know he is the right man for me."

What could she do? Jane was, quite frankly, the only friend she had apart from her sisters. Jane was a wonderful person, kind and generous. Though her romanticism did put one in mind of Becky, how could she not feel a pull to come to her new friend's aid?

On the other hand, she had already discussed this matter directly with her employer. Reed was the man who offered her this position in the first place, giving her the chance to prove herself on her own two feet. More to the point, Reed was the man who would assure that she was paid to do the job he hired her to do. What kind of trust could she build if she went behind his back, when he'd made his position about the Holdcrofts perfectly clear?

"I will not do anything covert or untoward," she pronounced. "Perhaps, over time, I can help you bring your brother around to your position. I can also find out if the Holdcrofts are good, honest people."

Jane opened her mouth to protest, but Hannah cut her off with a wave of her hand. "Yes, yes, I know that you hold the entire family in high regard, but I shall investigate them anyway. I consider it my duty to you as a friend." When she returned to Tansley, she would become as stealthy as a thief-taker, gathering clues without arousing suspicion.

Jane finally sagged against the back of her chair, as though their conversation had exhausted her. "Very well. I know it's a lot to ask of you, Hannah. I wouldn't ask if I didn't feel you were a dear friend."

Hannah's heart warmed. It was difficult indeed not to be swept off her feet by the sheer novelty of her new situation. Over the years, her position in the Siddons family had shifted. Once considered a vital part of the triangle of sisters, she felt increasingly left out and left behind. She was the scold, the nag, the voice of stolid reason. To her hotheaded siblings, she was the dousing of cold water being poured from a bucket. She was told what to do, expected to follow orders and often protested against her assignments. Her sisters loved her, of course, and she loved them. But it had been a long time since she felt welcomed in anyone's life.

At Grant Park, she mattered. Of course, she was being paid to do a job. But it was a pleasant change all the same.

"I like it here very much," she ventured. It was difficult to voice her opinion of the Reeds out loud, for biting back her own emotions had become second nature to her over the years. "I consider you a dear friend, too."

"Thank you. I feel so much better knowing that you will help me." Jane leaped from her velvet chair and trotted over to the window, throwing the lace curtains aside. "What a lovely day it is, after all."

Hannah laughed. "Now that we have the problem of your suitor under control, shall we turn our minds to your wardrobe? It is, after all, the reason I am here."

Jane nodded, and Hannah quit the room in search of her sketch pad. As she walked down the hallway to her own suite of rooms, the image of John Reed's burning eyes would not abate. If only she was a good artist, perhaps she could sketch a picture of him as he looked at that moment, as he clenched his hands so the knuckles turned white, his handsome face tense with suppressed rage.

Perhaps if she committed the memory to paper, it would cease to flicker in her own mind.

*Get ahold of yourself, man.* John paced the floor of his study like a caged tiger, unable to calm himself since he lost control of his emotions while talking to Siddons. Why had she driven him to a place that he had hidden so artfully that even he forgot it existed? She really could get under a person's skin. Small wonder, then, that her sisters had precious few kind words to say about her.

That wasn't fair. Nor was it gentlemanly. It wasn't Siddons's fault that he hated Grant Park and that he despised shouldering his burden. After all, she couldn't know that work and responsibilities and woes had been his mother's demise.

His thoughts shut down, as though somewhere in the recesses of his mind, someone had blown on a candle, causing it to gutter but not entirely burn out.

What could he do? There was nowhere to go. Grant Park was miles away from fun and frivolity. He could drink, but drinking alone was never much fun, and usually made him grow more maudlin and morose.

He had no friends here within visiting distance. Paul was two hours away, and he had just come from Paul's anyway.

Irritated beyond measure, he rang the bell.

Within moments, his butler, Forset, answered. "Yes, sir?" He had been in service to the family since John's mother and father were wed and had seen Grant Park through the difficulty of Mother's passing. He was the foundation of the house, and as such, always cast a decidedly baleful eye on John. Normally this would be the start of some great fun on John's part, but not today.

"What, if anything, is going on in my house?" He needed a distraction. Anything would be welcome.

"I beg your pardon, sir?" Forset's countenance remained impassive, save for a small twitch in the vicinity of his eyebrow.

"My sister. Siddons. Where are they and what are they doing?" The unreasonable feeling of anger simply would not abate.

"I believe they are working on Miss Jane's wardrobe, sir. Plans for her Season in London." Forset bowed as though he had fulfilled his duty and would now be on his way, off to check on something in the kitchens or whatever it was that butlers did.

"Just a moment, Forset." He struggled to curb the harsh edge that still gave his voice that bite. "What else is going on?"

"Going on? I don't quite understand your meaning." Forset faced him, a look of genuine confusion on his wrinkled countenance. "Not meaning to be impolite, sir. I just don't understand what you wish to know."

"Grant Park is a vast estate, full of all manner of things of which I am supposed to be master." Did Forset's eyebrow raise just a hair at "supposed?"

"Now, I wish to know if anything of interest is happening today. Something of which I should be a part." He lifted one shoulder defensively, as though someone might strike him. He should know all the doings in his own home. It was, after all, his business.

"Well, I am still not certain I catch your meaning, but there are a few interesting things that have transpired this morning." Forset nodded thoughtfully. He no longer appeared confused or annoyed, but merely absorbed with trying to recall all the minutiae of the morning's events. John's heart surged with gratitude. "Aside from Miss Siddons working with Miss Jane, there are some workmen building a new pigsty farther away from the barn. Another group of men are working out in the fields. Cook is preparing the afternoon meals, not just for the main house but also food to be carried out to the workers. There were a litter of puppies born in the barn, as well."

That was the only thing that sounded remotely interesting. He stroked his chin. "Very well. All right, thank you, Forset."

Forset bowed, his face returning to the same impenetrable mask of courtesy he always wore, and left.

John waited a reasonable amount of time after his butler left and then dashed from the room. He didn't want to seem overly enthusiastic about a litter of puppies, after all. Fawning over adorable fuzzy creatures was his sister's purview, not his.

As he passed through the back corridor, he grabbed a greatcoat off a hook. There were several of them in a row, waiting to be used by houseguests as they tramped off over the moors or through the pastures. Having several warm coats made in a variety of sizes had been his mother's idea, born when a houseguest neglected to bring his own cloak and the weather turned suddenly foul. From that moment on, Mother saw to it that all the comforts of one's own home were available to everyone who came to Grant Park.

She saw to everyone's needs, and not her own.

He tugged the warm wool around his shoulders and strode out the back door. The gentle spring sunshine gilded the pastures, highlighting the lingering frost on the grass, which glittered as though diamond dust had been scattered over the fields. He paused a moment, taking in the view. Yes, Grant Park was a pretty property. Anyone would agree that a man would be well-set indeed to have such a home. It was mildly prosperous, too. Large and with enough resources that it took care of itself, in a way. If only he could find a way to manage it from afar.

The horse stable was only a short distance from the house, and it was likely that one of the grooms had put the dog there to give birth. He continued on his way, breathing deeply the scents of hay and horses. There was something about those smells that banished all his bad feelings to the back of his mind, along with the anxiety, and the grief.

He spied the head groom as he drew nearer to the

redbrick barn. "Hullo, Davis!" he called, cupping his hands around his mouth. "Heard we have some new arrivals."

"We do indeed," Davis called back. He tugged at his cap. "Come and take a look."

When John got close enough to Davis, he held out his hand. Davis clasped it warmly, the wrinkles around his eyes deepening. He couldn't stand on ceremony with Davis—one of the best grooms not just in this county, but likely in all of England. The man could heal lame horses, mend broken stirrups, help puppies and kittens into the world and break green colts, all with a genuine kindness of nature that made him one of the most beloved denizens of the Park.

"It's our collie girl, Madge," he said, motioning for John to follow. "She had four this morning. Two boys and two girls, quite a little set of pups!"

John followed him into the barn, which was warm and sweet with the smell of hay and oats. There, in the corner of a stall, lay Madge. Her kind brown eyes regarded him warily. Four little mites, their eyes still tightly shut, mewed and rolled about in the straw.

"Easy there, Madge." John kept his voice soft and low. "I just came to see them. I promise I won't disturb you."

Madge put her head down and closed her eyes, but her ears remained pricked and at attention.

"She's a good mother. Those will be fine dogs, too. I think they would be good at sheep-herding, or perhaps even hunting. If they're at all like her, they could be trained to do anything."

John nodded, watching the mother and babies.

These little ones were learning their way about, just as he was learning his, stumbling along until he got the rhythm of life at Grant Park. "I'd like to help you with their training," he blurted. All at once, the thought of helping raise and train these dogs was interesting, an antidote to the blank disgust he felt with the Park and himself in general.

"Of course," Davis replied.

They stood in silence, John's arms hanging over the stall door as he watched mother and pups. This was a new beginning for them—and for him, as well.

## Chapter Seven

Hannah strode off over the pasture at Grant Park, a lady of leisure for the moment. Funny, she'd never had time to relax before. Not really. She had always worked, from sunup to sundown. If she wasn't doing needlework, she was stirring the fire to life, or helping to make meals, or mending her own clothing. The Siddons girls were industrious, because they had to be. At Grant Park, someone else stirred the fires and made the meals. Her sole responsibility was to make Jane Reed beautiful. Now that job was well in hand, she had time to herself, to enjoy the delights Grant Park had to offer.

They had worked on that together in Jane's room for precisely an hour before Jane turned to her. "I must go study my violin," she had pronounced, and then skipped off to do precisely that. Hannah could spend her time profitably, perhaps by organizing her sketches or going through her notions basket to come up with pieces of trim for bonnets, but somehow the outdoors just called her. It was a particularly fine day, and she would have plenty of time for work in the afternoon.

She picked up her skirts and made her way down a small hill, then turned and looked behind her. Grant Park stood majestically against the bright blue sky, rising up from the moor as though it was a mere extension of nature. She had never been particularly fond of big houses. When she looked at a big house, all she could usually see was work and expense. She and Becky often played a game she called "Other Lives" when traveling, and they would picture their lives being different in the different houses they passed by. She could drive Becky to furious distraction by merely commenting on the cost of glazing windows, but there it was. Big houses meant big expense, and in her heart of hearts she knew she must be thankful for the small houses that the Siddonses would come to call home. She knew even in girlhood that she must not grow enamored of an elaborate mode of living. There was no way on earth she would attract the master of a large house such as this. Better to be happy with her lot in life.

Grant Park was different, though. It called to her, for some reason. When she gazed at its lovely redbrick facade as she did now, she just saw the grandeur of it, and its proud tradition. Beautiful women had danced there, handsome men had come there for the hunt and adorable babies had been born there. This was a home for generations, a true family manor. It was strange and a little sad that neither Reed nor Jane seemed to appreciate what they possessed.

She set off at a brisk pace. Just a quick walk around

the grounds would help her feel more familiar with the Park, and would allow her some time to enjoy this glorious weather. She walked toward a squat redbrick building, built in a similar manner to the house so they matched one another nicely. It must be the barn. She wouldn't disturb the grooms as they went about their work, but it would be nice to see if the Grant Park stables had as many carriages and fine horses as her brothers-in-law had at their country homes.

As she skirted the edge of the field, John Reed came striding up from the barn, something small and furry tucked into the lapel of his greatcoat. When he caught sight of her, he paused, a sheepish look stealing over his face. He was like a schoolboy who'd been caught stealing apples.

She really wasn't prepared to see him, either. After all, the last time they spoke, he had been in a high temper, and she wasn't at her best herself. The only thing she could do was to brazen it out. Highly emotional scenes simply weren't her forte.

"What on earth are you doing, Reed?" she challenged, keeping her tone light. "You look like you've been caught in some mischief."

He held out the furry bundle, a grin crooking the corners of his mouth. "Well, our collie had puppies and this one seemed a bit sluggish. The other ones are fine. This one, though, I thought I could liven up a bit if I brought her to the house. Davis, my head groom, seems to think she's flagging."

Hannah reached out to touch the collie puppy's soft fur. "She's so tiny," she gasped. "Why, even her eyes are still closed."

"Yes. I thought I could try feeding her myself with a bottle." Reed tucked the puppy back into his jacket. "Madge, the collie, is a good mother. But the other three puppies are already taking up all her efforts, and this is the runt of the litter."

"You can't keep her out here much longer." The sun was shining, but frost still sparkled on the ground. A little thing like this—already fighting for life—couldn't last for very long in weather that was even mildly chilly. "Let's go inside. The kitchen is probably the warmest area of the house."

Reed nodded and tucked his hand around the puppy, closing her tightly into the warm wool of his jacket. Hannah's heart surged at this small gesture of kindness. Who knew that Reed, of all people, would have a tender heart where small creatures were concerned? She would have never guessed that he was capable of that level of sensitivity and compassion.

She struck off toward the house, then turned back. "I don't know where the kitchens are," she confessed. Honestly, she had only really explored Jane's side of the house, and this trek outdoors had been her way of broadening her horizons.

Reed paused, his brows drawing together. He shrugged slightly. "I must confess that I haven't been to the kitchens for ages," he replied. "In fact, it was so long ago, I had to stand on a stool to help Cook roll out dough for making cookies at Christmas."

For some reason, the thought of Reed standing on a chair made her chuckle to herself. How much he had changed since those days, surely. Now he was a grown man, easily over six foot tall, with the stubble of a beard already darkening his chin, though it was still morning.

"I am sure they haven't moved it since then," she replied. "Lead the way."

Reed sighed and then set off for the rear of the house. She followed, trying her best to keep her skirts clear of the frost. It was no use, though. Once they finally reached the back gardens, the hem of her skirt was well and truly soaked.

Reed hesitated for a moment after they climbed the back staircase. Then he squared his shoulders, lowered his head and opened the door.

Was he nervous? No, that couldn't possibly be so. What had he to be anxious about? This was his house, after all.

Hannah followed him into the kitchens, which hummed with activity. Scullery maids and kitchen maids dashed about, while a woman barked orders at the top of her lungs. The woman's red hair, which was fading to white, was tucked up under a cap and a large apron covered her ample form. She paused for a moment, wiping the sweat from her brow with the corner of her apron. When she dropped the fabric and glanced up, she spied Reed.

"Master John? Is that you?" She bustled around the wooden table she'd been working at, her arms outstretched. She gave Reed a quick hug, squeezing his shoulders. "Upon my word, it's been ages. Have you come to make cookies, then?"

Hannah chuckled, and the sound caught the cook's attention. "You must be the new seamstress working with Miss Jane. How do you do? My name is Mrs.

Hawkes, though this scoundrel always called me Mrs. H." She cast a fond glance at Reed.

Should she curtsy or nod? She had never been around servants for very long, for Uncle Arthur employed just a few. Then, of course, when they lost all their fortune, the Siddons girls had to make do for themselves. Unsure what to do, and with time dragging on, she finally just nodded. "Hannah Siddons, Mrs. Hawkes. So pleased to meet you."

Mrs. Hawkes nodded in return, a kindly light kindled in her brown eyes. "Pleased to make your acquaintance." She turned to Reed, placing her hands on her hips. "Well, then, are you here to filch something to eat? You know very well that I'll be serving a meal in less than an hour."

"Actually, Mrs. H., we need someplace warm and cozy for this mite." He opened his jacket, revealing the puppy.

"Oh, the poor thing! Of course, let's set the beggar inside here." She flew over to a vast cast-iron oven, opening one of the many compartments with a quick turn of her wrist. She removed a pan of bread, which had risen beautifully, and tucked several thick towels inside. "There's no real fire in here," she explained, taking the puppy from Reed and placing it on the mat of towels. "But the heat from the stove reaches it just so—perfect for helping bread to rise quickly, and for bringing puppies to life."

She closed the door just a bit, so that they could still observe the puppy. Hannah smiled. This was the best place in the world for that little one to be. She breathed deeply of the scents of newly risen bread dough, yeasty and warm. Her stomach rumbled in acknowledgment, and she pressed her hand over her middle. How embarrassing, or, as Susannah would say, how perfectly perfect.

She would never pass for an elegant young working lady, that much was certain. Surely Reed would tease her mercilessly.

If he heard, though, he gave no sign. Instead, he was staring intently at the puppy as she slept.

Mrs. Hawkes smiled, taking both Hannah's hands in hers. "Would you like a bite to eat while you wait to see how the puppy takes to the warmth? I've a new loaf of bread, some fresh butter and honey. And I can have some tea ready, as quick as a wink."

"That sounds marvelous, Mrs. H., thank you." Reed spoke up in an abstracted fashion from his place in front of the stove.

Mrs. H. swatted him with a towel. "I was speaking to the young lady, Master John. Not everything is tied to your well-being, you know." Her tone was light and playful, but even so, what cheek for a servant to give her master! The cook must have been employed by the family for ages to speak so freely.

John smiled and stirred himself from his absorbed state. "You are entirely correct, Mrs. H."

The cook laughed and beckoned them over to a long oaken table in the middle of the kitchen.

"May I help, Mrs. Hawkes?" Hannah hated to sit down and be waited upon when there was obviously so much going on. "I miss cooking with my sisters. The busyness of this kitchen puts me in mind of home."

"Bless you! Yes, please. I'll boil the water for tea if you will slice the bread." Mrs. Hawkes presented her with a loaf of golden-brown bread on a wooden tray and handed her a sharp knife. "And it's Mrs. H. I don't mind if you are cheeky with me, my dear. You have the look of a girl with a sharp wit and common sense."

Hannah glowed under this unusual praise and set the tray on the table. As she sliced the bread, she caught Reed's smiling glance. "What's so amusing, sir?"

He shook his head. "Just—I can't really say."

"You had better say," she commanded. Something in Mrs. H.'s free and easy manner caught in her attitude. "After all, I am wielding a knife."

John laughed. "Ah, I see. I am bested by your ferocious nature." Some of the pleasure faded from his heart as he glanced around the kitchen. "It's just really…nice…to be here." There was no real way to say it aloud, especially to someone as unfamiliar with his past as Siddons was. The warmth and ease of Mrs. H.'s ways, the good smells emanating from the kitchen, made him feel as though everything would be all right. Even the puppy, tucked away in its warm bed, would revive.

Siddons sliced the bread with the efficiency born, surely, of much practice. "It's very pleasant here," she agreed. "I can imagine, as a child, how this must have seemed like a wonderland."

"It was." He nodded. Siddons understood his fumbling explanations more than he did, even. "The scents, the sights, being so warm and cozy on a chilly day—it was easily my favorite part of the Park. Save, perhaps, the stables."

"Ah, yes." Mrs. H. brought over a stack of plates—sturdy pottery, not the fine china she sent upstairs. "Master John would come through here, grabbing a basket of apples on his way out to the stable. If I saw him, I would demand he bring them back. Many's the time, however, that his mother's guests were denied an apple tart because this rogue had fed them all to the horses."

John's heart caught in his throat. Yes. Mother would invite everyone over to the Park at the slightest excuse, sharing the bounty of the kitchens and the estate with all the families in the county. Or, she would grab a large willow basket, stuffing it with provisions, on her way out to visit the tenants. Always, her thoughts were on making others comfortable.

She thought of everyone else, especially of her family. She had given up everything she had for him. If there was a God, why had He allowed that to happen? He, John, was not worthy of her sacrifice, not at all. Though he had tried to live as he would have wanted for her to live—enjoying herself and taking pleasure from life—it was painfully obvious that a great lady like his mother would never have approved of his high jinks.

Could he dwell on this thought of Mother without breaking down into tears like a child? No. He focused his full attention on Siddons as she placed a slice of bread on the plate and handed it to him. Then he gave the butter and honey as much of his focus as he could. By forcing himself to think only of the mechanics of his movements, he could banish the memory back to its hiding place until it was safe to blink again.

He took a bite of the bread, savoring its warmth.

The moment had passed.

Siddons sat in the chair across from him, pouring tea into a sturdy mug and handing it to him. "Here. Take this. It's been quite a morning, hasn't it?"

Did she suspect how close he'd been to acting like a fool? He shot her a glance from under his eyebrows, but she seemed to be casually intent on sipping her tea.

"Yes, it has." He had to say something, take control of his own life once again. If, of course, a conversation with a seamstress in a kitchen could be considered his life in miniature. "So. Once the puppy is revived, I suppose I need to feed her?"

"Yes. I would think warm milk." Siddons took a bite of her bread.

"Mrs. H, can you please warm some milk for me?" He raised his voice to be heard above the kitchen din.

"The milk is warm, and you can feed it to the pup with this bottle." Mrs. H held out a glass bottle, which she had fitted with some kind of stopper.

"Is that the finger of a glove?" Siddons applauded. "Mrs. H, you are a brilliant woman."

"Well, it's been many years since we've needed a baby bottle around the house," Mrs. H. explained with a warm smile. "But perhaps we will need one someday soon. Eh, Master John?"

John forced a smile, but it was hard indeed. *In due time, Mrs. H, in due time.* It was difficult enough to reconcile himself to the role he had to play as master here. Doing so meant taking full responsibility for all he had done. That would have to occupy his thoughts for the next several months. There was no room in his heart yet to think of love.

## Chapter Eight

Hannah put the final touches on her sketch and then turned the pad about so it faced Jane. "What do you think?"

Jane, who was sitting in the window seat, put aside her violin and squinted. "Oh, yes. Very pretty." Then she picked up her bow and continued practicing.

Hannah tried not to sigh in frustration. She had been sketching some truly fetching costumes for Jane all morning, while Jane sat and played, making pleasant but noncommittal remarks about each drawing. She turned the sketch pad back around and deepened the shade of a ribbon with a few broad strokes of her pencil. "Oh, come now. This is much more than pretty. This is an organdy gown with a deeply embroidered skirt in a pale shade of pink, just the right color to heighten your complexion. It is topped off with a simple velvet Spencer jacket in a darker shade of blush pink and a fetching straw bonnet that ties under the chin."

Jane laughed, drawing her bow across the strings

with a lilting touch. "You sound like a High Street dressmaker."

"I am a dressmaker." Even though Jane was protesting a London Season, how could anyone protest such lovely clothes, made expressly to enhance her natural beauty? Why didn't Jane take this venture seriously? Or at the very least, why didn't she take a sincere interest in Hannah's role? This was an amazing opportunity for anyone. In her own case, making this wardrobe was the start of something she could call her own, something that had the potential to make her independent.

"I apologize." Jane sat up, putting her violin and bow aside once more. "I don't mean to sound unappreciative. You must understand how this seems to me—all these frills and furbelows. I never had to worry about my appearance before. Now that all this emphasis is being placed on how I look and what I should wear, it's difficult indeed not to feel like I journeyed to a new world."

"Didn't your mother prepare you for this?" Hannah turned her head to one side, regarding her sketch from a slightly different angle. Perhaps she should lengthen the jacket just a tiny bit. Jane needed to raise her arms often when playing, and each piece must be designed with that in mind, for Jane was as likely to break into a solo when wearing a riding habit as when wearing a ball gown.

"No. I was too young when she passed away. I was only eight years old. John was eleven, just a lad." Jane sighed. "I am sure Mother would have seen to it, but when she died, Father was heartbroken. Indeed, our entire family was. Father didn't force me to do anything I didn't wish to—he said it broke his heart to see me unhappy." She drew her knees up to her chest, wrapping her long skirt around her legs. "I wish my brother felt the same way."

"I suppose he's just trying to do the best he can," Hannah pointed out. Jane was a dear, but so focused on her own thoughts and feelings that it blinded her to all her brother had done for her. Not many other men would have hired someone to guide a stubborn younger sister's debut.

"He could save us all a lot of trouble and just let me wed where my heart has led me," Jane replied, her gentle voice sharpening. "I do love your dresses, Hannah. Please don't think that I hate your work. But every sketch just shows me how little regard my brother has for my feelings and wishes. It's like every dress is a cell in a prison."

"Don't be ridiculous." Hannah fought to keep her tone light, but Jane's attitude grated on her last nerve. Like her brother, Jane was rebelling against a very luxurious gaol. These were people who never had to worry about where their next meal was coming from, or how they would stay warm at night. It was difficult indeed to sympathize with either of them. "Why don't you just enjoy having lovely clothes and attending dazzling parties? After all, if the Season ends without your engagement, then you can say you held up your end of the agreement. You would be in a much better position to persuade your brother that you should marry Timothy Holdcroft."

"I suppose that's true," Jane murmured in a distracted fashion. After a moment's pause, she added, "Will you help me get word to Timothy? You leave to visit Tansley in a week, do you not?"

"I do." Hannah put aside her sketch, drawing in a deep breath. "But I have already made it clear that I will respect your brother's wishes in this matter. He is my employer, and has given me orders not to interfere." It was so sad to be put in this kind of position with Jane, who was a lovely person and someone whose friendship she enjoyed very much. In fact, Jane remained the only friend she had, and telling her "no" about anything was daunting. Somewhere, in the back of her mind, Hannah expected Jane to simply end their friendship over her refusal to help foster her budding romance. She was resigning herself to losing this delightful closeness with Jane with each passing minute.

"I understand. I just wondered." Jane gave her a sweet smile. "It will be nice for you to go home and see your sisters again. I imagine you miss them quite a lot."

Hannah nodded, for that was the correct reaction to Jane's words. But in truth, she did not miss her sisters as much as she had thought she would. She could be frank in her own mind. It was actually very nice to have few responsibilities and no one holding her back, commenting on how she did what she did and how she should improve herself all the time. "I'm actually more worried about how my hat shop is faring. I haven't received word from Abigail, and I left her in charge."

"Then you will definitely want to visit your shop,"

Jane agreed. "Perhaps you will even end up staying there, rather than in one of your sisters' homes."

"I certainly hope so," Hannah blurted. Not that she didn't love her sisters, but after her brief taste of freedom at Grant Park, staying at Susannah's or Becky's would be stifling.

Jane smiled and picked up her violin once more. She began playing a piece by Lully that she had been working on for the past several days. With each practice, the song took on a little more life. What had been hesitant at first was growing more assured and dynamic with each playing. With each playing, too, Hannah had learned to respect Jane's space. She could not continue to interrupt and ask questions or opinions of each gown she sketched. She was quite on her own.

Hannah squinted at the sketch pad with a critical eye. There was nothing more to be done with this sketch, for the gown was as perfect as it could be. All that remained was purchasing the fabric and cutting out the pieces. Perhaps when she went home to Tansley, she could find several bolts of fabric at the village shop. It wouldn't hurt to see how the French milliner was doing, either.

Somehow, though, the thought of the milliner stealing her business no longer stung. In point of fact, it was difficult for her to work up the same fire to continue fighting that had burned within just a few weeks ago. She flipped over to a fresh page on her sketch pad and picked up a pencil. The urge to sketch dresses had utterly fled. Instead, she allowed her mind to drift along with the sweet violin music, like a leaf catching the current of a small stream, and she merely sketched as she floated along.

With a few broad strokes, she outlined the figure of a man, tall, broad-shouldered, with a square jaw. He was bareheaded, and his hair was ruffled by the wind. She roughed out his greatcoat, and with a few quick lines, added his hands. One hand protected a small puppy, cradling it against the shelter of his chest.

She could no longer hear Jane playing, for her sketch commanded all her attention. She shaded carefully around the gentleman's face, playing up the mysterious shadows around his eyes. For a man who made such a show of being a joker and a scamp, he had an enigmatic look about him that made one step back and search for more answers. She filled in the puppy, too, using short, fine marks to delineate her soft fur and delicate ears.

"Why, it's John!" Jane spoke up from behind Hannah's shoulder.

Hannah dropped her pencil.

"What a lovely sketch," Jane continued. "You've captured him, you know. He looks like he could speak at any moment."

"When did you stop playing?" Hannah took a deep breath, trying to calm the hammering of her heart in her chest. How long had Jane been sitting there? Not too long, surely. She never meant for anyone to see this sketch. In fact, she never really meant to sketch it herself. She was merely floating along to the music.

How ridiculous that sounded, now that Jane's song had ended.

"A few moments ago. I saw how absorbed you

were in your sketch and I came over to see what you were working on. You have the soul of a painter, you know. This is quite astonishing." Jane turned her head slightly, examining the drawing more closely. "You could be a portrait artist."

"Oh, no." Hannah gave a nervous laugh. No one knew about her sketches, because she kept them well hidden. Even her sisters never suspected that she could sketch anything beyond a bonnet or a gown. "It's just a squiggle. I don't really indulge myself. It's not practical, you see."

"Well, I don't know if it's practical, but it certainly is beautiful," Jane pronounced. "My brother will love it, I am sure."

"I shan't show anyone else, and you mustn't tell him." Oh, mercy, the teasing that she would endure if John knew she'd been sketching him. She would never hear the end of it. To be caught sketching a handsome rogue—why, the humiliation would be unendurable. "My sketches are a mere hobby. I don't wish anyone to know."

Jane nodded, her dark eyes kindled with a gentle light. "Of course. I understand. I don't like to play violin in front of everyone." She patted Hannah's shoulder and then settled herself back in the window seat, drawing her chin up to her knees as she stared out the window.

Hannah's face burned as though she sat too close to the fire. With trembling fingers, she picked up her pencil. *Control yourself, you fool.* She turned over to a fresh page. There was no time for indulging herself in any kind of reverie. She was at Grant Park for one purpose only—to create lovely ensembles for Jane Reed. John Reed was not the kind of man who would like a plain girl like her, for that's what she was. Her place in life had been ingrained in her as long as she could remember.

With renewed dedication, she clenched her jaw and began roughing out a sketch for a riding habit. This was her purpose in life, and this was why she was here. Anything else was mere folly.

John held the puppy gently, feeding her with the bottle that Mrs. H had devised. He had been feeding the pup every few hours since bringing her home. Sometimes he could coerce his valet, Williams, into feeding her. Sometimes, he could ask Mrs. H for help. But for the most part, it had been him, every few hours over the past few days.

He could fall asleep right now, if he could but close his eyes—

A gentle knock at the door roused him. It must be Jane. She always knocked so quietly. Sometimes he could barely hear her.

"Enter," he said, stifling a yawn.

Jane popped her head around the door frame. "Oh, you have the pup with you. How sweet." She came over and sat beside him. "May I feed her?"

"Please, do. I am like a man dead on my feet." He shifted the puppy over to her. Jane held the pup with the same tender care as her prized violin. He stretched his limbs, giving way to a hearty yawn. Who knew taking care of a dog would be so much work?

Jane smiled. "You are exhausted. Why don't you

let Hannah and me help? We can work together, taking turns. At least until she's old enough to drink on her own."

"I daresay, that is a good thought." John rubbed the stubble on his chin. Here he was, exhausted, rumpled, unshaven—as bad as the time he spent a week in the gambling halls, moving from game to game. Only this time, his exhaustion was the result of taking care of another, not in indulging his own whims. "Where is Hannah, anyway? I haven't seen her. Of course, I've been rather occupied."

"She's been working with me, you ridiculous man," Jane replied with a soft laugh. "She is turning out sketch after sketch of gowns that should grace a princess. I will feel like a donkey passing herself off as a fine pony in those gowns. It's really not for me, John. It's really not."

"I know. I, too, feel like a fish out of water." He did not fancy another round with Jane. She never screamed or fussed, but her tears and gentle squabbling were enough to make him lose his reason. "We must become what Father and Mother meant us to be, Jane. You know that as well as I." Perhaps by reminding her that it wasn't a mere Draconian decision on his part, he could stave off her weeping.

Jane lapsed into silence. He rolled his head from side to side, trying to work the stiffness out of it. Should he bathe or eat first? Both were appealing at the moment. Or should he sleep? If only a man could find a way to do all three at once.

The puppy made a mewling sound and Jane cradled her closer. "She really is talented, John."

"Who?" He looked at the puppy, drawing his brows together. The pup? Surely it was still too young to tell if it was going to be a good hunter or sheep-herder.

"Hannah." Jane chuckled and shook her head. "I've seen her sketches. You know, she could have a career as a portrait artist. She has that gift. Even her sketches of gowns look as though they have movement in them. I can't imagine how she ended up as a milliner in a little country store. She could have royalty clamoring for her work."

"Well, as I understand it, the family was destitute. The millinery shop was their last stab at independence." Everyone had their roles to play, whether they liked it or not. Of course, he had never been destitute, but he had been desperate. He ran and ran until he could run no longer. Had Hannah faced that same sort of hunted feeling? No, probably not. She was so eminently practical and well-grounded that she had plodded along as best as she could.

"I want you to promise me something." Jane shifted slightly so the last bit of the milk could drain out of the bottle. "No matter what happens with my debut, I want you to make sure that Hannah is all right. She should have every opportunity to make something of herself."

"Well, we've given her the chance now," he replied. He rose, stretching once more. "This is better than toiling away at her country shop. Her competition will likely shut them down. She's establishing independence now."

Jane fixed him with her soft, yet rebuking, glare. "You must promise."

"Oh, very well." He was ready for bed, a bath and a meal. He would pledge anything to end this conversation, which, once more, was adding to his already sizeable pile of responsibilities. "I shall see to it that Miss Hannah Siddons has every chance to make something of herself."

## Chapter Nine

Hannah followed Jane into her brother's wing of the house. It was rather abashing, not just because he was a gentleman, but also because he was her employer. Of course, this entire estate was his to govern. Every inch of space in the house belonged to him. There was just something—not really troubling, that wasn't the emotion—just something *more* about seeing Reed's part of the house. This was where he spent his time eating, sleeping and reading. This was where he spent his intimate and quiet hours. Of course, she would never dream of setting one slipper in this side of the house, were it not for Jane's insistence that they would all help with raising the puppy.

In truth, she was glad of a little distraction. She had spent the past several days designing every kind of ensemble imaginable for Jane, and Jane had given her approval to everything. There was nothing more to do except begin the actual work. Provided, of course, she also had Reed's approval. She tucked her sketch pad closer to her body as Jane opened a door and ushered her into a pleasant little sitting room.

Reed was there, on a settee that was upholstered a deep shade of blue. The entire room was done in varying hues of blue, with heavy oak furniture, giving it a decidedly masculine feel. She curtsied briefly as Reed caught her glance.

"Don't stand on ceremony, Siddons. After all, you are seeing me at my absolute worst." Reed's voice sounded tired, and his smile was wan. "Here. Take her."

Hannah dropped her sketchbook on the settee and accepted the warm, furry bundle from Reed. The puppy had grown so much. In fact, she was fast becoming more than just a tiny little creature. At any time, her eyes would open, and then she'd be off, gaining independence with each day.

"Have you named her?" Jane came over and stroked the puppy's fur.

"No," John replied. He scrubbed his hand over his face.

"What?" Both girls cried in unison.

"I've been too busy keeping her alive," Reed protested, holding his hands up in a defensive gesture. "I don't have time for that responsibility, too."

"Fine. Then we shall name her." Jane shot her brother a scolding look. "What do you think, Hannah? What about Princess?"

"I refuse, under any circumstances, to baby a dog named Princess," Reed growled, his eyes tightly closed.

Despite herself, Hannah's mouth twisted in amusement. He was right. The dog was his, and it would be ridiculous for a young man to be calling for "Princess" while out hunting.

"What about Jill?" She shrugged, gently stroking the pup's fur with her forefinger. "It's short and feminine and you shan't worry about your masculinity if you call her when your hunting friends are out shooting with you."

Reed chuckled. "Too many *J* names in this house. Jane, John and then Jill. Somewhere someone would throw their hands up in horror at the alliteration."

Hannah smiled. "I suppose that's true. Molly, then."

Reed nodded thoughtfully. "Yes. I like it."

Jane beamed. "Molly it is."

Molly had finished the last of the bottle and was now snoozing comfortably in the crook of Hannah's arm. She hated to wake Molly, but it simply didn't do to sit around in Reed's study. She must show him her work and gain his approval. Then, when she journeyed to Tansley the next week, she could purchase the fabrics and begin the actual work of making the gowns.

She handed Molly over to Jane, taking care not to jostle her too much. Molly stretched one paw lazily toward the ceiling, but remained sound asleep.

"Reed, I have gotten Jane's approval on her wardrobe, and now I feel I should have yours." She scooped up the sketch pad and held it out to him. "Would you please look through my ideas?"

"Come, sit." He patted the seat beside him.

Hannah hesitated. Sitting next to him? That seemed a trifle forward. On the other hand, his sister was standing right there, and he looked absolutely fatigued. Her virtue was certainly not in any danger, so there was no need to be missish.

Even so, her pulse quickened as she took her place beside him. Could he see her heart racing or hear it pounding in her chest? She coughed loudly to cover the moment.

"Are you quite all right? I can ring for tea." John reached over and gave the bellpull a tug. "Now, let us see your work."

Hannah held her breath as he began examining each drawing with an interested, absorbed expression on his face. She had removed the sketch of him with Molly, so there was no need to worry about him stumbling across it. She had tried to throw it into the fire but couldn't bring herself to go that far. It was a good sketch, even if the inspiration had been John Reed. So she had tucked it away in a drawer, safe from anyone's sight.

"As you can see, I kept all of the garments very modest," she began hesitantly. It was easy enough to describe the gowns and her vision to Jane, but quite different to tell a gentleman about them. "The necklines are high but still accentuate Jane's natural beauty. I also use a lot of pink. I feel pink sets off her complexion perfectly."

They were briefly interrupted by the butler, whom Reed asked to bring tea. When the butler had respectfully bowed out, he continued his perusal of the sketchbook.

"Yes, of course, I can see how much you've tailored the dresses to my sister's tastes." Reed finished leafing through. "You've done excellent work. What do you need now?"

Hannah blinked. Always she had to find everything on her own. Having someone offer to help was so unusual. "I suppose now I need to gather together the fabrics, the notions and so forth. I had planned to do so when I returned to Tansley."

"When do you go back?" He handed her the sketch pad.

"On Monday. I decided that I would pack my trunk on Sunday after we attend church. Well, I assume we shall attend church services, as we seem to have missed them last week, and then I shall leave at first light." She had made the plan in her mind without consulting him, and now it all sounded rather bold. "Provided, of course, that this is acceptable to you."

"Yes, I'll provide you with the traveling coach," Reed replied. "We don't usually attend Sunday services. The church is in Crich, which is quite a drive, and I am not enough of a believer to make that journey every Sunday." He gave a bitter little laugh.

"My brother makes certain that any conversation about our Lord ends in ill feelings for all," Jane added, her normally soft tone taking on a hard edge. "I apologize if he has offended you, Hannah."

"I don't aim to make people uncomfortable." Reed rose from the settee. He looked distinctively uncomfortable himself. "I just don't have much use for a higher power."

The butler showed himself in, carrying a large tea tray. The moment was broken. Jane set Molly into her basket by the hearth and bustled about readying the tea. No more was said about church services or about Reed's lack of faith. Like his sudden, deep-seated rage, this was a surprising development. Not so much that he had a lack of faith, for there were plenty of young bucks milling around the gaming halls of London who had surely lost their way. Just that, once again, he seemed to have more depth than she had ever expected. A typical young man might say he had no time or had forgotten God. What Reed implied is that he had made a deliberate decision to set aside his religion.

Hannah accepted a cup of tea. Reed also took tea and a biscuit, and sat beside her. "Anyway, as we were saying, you shall travel on Monday. How long will you be gone?"

"I had hoped a week, if that is quite all right with you," she responded. She stirred her tea with the small silver spoon Jane had given her.

"Yes." He paused for a moment, taking a bite of the biscuit. "You'll return, though. Won't you?"

She laughed. "Of course I shall. I will have a lot of work to do. Once I have purchased what I need from the village shops, I will spend all my time sewing."

"Don't spend all your time working," he admonished. He turned in his seat, eyeing her frankly. "Write down a list of everything you will need for the wardrobe. I have a man in London who can arrange to purchase everything and send it down. Once you return, the materials will be here. I will also ask our housekeeper, Mrs. Pierce, to press two maids into service for you. You can use them to help sew, trim, baste—whatever you need."

He had thought of everything, and she would have very little to do on her own. How nice it was to have some of the burden shouldered for her. "Thank you."

"No, thank you." He leaned forward, his tired eyes kindled with a warm light. "Jane depends on you entirely, and I know you will help me in this endeavor. Anything you need, anything at all—you have only to ask."

For some ridiculous reason, the closeness of his person and the confidential tone in his voice caused a frisson of awareness down her spine. How absurd. She made a deliberate move to set herself away from him and capsized her teacup in the process. The commotion of cleaning her gown, setting the teacup to rights and apologizing for her clumsiness erased any illusions she was gaining about herself.

She was no swan. She would always be the plodding and predictable Nan.

After the girls left and Molly lay snoozing peacefully in her basket, John made his way to the barn to check on the other pups. It was a good idea to see how the mother and babies were doing, though if anything had gone wrong, he was sure Davis would have told him. Too bad Hannah was gone. He would have asked her to accompany him. Her company was becoming most satisfactory to him.

The barn was humming with activity as he drew near. A farrier was working with one of the draft horses, and several grooms were holding the Percheron steady. Stable lads were using the excellent weather as an excuse to muck out all the stalls and whitewash the stone walls. Davis was supervising their work, barking orders as the boys scattered to and fro.

"Davis," he called as he came close enough for his head groom to hear. Davis smiled and lifted his hand in greeting. John returned the wave. It felt strangely good to be near the barn, as if he had a purpose on this vast estate. Something more than that vague title of "Master," which meant heavy lifting, but it often felt like no real work.

"Madge and her pups are doing very well, sir," Davis began, tugging at his cap. "And how's the little one?"

"Hale and hearty." John clasped the groom's hand in greeting. "We've decided to call her Molly. Already she's the favorite of the house."

Davis chuckled. "Glad to hear that. They're all fine puppies. If they take after their mother, they could be the finest litter in the county."

Was this mere hyperbole, or was the groom really sure that they were an above-average group of pups? "Do you really think so?"

Davis nodded thoughtfully. "Come into the barn. I'll show you." He turned to one of the stable lads. "Jim, I expect this wall to be done by the time I get back. No idling or you'll catch the rough edge of my tongue. You hear?"

The boy nodded, a grin crooking the corners of his mouth. "Aye, sir."

Davis led the way into the barn, which hummed with far more commotion than it had during his previous visit. "Upon my word, you are turning the place inside out, Davis."

"Spring cleaning—we do it every year. During the winter months, it's difficult to keep the place as clean as it should be. Now that the weather's warm, we can get everything spick-and-span. Ah, here we are." He motioned John over to the same horse stall, where a fresh, bright layer of straw had been laid.

Madge lifted her head at their approach and wagged her tail. The puppies slept in a heap together, hardly stirring except for the rise and fall of their breaths. It was a cozy picture, to be sure.

"Now, Madge is the offspring of two magnificent collies that were your father's pride and joy. I am sure you remember them—Bah and Cleo. Cleo was an exceptional mother, as good as Madge here. Bah was your father's best hunting companion. Both of them the products of many generations of fine breeding. Grant Park has always produced the best dogs in Derbyshire."

"Have we really?" He was shockingly uninformed about this part of his estate. Of course, he remembered Bah—what a good old dog he was. But John had never stopped to consider more than that. Bah was just a dog. He was excellent on the hunt. That's all there was to it. That there could be more to the story, or that there were a few generations of history behind each pup—well, who knew?

"Yes. I always wondered why your father didn't go in for dog breeding in a big way. After all, the pedigrees at Grant Park have been excellent. He didn't really care for it overmuch. He thought of it as a mere pastime, I suppose." Davis shrugged and fell silent.

The germ of an idea grew in John's mind. Could this be something he could try? Something of Grant Park that could be uniquely his contribution to its well-being and its reputation? "What about training?"

"Ah, well. I never got much beyond trying to convince your father that he should breed dogs and sell them. Training them is another excellent idea. These dogs are all going to be bright and quick. They could be trained to do almost anything." Davis smiled. "I'd even say one or two of them could learn to dance, if we taught them."

John laughed. "They're that smart, then? Smart enough to dance their way through a crowded ballroom? Well, that is quite a feat, indeed." He stared at the pups. This could be his way of easing into life at Grant Park. He had, already, done well with Molly. Raising puppies was interesting, and training them could be, too. "Let's do it, then. Let's start with this litter. As they grow, we shall see which of them would be best bred for hunting, others for sheep-herding. We can continue to breed other litters. In time, this could become quite an interesting enterprise."

Davis clapped him on the shoulder. "Excellent thought, sir."

John's breath caught in his chest. Was he accepted now? There was something of respect in the old man's manner, something that went beyond the reserved, expected kind of deference he would receive as master. He was being accepted as a man in his own right, and it meant more to him than he cared to admit.

A sudden thought seized hold of him. What would Hannah have to say to all of this? He could hardly wait to tell her. She, of all people, would understand the importance of carving out one's own place in the world.

## Chapter Ten

"There, that should do it." Hannah closed her valise and turned to Jane with a smile. Ever since they had left her brother's suite yesterday, Jane had kindly helped her prepare for her journey. That morning, since no Sunday service was being held nearby, Hannah and Jane had read the Bible together and prayed. Then the quick business of packing had been accomplished, thanks largely to Jane's assistance. She had done everything, from folding Hannah's nightgowns to packing her handkerchiefs. She had even loaned Hannah a lovely leather case to carry the handkerchiefs in. Hannah protested Jane lending her the case, for what if she lost it or damaged it?

"Nonsense. Besides, I insist you leave it out in the shop as part of a display while you are gone. Who knows? Perhaps someone will see it and decide to order a bunch of embroidered handkerchiefs," Jane replied. Then she dropped the handkerchief case into the side pocket of the valise and gave it a little pat.

"Thank you so much, Jane. I must confess I could

not do all of this without your help." Hannah lugged the valise over to the doorway of her room.

"Don't worry about doing that," Jane admonished. "I am sure that one of the footmen will carry it downstairs for you."

"I know. It's just that I need to become accustomed to doing things on my own again," Hannah replied. "Everyone here is so helpful. I've never had this kind of aid. I am used to cooking my own meals, making my own bed, mending my clothes and stirring my own hearth to life every day." Going back home meant going back to being Nan, to working and toiling away for an uncertain future. She suppressed a shiver. She really wasn't looking forward to it, but the trip had to be made.

"Hopefully, all that work will make you hurry back all the sooner." Jane sank onto the window seat. "I shall be desolate without your friendship."

A knock sounded on the door, and one of the servant girls entered. "I beg your pardon, Miss Jane, but your brother says it is your turn to take the puppy." She brought in a large wicker basket, and as she set it on the hearth, Molly's fuzzy little face popped up over the basket edge.

"Oh, the darling thing." Jane rushed over to the basket. "Does she need another bottle?"

"The master said that she had just eaten an hour ago. I'll bring another bottle when she's ready for one," the maid answered, and then she bobbed a brief curtsy.

"I need to leave a list of the fabrics and notions I require for your wardrobe, Jane." Hannah turned to the maid. "Is the master available, if I take this list to him?"

"I believe so, miss. He was in his study when I brought the puppy here. Shall I take the list to him?"

"No, thank you." Hannah grabbed the sheet of paper, which she had torn from her sketch pad. "I need to explain some things to him. If he's available."

"Yes, miss. I believe he is." The maid looked over at Jane. "Shall I bring the bottle in an hour?"

"Certainly. She has been eating every two hours, so that should be perfect." Jane cooed at Molly and brought her out of the basket.

Hannah followed the maid out of the room, but when the maid turned to go downstairs, she continued across the landing. Butterflies seemed to have permanently settled in her stomach, and her hands had already begun to perspire. She must take care, or she would smudge her list. Perhaps she should entrust the maid with her list—but, no. This was her job, after all. She wanted to prove that she had planned everything out. Every piece of trim, every bit of fabric, was carefully accounted for. Not only would she create a gorgeous wardrobe, she would do so with efficient attention to the Reed fortune.

When she finally came to his study door, she paused for a moment. She must pull herself together. If going home was terrifying her so much, then she must do an outstanding job for the Reed family. There was no other way to save herself from a life of spinsterhood.

She wiped her hands on the front of her skirt and

knocked, then assumed the air of brisk competence that had served her so well all these years.

"Enter." He sounded tired. She must not take up more of his time than absolutely necessary.

She showed herself in. "Sir, I wish to give you the list of materials I will need for Miss Jane's wardrobe."

"Is that you, Siddons? Upon my word, I am glad to see you. Come, sit." He was stretched out on the settee, his long booted legs hanging off the end of it. "Forgive my dishabille. I am utterly exhausted."

"Um, yes. I understand." She bustled over and sat opposite him. "I shan't take up much of your time. I just wanted to show you what I need and how much. You see—"

"Yes, yes." He ran his hand over his eyes. "Just put it there, Siddons." He nodded to a nearby table.

She stared for a moment at its polished mahogany surface. Really? Just leave it there? "I did want to let you know how I had planned everything out."

"My dear Siddons, at present I am so fatigued that I can hardly bring myself to pronounce the second syllable of your name, much less feign interest in calculations about furbelows." He yawned hugely. "Just leave it there."

She must do as she was told. There was no sense in pushing harder. If she did, she could easily lose the foothold she had gained. "If you are certain, sir." She flicked the list over onto the table and sat, clasping her hands in her lap.

He rose up on one elbow. "Why are you calling me sir? Just for that, I am shortening your name. Henceforth, you shall be known as Sid."

"I am trying my level best to be professional," she snapped. *Temper, temper. Count ten, just like Susannah would recommend.*

"Well, don't. It doesn't suit you. Come on, be the jolly girl I know you can be." He lolled back, reclining against his pillow once more. "At least take pity on me, the poor substitute mother for the runt of a litter."

"Poor man." She fluttered her eyelashes as though really taking sympathy for his plight. "With an army of servants to help you warm bottles and carry the pup to and fro."

For a moment his expression darkened and he raised himself up once more. She kept her countenance, though she had overstepped her bounds. When would she ever learn to curb her dry comments? Her lack of control was going to put her entire hope of independence in jeopardy.

"Sid, you will be the death of me." He chuckled, his shoulders shaking. His laughter was, strangely, not as annoying as she thought or remembered. "I trust very few people, I can assure you of that. I do, however, have great conviction in you. I will buy every single thing on the list and I don't need to know why you've ordered what you've ordered."

"Thank you." She was unsure what to say. Although his words had a bit of a sting to them—after all, no woman enjoyed being told that she would be the death of anyone, and she certainly wasn't sure about being referred to as "Sid"—he was laughing, at least. That meant she still had a job.

"You'll only be gone a week. Is that correct?" He

sat up fully, his powerful form dwarfing the back of the settee.

"Yes. I thank you for your generosity." She found herself on the defensive once more. There was something about him, something that made her feel less like a decisive woman and more like a silly girl, and she despised that loss of control.

"I'm no Lord Bountiful. This was our bargain. I knew you would need to go home to see to matters at your shop." He rubbed his hands together. "Besides, when you return, I hope to have a new venture started."

"Oh. That's nice." She really didn't know what to say. Venture? What on earth would a man like John Reed do as a venture?

"I know this may sound ridiculous, but I am going to try my hand at training dogs," he began. His expression softened and he glanced from under his eyebrows at her. "I had no idea that our dogs' pedigrees were so fine here at Grant Park. Apparently, though, we have the makings of champion collies. I talked to my head groom, Davis, about breeding and training dogs and he thinks it's a fine idea."

For a moment, she was stunned. Was he actually talking about doing something at the Park? Something that involved his own active participation? "Is this not another responsibility?" As soon as she said it, she wished it back. Again, that sharp tongue of hers...

"It is a responsibility. A large one." If he was offended, he wasn't showing it yet. "It's just the seed of an idea, really. I hadn't thought of it until yesterday, when I went to see the rest of the dogs with Davis. He mentioned that it was something my father wouldn't do, and for some perverse reason, it took hold with me." He sighed. "I suppose it's because I know it would be something of my own."

She nodded. "I can see that. In some ways, you face the same dilemma as I do with the shop. Here is a great responsibility, built up by other people, me with the shop and you with the Park. But we would each, in our own way, be making it into something we could call our own."

"Exactly." He snapped his fingers, and his posture and bearing became more invigorated than she could recall seeing before. He was not a lazy young buck any longer, but a young man enlivened with purpose. It was an attractive change, that much was certain. "I value your opinion of this more than anyone, because I know you will be honest with me. I also know that we are akin in our business lives, as you pointed out." He leveled his glance at her, and being fixed with those piercing brown eyes played havoc with her sensibility. "So? What do you think?"

For some reason, Hannah's answer mattered more than he cared to admit, even to himself. He affected the position of a young buck, lolling back against the settee with studied insolence. Inside, though, he was on edge. Hannah would never lie to him. Of all people, she would tell him the truth. If she felt as if he couldn't make a go of it, then she was likely correct and he would have to go back to his old life and the old way of doing things.

"I think it's probably a sound endeavor." Her blue eyes grew a shade deeper as she regarded him. "Of course, it will take a great deal of hard work, and that seems to be the one thing you dislike most in this world."

His first thought was to be angered. Who was she to say he didn't like hard work? On the other hand, he had played the role of the lazy young rogue about town for so long, it was difficult even for him to accept that he could be anything else. "I don't hate hard work," he protested. "What I loathe is hard work without any respite."

"Some people cannot afford rest," she replied tartly. Already she was getting worked up. He liked this side of Hannah. When she was too professional, too precise and too polite, he wanted her to loosen her hold on her temper. For even though she had a sharp tongue, her thoughts were clear, concise and invigorating—like a long draught of cool water from a mountain stream.

"Everyone can afford to have time for relaxation and for fun," he countered. He leaned his elbow against the arm of the settee and regarded her frankly. "You don't have enough fun, do you?"

Color bloomed in her cheeks and her eyes sparkled with a feisty light, and she clasped her sketch pad in her hands until her knuckles turned white. "I have more than enough hilarity for a woman in my situation."

"You do not." He spoke the words flatly, glaring out at her from under lowered lids.

She pursed her lips together as though she were

biting back harsh words. He pressed his advantage. "Come, then. Stand up. Dance with me."

She shook her head, her eyes wide. "No indeed. There's no music, for one thing."

"I shall hum." He stood, holding his hand out to her.

She clasped her sketch pad to her chest. "That would be ridiculous in the extreme."

"But it might be fun." He gently pried the sketchbook from her and placed it on a nearby table. Then he held his hand out once more. "Shall we?"

She shook her head again. He bent down and took her hand in his. It was cold as ice.

"You are a graceful dancer and should indulge in the pastime more often, Sid." He drew her to her feet and took her other hand. "Physical activity can, after all, sharpen your mind. Perhaps you will find your productivity enhanced." He began to hum a familiar tune, leading her through the figures of a country dance.

He hadn't danced with Hannah in weeks, but she responded to the figures with the same grace and poise as though she had been practicing with him every day. She kept her eyes stubbornly turned down toward the carpet, and her hands did not grow any warmer.

After a few moments, he paused his humming, but he didn't let go of her hands. "So. You think my idea is sound enough to try?"

At last, she looked up at him. He must be a little winded from the dance. That was the only way to account for the sudden catch of breath he experienced when she lifted her chin and looked at him squarely.

"Yes. In all seriousness, and assuming you can also be solemn, I do."

"Excellent." He resumed their country dance. It seemed the celebratory thing to do, after all.

"Tell me, why do you insist upon so much amusement in your life? And in the lives of others? Why is having fun so important to you?"

He enjoyed her honesty. She compelled the truth from anyone. Now, though, she had turned it on the ugliest, most vile part of his being. If he told her why, she would hate him. Everyone would.

"Let's just say I've seen too many people who've been hurt by too much work and not enough play," he replied, struggling to keep his tone light. "I find that it's too vital to ignore."

She eyed him candidly, even as she executed the difficult turn he led her into. "I see. I don't suppose I will get more of an answer than that. Even if I am dancing like a puppet on a string. You see, I do what you ask. You don't seem to return the favor."

She was right, of course. She always was. "There's a real difference between the two," he managed, drawing them both to a halt. "You ask the most difficult questions, while I merely want you to indulge the lighter side of your nature."

She quirked her eyebrows at him. "Very well. I shan't press." She broke away from him and gathered her sketchbook. "Thank you for approving my list and for ordering the supplies from London."

"Not at all." Suddenly bereft of her touch, he

jammed his fists into his pockets. "You'll be back in a week, then."

She tossed him a blank, efficient smile. "Of course." For a moment he thought she was going to add "Sir." That would never do.

"I'll hold you to it, Sid," he pressed on.

She nodded, her coronet of braids catching the light that streamed in through the open window.

Then, with a swish of skirts, she was gone. A strange heavy feeling settled over him as the door shut behind her.

This would be the longest week of his life.

## Chapter Eleven

Had the shop always been this small? Hannah looked at it again, as though by blinking she could return the millinery shop to its former rightful glory. Perhaps she was just used to the grand size of Grant Park. The shop did appear rather forlorn, with the sign proclaiming Siddons Sisters Millinery Shop still propped against the outside wall. Of course, its location was never ideal. Here, on the very edge of the village where the main road trailed off, it popped up unexpectedly, like an exclamation mark at the end of a very long sentence. The building was all they had when they first arrived. Now, with its dejected appearance, it was a symbol of how very far the Siddons sisters had moved.

Hannah lowered her head and pushed open the front door. Abigail and Mercy glanced up from their work. "Good afternoon, Miss Nan," Abigail said, laying her handiwork aside. "Did you have a pleasant journey?"

"I did." She would have to get used to being called

Nan again. No one in Tansley Village would refer to her as anything else. "I'll take my valise upstairs and then I'd like to hear about how the business has been while I've been at Grant Park."

The two girls nodded and went back to their work. Hannah hefted her valise up the stairs, remembering every creak and groan with each footstep. Her bedroom smelled musty. She dropped her valise on her woebegone cot and hurried over to the window, flinging it open. She then prepared to wash her face, but there was no water and no soap in the basin.

She resisted the urge to heave a gusty sigh, for she knew full well that returning home would mean a return to work. Not just the kind of focused, friendly labor of working with and for Jane Reed, but the heavy work of cleaning, cooking and readying herself each and every day.

In a moment, she would draw water from the well and fill her pitcher. She would find some linen in the cupboard and hang it on the line to air out so that she would be able to make her own bed this evening. For now, she needed to talk to her workers and find out how the business had been faring while she was gone.

Before she left her room, she pulled the leather box from her valise. Having it out in the shop would surely remind her that she had another existence far away from here, an existence that was hers alone. She tucked it into the pocket of her apron and trudged downstairs.

"So, how goes our sales?" Hannah sat in her usual spot, a worn-out chair near the hearth. It was a fine, warm day so there was no need of a fire, and the hearth smelled of ashes. Everything was smaller, dirtier and mustier than even she had pictured during the long carriage ride home.

Abigail, the more talkative of the two workers, spoke up. "We've sold one or two bonnets since you have been gone, Miss Nan."

Had she heard aright? She sat up straight in her chair, fear charging down her spine. "One or two? That is all?"

"I'm afraid so." Abigail put aside her work and looked over the ledger book nearby. "We did have another order come in today, though."

One or two bonnets in a fortnight? Hannah struggled to breathe. That was a paltry sum, far worse than she had imagined. She would never gain independence, relying on one bonnet sale a week. The profit would hardly pay for her workers, much less her own wants. *Dear Lord, please help me. I'll fail for certain.* She thought of John, lounging in his study. How nice it could be to go to him right now and tell him about her troubles. He might understand. He would tease her, certainly, but somehow, unburdening her fears to him might make them seem smaller and more manageable. He was back at Grant Park, though, and she was here. There was nothing to be done but to get to work. This was her problem to solve, and not his concern.

She stuffed her hand in her pocket, clasping the box for strength. She had better do well as Jane's seamstress, otherwise she would be stuck as an old maid in Susannah's house for certain, or playing nursemaid for her newborn niece or nephew at

Becky's house. "Who have our faithful customers been?"

"The Honorable Miss Glaspell. She ordered two fine silk bonnets. She's remained loyal to the shop, even though everyone else seems to have deserted us." Abigail flipped through the pages of the ledger, eyeing the columns written in Hannah's handwriting.

"Yes. She was our first customer and really gave us our start." Hannah resisted the urge to jump from the chair and pace. If her workers saw how agitated she was, then they might worry about their own jobs. That would never do. "So is it certain, then? Are all of our customers going to the French milliner?"

"Well, old Mrs. Hugh Holdcroft came in yesterday. She was with her son. He promised to purchase a bonnet for her within a few days. I suppose he was waiting to be paid for a job," Mercy piped up from her place in the corner.

Hannah glanced over at Mercy. "Are you certain?" Mrs. Holdcroft usually only ordered one bonnet a year, and she had ordered one just after the Christmas holidays.

"Yes." Mercy paused at her work, looking over at Hannah. "Not to be cheeky, but there have been very few customers. I remember every single one."

Hot tears pricked the back of her eyes, but she refused to let them fall. Not now. Tonight, on her musty cot, she would allow herself the luxury of crying her eyes out. "Well, I am here for the entire week before I must return to Grant Park. I shall see what can be done about drumming up more business."

Mercy raised one eyebrow but turned back to her

work. Abigail nodded, her lips pursed, and picked up her handiwork once more.

Hannah rose and walked over to the window display. The bonnets in the window were faded, and a few traces of cobwebs graced the brims of one of them. This would never do. She hadn't given much thought to displays in the past, for who cared? After all, at one time, this was the only millinery in the village. Why waste precious materials on a silly display?

Now, however, times had changed. She was engaged in a fight for her very life. She was not the only milliner in town, and her entire business was doomed if she didn't engage in the battle. Silently, she pushed aside the table and began working, ripping down drooping fabrics, tearing away faded ribbons and sweeping aside tattered trimmings. The task at hand demanded her total absorption. She went behind the shop and drew water from the well, then began scrubbing the windows and the front table.

When they shone brightly, she went back through storage at the rear of the shop and brought out a length of rose-colored silk, which she draped from the ceiling rafter and allowed to pool on the floor. In front of the silken waterfall, she placed the table. Then she added three of the very finest bonnets from the back storage area, still left over from when Becky had indulged her artistic bent.

She stepped outside and squinted at the display through the sparkling windowpane. It was arresting, to be sure, but not ready. Something was missing.

Hannah hurried back inside and rushed up the stairs. Some of her drawings were still tucked into her valise. They were pretty sketches, but the bonnets did not pass her rigorous approval for Jane's wear. Jane needed something delicate, almost whimsical. These bonnets were a trifle too bold for her subtle beauty.

Hannah took them downstairs and pinned them to the waterfall of silk. It was almost perfect, a delicious display of vibrant colors and textures.

"I must say, Miss Nan, that looks lovely." Abigail spoke up from her corner of the room. "A new display is just the thing."

"I agree." Mercy nodded. "We didn't want to change anything, because it's not our shop. But that makes all the difference in the world. Even just to me as I sit here and work."

"Yes." Abigail smiled over at Hannah. "That silk sort of filters the sunlight as it comes through the window. It gives our whole work room a rosy glow."

Hannah glanced up. "You are right." The whole attitude of the room had changed. It no longer had a neglected, desperate feel. It had come back to life.

She eyed the display critically once more. There was still something missing. In fact, she needed some sort of talisman, something to remind herself that she was going to be all right. She dug her borrowed handkerchief box out of the pocket of her apron and placed it on the table. She opened it slightly, tugging out just the corners of a few of her most elaborately embroidered handkerchiefs.

The leather case, richly embossed with wild-flowers, added just the right touch. Any fashionable woman would want to shop at the Siddons Sisters Millinery Shop after seeing a display like that.

She still had the touch. She still had the gift.

Now she just needed to convince the rest of Tansley of that truth.

Sid was gone. She was gone to her shop in Tansley, and somehow, the life of Grant Park had gone with her. John eyed his sister across the dinner table. Jane had been dreamy—well, more so than usual—ever since Sid had left. It was as though no one around could talk plain sense anymore.

"I am thinking about breeding collies," he began. Maybe Jane would help him mull over this venture.

She started as though he had stood on the table and yelled. "Beg pardon?"

He sighed. "I am thinking of raising puppies."

"But, you are raising puppies. What about Molly?" Jane eyed him with bewilderment.

"Not just one puppy. Several. Entire litters, in fact." He poked at the chicken on his plate with his fork. "The stock at Grant Park is excellent, you know."

"No, I didn't know. But thank you for telling me." Jane sank back against her chair with a sigh.

"Aren't you going to eat anything?" Jane's plate was still heaped with food.

"I am eating." Jane took a tiny bite of a piece of bread. "See?"

"Honestly." John pushed his chair away from the table. "Country life is the absolute worst. I am fairly itching for London right now." The urge to do something, anything, was overwhelming. It was far too quiet and dull without Sid around.

"Then go to London." Jane glanced at him evenly.

She, of all people, had seen this mood come and go in him since childhood, and as always, she remained unimpressed by it. "But don't take your lack of ability to stay calm and quiet out on the country. Grant Park is lovely. The only prettier place I've seen is Tansley Village."

"I can't go to London. You know that." He was pacing now, like a caged tiger. "If only you would agree to go to London—"

"Not until I absolutely must," she broke in. "You know how much I hate it. If you pursue this line of conversation, then you know full well I shall berate you about forcing me to make my London debut. Shall we venture down that path together?" Jane cocked her head to one side and glared at him.

"No." He knew when he was beaten. He would do anything else. He could not have that discussion with Jane once more.

"Then go find something else to do," Jane chided. "You don't need London to have fun. You, of all people, always on the hunt for mirth, should surely be able to find it wherever you go."

He shot Jane a baleful glare but said nothing. Instead, he picked up his plate and silver and stalked out of the room. Better to eat alone, really. Jane was in quite a mood and he was no better. Sid, it seemed, brought a great deal of balance to their home.

But where to go? If he went to his study, he could work. Should he write Sid a letter? No, she wouldn't receive it until the end of her stay. He could send a runner up to Tansley with a message, but that might make her feel as though she should hurry back. Part of their bargain was that she could return home and work on the shop without interruption. He must uphold his part of the agreement.

Instead, he walked across the house to the library. He hadn't been in that particular room in years. It was his father's favorite place. If he met Father in the library, he was usually being called to task for his failings.

"Have you met a young woman yet?" Father would say.

"Oh, I've met many," he would reply, stuffing his fists down deep in his pockets.

Father would glare disapprovingly and then shrug his shoulders.

"Decent women, I should say."

"A fair few, but none who suited me." Then on and on the interview would stretch, as Father reminded him of all that was expected of him as the heir.

The walls would close in on him, and the portraits lining the wall would glare disapprovingly down at him.

Why was he going there, then, if all he had were bad memories of the place?

He opened the door with great caution, as though Father might still be there, waiting for him.

Father wasn't there, though. The room was empty. Even so, a fire flickered in the grate, warding off the spring evening's chill. Out of habit, he wandered over to the chair that was usually his seat during his father's many lectures. He balanced his plate precariously in his lap and stared, brooding, at the fire.

"You have too much fun," Father would reprimand.

"Better than having none at all," he would return, his temper beginning to rise.

That's when the conversations would end. Father knew when not to push the envelope. That is how matters ended as they did, with Jane allowed to indulge her passion for violin and with John allowed to fritter away his existence in London. Father knew his boundaries well.

John forced himself to look at the ancestral portraits on the wall. They were all well-dressed and well-taken-care-of people. More to the point, they knew how to take care of others. Responsibility and duty were the hallmarks of Grant Park.

He eyed them carefully, forcing himself to confront his family. Had they ever wanted to run away? Had they ever wanted to be done with obligation? No, that was hardly likely. He passed a weary hand over his forehead.

There was one portrait he couldn't look at, and it hung on the opposite wall. It was Mother's picture, painted just after she and Father had married. The likeness was so realistic, Mother looked ready to speak. The gentleness of her character was evident in every line. Even when he would come in to get a lecture from Father, he couldn't bear to raise his eyes to hers.

She knew all too well the price one had to pay for caring for others, for because of him she died an early death.

He lived, while the light dimmed in her beautiful eyes. He lived and he continued to thrive through selfishness. It would be better to examine the issue as he would an algebraic equation. Assuming there was a God, why did He play so fast and loose with John's life? Why did God take her when He allowed John to live?

A pang of self-loathing shot through him like an arrow. His debts were so great, he could never begin to make amends. That was one of the reasons why he had turned away from the Lord. If he couldn't forgive himself, surely God wouldn't either. Over time he convinced himself that there was no God, because at least that way, there was no eternal Father looking down on him in disapproval.

He was better off in the study.

He took his plate and left the room, leaving it to its silence and its painful memories.

## Chapter Twelve

Hannah stifled a yawn as she toiled away at a bonnet. Already she had been in Tansley long enough. She would leave tomorrow, in fact. Yet her brave attempt at refashioning the millinery shop had not made any difference, at least as far as she could see. No customers had come in while she had been home, and she finally dismissed Mercy and Abigail, giving them a respite while she was in residence. No sense in paying the girls to be bored, when she could do that quite well on her own. She would bring them back to the shop when she returned to Grant Park.

She was utterly alone in her feeling of misery, for no one else seemed to care. Of course, her sisters had been no help. Totally absorbed in their own families and their own troubles and triumphs, neither sister had offered any wisdom about the current state of affairs. Becky, becoming prettier and rounder with each day of her pregnancy, had simply said, "Perhaps the other milliner is more artistic, and it is her calling to dress the women of Tansley. Your calling may lay elsewhere, Nan."

Susannah had rolled her eyes as she chased after her scampering son, Charlie. "Nan, you are being far too dire about the situation. There are ups and downs with every business. You've enjoyed success for many years. Adversity is good for you. It keeps you from resting on your laurels."

Fine words for both sisters to say. They had roofs over their heads, and security in knowing their own place in life. While she, Hannah, still floundered about, trying to keep her precarious foothold.

So absorbed was she in these gloomy thoughts that she hardly noticed a flutter of activity outside. The door to the shop opened and an older woman stepped over the threshold, followed by a tall young man, so tall he had to duck under the door frame.

"Mrs. Holdcroft," Hannah said with a smile. "I was told you might come in soon for a bonnet."

"Upon my word, yes," Mrs. Holdcroft replied. Her bearing was graceful and her smile charming. Funny, one couldn't tell right away that Mrs. Holdcroft was from a poorer background than some of their genteel clients. Hannah's practiced eye caught the finely mended hole in one of her sleeves and the lack of truly extravagant trimming on her bonnet. Of course, she had made that bonnet and remembered how much it had cost, down to the last penny. "Timothy has insisted on buying a new one for me, though I daresay I don't need it. The one you made me earlier this year is just lovely."

Timothy ducked his head and shrugged. "You deserve it, Mother." He wandered over to Hannah's new display, his hands clasped behind his back.

Hannah was in an odd predicament, for she remembered all of Jane's confidences. She wondered if, for example, she were to utter the name Jane, would Timothy show any interest? She had played the role of confidante before, but only for her sisters and none of their beaux had been customers.

"Well, I should be happy to start one for you, and then I will leave it to Abigail and Mercy to finish it." Hannah made her voice a tiny bit louder. "You see, I am leaving for Grant Park tomorrow. I am working as a seamstress for Miss Jane Reed."

Did Timothy's shoulders rise as she spoke? It was difficult to tell. Mrs. Holdcroft did not look the least bit baffled. She merely smiled. "What a good position to have, Miss Siddons. I certainly hope you aren't leaving Tansley forever, though. We would miss you so much."

"Would you really?" She blurted the words before she could check them. Mrs. Holdcroft was merely being polite. Her presence in Tansley made no difference to anyone.

"We would. The entire village would. You know, the Siddons sisters brought so much life to the village. Before you were here, there wasn't anyplace a woman could go to purchase anything fashionable. When you and your sisters opened this shop, it was as though the world had been brought to Tansley." She reached out and patted Hannah's arm. "Of course, with your elder sisters married, I am certain the burden of running the shop must get tiresome."

Hannah nodded. She couldn't trust her voice just then. It was just so nice to have someone sympathize with her and say such complimentary things about the shop and all they had accomplished. Why, they *had* accomplished a lot, for three unmarried girls with no fortune and no family connections. They had much to be proud of, and God had been good to them.

"I don't know that I can be here forever," Hannah finally managed. "Business is not very profitable now that I have a rival in the village."

Mrs. Holdcroft shook her head, clucking her tongue. "Tut, tut. Never mind what she may be doing. My thought is this—you will get all your customers back once the novelty of her presence wears off."

Hannah gave her a weary smile. That was an unlikely scenario, but pleasant to hear all the same. "Thank you, Mrs. Holdcroft. Now, shall we discuss your bonnet?"

Hannah worked with the older woman to plan a nice, simple spring confection—nothing too elaborate, but something that set off Mrs. Holdcroft's refined features and graceful bearing to perfection. Timothy waited patiently by the display, saying nothing.

As they were finishing the order, Hannah glanced over at him. He was a handsome lad, with dark hair and eyes like his mother. He also possessed that same dignity of manner that characterized Mrs. Holdcroft. One could see at a glance that the Holdcrofts were no mere country farming family. They came from an aristocratic background, despite their current state of poverty.

"Timothy is so kind," Mrs. Holdcroft confided in a whisper as they finished her bonnet order. "He sold a prized calf of his and insisted on buying something special for me. I wouldn't hear of it at first, but he kept saying that it would give him great pleasure. I feel so fortunate to have such a good son."

"You are fortunate indeed," Hannah replied, her heart warming as she glanced over at Timothy. He was a good man and would be a good husband and father someday, surely. Would Jane be able to persuade her brother that she should marry where her heart led her?

If only she could. Timothy Holdcroft would take care of Jane Reed, no matter what befell them.

She finished Mrs. Holdcroft's order and watched them leave, the mother leaning on her son for support as he opened the door for her. She made a few notes on the order for Abigail and Mercy so they would understand what should be done once she left in the morning.

Then she spent the rest of her time cleaning the shop. Perhaps if she gave it a thorough cleaning each time she came home, it wouldn't look so forlorn. As she swept and scrubbed, her mind drifted down a trail of thought sparked by the Holdcrofts and the Reeds. What would it be like to be cared for by someone?

No one had ever bought her anything simply because she deserved it. Gifts in a poor household were rare indeed, and the few she had gotten over the years had been given to her by her sisters for the holidays. Jane would be blessed indeed to have a young man so thoughtful and so caring.

A sudden wave of jealousy swept over Hannah, leaving her so dizzy that she had to sit, abruptly, in a chair nearby.

She should be happy for Jane, but she wasn't. If Jane didn't marry Timothy, she would marry someone else, for her place in life was secure. She would live in a beautiful home and have someone to care for her. She would have children. She would never suffer from loneliness and she would never have to worry about making herself useful in order to earn a place in someone else's house.

Neither would her sisters.

Hannah alone was the unattractive one, the plain one, the unwanted one.

No man would want her. John's elaborate apologies after his mistaken proposal just rubbed salt in a wound that had existed for years. The thing of it was, John was actually turning out not to be such an odious swine as she had originally suspected. He was a good man, beneath all his pretenses at laziness and pleasure-seeking. If he thought her an unlikely candidate for marriage, then likely other men felt the same way.

For some reason, that thought caused her heart to lurch heavily in her chest. Who cared what John Reed thought of her marital prospects? It didn't matter one whit.

Hannah balled her fists in her lap and squeezed her eyes shut.

She must focus. She must.

She would be scrambling after crumbs from another person's table for the rest of her life if she didn't earn her independence.

Why was this journey her path? What possible use could God have for an unloved, unwanted spinster? "I know You care for the smallest of the small, for the weak and for the poor," she said aloud, spitting the words out as though they tasted foul. "Why do I feel so abandoned, then? So forgotten?"

She gave vent to hot, uncontrollable tears, the kind that seemed to tear through her very soul. She mustn't take on this way, for Jane deserved happiness, as did her sisters. If only a few drops of joy could also come her way, what a difference it might make.

Grant Park must be the answer. God was calling her there for a reason. He wouldn't abandon her.

She dried her eyes on the corner of her apron and walked across to the display she had created. It was time to pack her valise, and she must take the borrowed handkerchief case home to Jane.

Sid would be home today and life would return to its even pace. John took the stairs two at a time in his haste to get to the barn. All week he had thrown himself into work, because he wanted to have something to show for the time she was gone. He craved her approval, for her good opinion was not easily won.

Molly had opened her eyes this week. That was something new. He had set her in with the other pups as she gained strength, giving her time to play with her siblings. That had gone well. Madge accepted the puppy but also made no move to stop John when he took Molly away. It was as if the mother knew that he was taking care of the runt so she could focus her energies on the rest of the litter.

He nodded to Davis as he drew closer. He no longer felt the need to consult with the head groom on every detail of his visit. With each day this week he had become more of his own man, more of the master and less of the guest merely passing through.

He made his way into the barnyard, where the puppies were rolling around in the lush grass. Madge stood guard nearby, eyeing the puppies while sunning herself. A pleasant enough pastoral scene, and one in which he felt a sneaking sense of pride. This was his.

"So, what will you be?" He questioned the puppies as though they could really answer. "I wonder what I shall train you for. Would you prefer the life of a shepherd or guard dog?"

Davis chuckled appreciatively as he wandered up from the paddock. "I suppose, right now, they would all prefer to live a life of luxury."

John nodded. "It is an addictive lifestyle, I must say. However, as one who is developing a newfound appreciation for work, I must say the joy of doing nothing palls after a while." He stared intently at the mother and pups. "What should we breed these dogs for, Davis? Any thoughts?"

"Well, Bah was as good a sheep-herder as you could imagine." Davis rubbed a handkerchief over his brow. "Cleo was good at herding, too. Not as good as Bah, but very close. I haven't had Madge out in the field yet, for she has been hanging about the barn, working with the horses. She's a good lass to have around skittish animals. Always calms them right down."

"I could see that. She has a tranquil nature, even around these wriggling pups." So how were they to proceed? He had all the enthusiasm of someone delving into something new, but no idea how to turn this zeal into something permanent. "Is it impossible to tell now how best to train these pups?"

"I would consider a few things while they are still too young for training," Davis replied. "First, I would think about what kind of dog is in demand in Derbyshire. What do we need most? What would be the most popular? After all, we want to create the kind of dogs that are sought after throughout the county."

"True, true." He could begin by writing to his landed friends, those who already managed their estates, and see what kind of dog they used most often in their daily work. Paul and Daniel would certainly know, and other friends might be able to put in a few words, too. "What else would you recommend?"

"We will have to see what each pup can do best, once they are older. Use their natural talents, so to speak." Davis shrugged. "There was a book, I believe it is housed in your father's library." He paused, looking distinctly uncomfortable. "I should say 'your library.' I beg your pardon, sir. I didn't mean to be disrespectful. It's just that I am still adjusting to the loss of your father."

"No harm done," John reassured the groom. After all, he was just now showing an interest in the doings of Grant Park. It would take a long time for everyone to get used to his newfound concentration.

"Thank you, sir." Davis's shoulders relaxed. "There should be a book in your library, devoted to the history of all the creatures at the Park since it was first built. Horses, dogs, cattle, sheep. If you find that book, it could do a great deal of good in helping us establish a breeding business."

"I shall look for it later, I promise." John straightened. One of the lower grooms was approaching, needing Davis's help, no doubt.

"Mr. Davis, a carriage was spotted coming through the main gates. I believe Miss Siddons has returned. Shall I go and meet the horses?" The young man stood patiently, awaiting Davis's instruction.

"I'll go," John interjected. "Have a horse ready, Davis?"

"In two seconds, sir," Davis replied, tugging at his cap.

True to his word, within a matter of seconds, John was seated on one of the Park's impressive stallions, riding out to the main gates of the Park. For some reason, this felt like the right thing to do. During Sid's absence, he had gathered together all the materials she needed, plus some additional items she had not requested. Everything had been piled into her sitting room, making a striking display. Of course, she would not have room to work in her sitting room, so he had made sure that one of the studies downstairs would be put into service as a workroom. Would Sid like it? He certainly hoped so.

Over the course of her time in Tansley, he had realized how much the house depended on Sid and her good sense. He had a plan in mind for her, if only she would agree to it.

Would she agree to it? He was struck with self-doubt. Perhaps she had seen how much she missed in Tansley, and was eager to return. He spied the carriage through a break in the line of oak trees and hastened over.

He drew up alongside the carriage and motioned for Sid to open the window. She waved a gloved hand and did as he asked.

"Welcome home!" he boomed, and then realized how ridiculous he sounded. Embarrassment—a rare feeling for him—filled his soul. "I'll see you in a few moments!"

He rode off, thoroughly disgusted with that fulsome display. Why the awkwardness and indecisiveness all of a sudden? She was just Sid, after all.

Perhaps a good ride through the Park was in order before he allowed himself to see Sid's reaction to his arrangements. He needed something to clear his head. There was no need to take on so about a chit like Hannah Siddons.

## Chapter Thirteen

"Upon my word, this is astonishing," Hannah blurted as she walked into her study. She dropped her valise in startled wonder. The sight of roll upon roll of fabric was well-nigh overwhelming. Baskets of notions overflowed in one corner. She caught glimpses of lace, of flowers and of carefully crafted birds that looked ready to take flight. All that she had requested must be here, along with a great deal that she hadn't even considered.

"Surprise!" Jane called, laughing, as she rose from the settee. "You see, my brother took your request quite seriously. Everything you need to turn me into a diamond of the first water is here, right in this room."

"I must confess, I am quite amazed." Hannah smiled as Jane embraced her. "I could turn this room into another location for the Siddons Sisters Millinery Shop, so great is our inventory of supplies."

Jane walked over to the corner of the sitting room and pulled the embroidered bellpull. "We won't, of course, leave all of this in here," she stated matter-of-factly. "John has had an entire room downstairs cleared out for storage. This was just set up to surprise you."

"Well, it certainly worked." Hannah removed her bonnet and cast it aside. "I cannot wait to start your wardrobe." In fact, her fingers fairly itched to open all the boxes and baskets, to touch all the fabrics and to begin the hard work of cutting and laying out each garment.

The sitting room door opened, and a maid came in. She bobbed a curtsy at Jane. "You rang, Miss Jane?"

"Yes. Go and fetch the footmen, and have them start moving all of this to the room Mr. John set aside downstairs. Then please send Lucinda and Amelia up here as they need to meet Miss Hannah."

The maid bobbed a respectful curtsy and left to do as she was asked.

Jane turned to Hannah. "Amelia and Lucinda are the maids that John has assigned to help you with my wardrobe. They are skilled seamstresses, though they lack your talent. After I've introduced you, you may order them about as you see fit."

"I am not sure where to begin," Hannah murmured, wandering over to a bolt of fine lavender silk. "There's just so much to do, and so much to choose from. I shall have to make a list."

"Well, I am certain that you will be working away busily in no time at all." Jane paused for a moment, pursing her lips. "Did you enjoy your time in Tansley?"

"I did." Hannah flicked a quick glance at her friend. Was Jane actually interested in her trip, or more concerned about whether or not she'd caught a glimpse of the Holdcrofts? "I saw many familiar faces, including your particular friend, Timothy Holdcroft."

Jane paled a little. "Did you really? How was he? Did he say anything?"

"Not much, to be perfectly honest, though he seemed well." There was surely no harm in telling Jane about his visit. She was agreeing to a London Season and had made no more demands to change her brother's plans. Perhaps she had finally come around to his way of thinking, or had at least agreed to the inevitable. "He brought his mother in to buy a new bonnet. She said he was purchasing one as a special treat for her." Somehow, the sting of not receiving any gifts over the years lessened as she was surrounded by more fabrics than she could ever hope to use. Even if this extravagant display of largesse wasn't for her personal benefit, it was still quite comforting to be surrounded by luxury. "He seems a nice enough fellow. His mother is lovely. She said so many nice things about my shop. I sincerely appreciated her thoughtfulness."

Jane's dark eyes glowed. "I only met her a few times, but I agree. She is a most pleasant woman."

"Yes." Hannah could think of nothing more to say. There really wasn't that much about the Holdcrofts' visit that was worthy of note. Indeed, if she had not been aware of Jane's affection for Timothy, she would not have remarked on it at all.

Jane turned and walked toward the window. "Was my handkerchief box a nice addition to your shop? I do hope you brought it back with you. I realized after I loaned it to you that my favorite handkerchief was still in it."

"Oh, no. I didn't see anything in there." Hannah grabbed her valise and pulled out the box. "I had my handkerchiefs in here, but I removed them." She handed the box to Jane. "Here. If I find yours mixed in with mine, I'll be sure to tell you."

"Oh, thank you." Jane took the box. Were her hands trembling? Surely not. Hannah shook her head. There was nothing upsetting in their conversation, and she had returned the case, after all. Was Jane really that upset over a missing scrap of linen?

"Do you want me to help you search for it?" A troubling feeling gnawed at her insides. Perhaps there really had been something in there and she missed it? She didn't want to lose anything of Jane's, especially after her friend had been so kind to lend it.

"No, no." Jane waved her hand with a dismissive gesture. "I must have left it somewhere else. I'll find it, I am sure."

The door to the sitting room opened again, and four footmen entered. Hefting bolts of fabric on their shoulders, they began the first of many trips downstairs to Hannah's newly established sewing room. Amelia and Lucinda entered next, ready to do Hannah's bidding. It was a whirlwind of activity after the quiet dullness of a week at the shop, and it energized her. She was so ready to do good work and to prove herself worthy of her new position at Grant Park.

Jane waved a cheery goodbye as the two maids, pressed into this new venture by John, began inquiring about their positions. Hannah gave a distracted wave in return and turned her full attention to the matter of organizing and directing the greatest challenge she had yet faced. Purpose filled her soul and gave quickness to her movements. She never gave much weight to anything Becky said, but perhaps her elder sister had been right. Perhaps this was her new calling.

Once they had moved everything, she would set Lucinda and Amelia to work cataloging the items in the new workroom, assigning each bolt of fabric and each basket of notions a place so that items could be found quickly when needed. She followed the last of the footmen into the room and gasped. Never had she worked in such a pleasant place. Arched windows reached from the floor to the ceiling, flooding it with light. She would not have to squint as she stitched, that much was certain.

Large, long oaken tables crisscrossed the room, giving her ample space to lay out fabric and cut patterns. Comfortable chairs beckoned her to sit and work. Shelves lined the walls, filled with all the fancy goods Reed had sent down from London. Lucinda and Amelia bustled about, organizing everything as she had requested.

It was, in brief, as different from the dusty, neglected shop in Tansley as night was from day. She clasped her hands over her heart and forced herself to stay calm when all she wanted to do was dance around the room, clapping her hands with glee.

"Do you like it?" A familiar voice spoke up behind her.

She turned, smiling, to Reed. "I love it."

Reed stared at her for a disconcerting moment, as though he'd finally noticed something different about her. She put a hand up, defensively touching her braided coils of hair. She must look a sight, after all the traveling she had done and now moving everything into her workroom.

"That's good." He still regarded her as one might gaze upon a strange insect.

She nodded and turned away. Some of the gloss had dissolved from her day. It wasn't nice, after all, to be regarded so closely. She had to be polite, of course, because he was the agent of this transformative change in her life. But she didn't have to like it.

Behind her, Reed cleared his throat. "Well, I am glad to hear it. I ordered extra fabric and notions so that you could sew some new gowns for yourself, too."

Hannah whirled around. "Why?" She would have her hands full with making clothing for Jane—there would be no time to make her own. Her dresses looked nice enough, didn't they? She glanced down at her skirt. It had been mended, but she'd done a good job of it. Only a practiced eye could see the darning.

"My dresses are good enough," she rejoined shortly. Reminders of her own poverty and precarious situation in society were intolerable at the moment. "I do thank you, though," she added. She must continue to be polite, no matter what happened.

"Yes, they are," he agreed. Then he came around to stand before her. "You are quite well dressed at all times, Sid. However, I am bribing you with copious amounts of fabric for two reasons."

The sharp edge of her temper began to dull. She didn't mind teasing nearly as much when it wasn't so personal. "Give me your reasons."

"First of all, I want to have your help with my puppy training business." He clasped his hands behind his back and began to pace, looking for all the world like a young man pretending at being an old, entrenched master. She resisted the urge to laugh, for he was being serious. "You have a vast amount of common sense, which I need, and an absolute inability to couch the truth in pretty nonsense. Therefore, I would consider you an invaluable assistant as I begin this endeavor."

Hannah hesitated. On the one hand, it was difficult not to feel a trifle insulted, for who liked being told that she was too blunt for words? On the other hand, it was the truth. She was known throughout her family as being one who would never dissemble. She sighed. "Very well, I shall help you in any way I can."

"The second reason is simple. My sister likes you very much, and you have played no small role in convincing her to listen to me and take advantage of a London Season." He paused in his pacing and faced her squarely. "You'll need a new wardrobe if you are to accompany us to London. Will you?"

John's heart skipped a beat as he waited for her response. Somehow, this meant a great deal to him. He'd come up with the idea just a few days ago, and now he didn't know how he hadn't thought of it before. Bringing Sid to London was a fantastic idea. She would help curb Jane, and she was a fine dancer herself. With a new wardrobe, who knew? She could certainly pass for a gentlewoman. Her straightforward demeanor would be the stuff of legend at many fine gatherings.

"I don't know what to say." Sid, who had an uncanny directness in her gaze, turned her eyes toward the floor. "I hadn't thought about that at all. I assumed once I got the dresses done, I would return to Tansley."

"That was the original agreement, of course." He stepped aside as two of the footmen walked by, moving a large bolt of fabric from one end of the room to the other. "But I don't know why I didn't extend the plan further when we first discussed it. You are a natural fit for London, Sid. Moreover, you will keep my sister and me from killing each other." He said the last with a hint of laughter in his voice, for she looked so utterly serious and yet he knew that he could only lighten the mood so much before he annoyed her.

"Have you discussed this with Jane? She may not want a duenna," Sid replied, her eyes still fixed on the floor.

"What nonsense. Jane will think it's a capital idea, and you well know that," John said, stuffing his hands in his pockets. Why was Sid acting so oddly? "Just say you will go and let's have an end of this. I want to celebrate your return."

"I suppose." Sid sighed and turned to look at the buzz of activity in the work room. "I'll be so busy sewing, I am not sure I can finish Jane's dresses and do mine. But I will try to make one or two so I can be presentable."

"Excellent." He rubbed his hands together. "Now, tell me, what do you prefer for supper? Our man has caught fish from the lake, and we also have chicken. Mrs. H awaits your decision. After all, we must kill the fatted calf for your return."

"I thought you weren't particularly religious," Sid countered, finally turning and giving him one of her looks. "How, then, do you know that Bible story?"

"My dear Sid, I am the original prodigal son. Have I not returned to Grant Park after years of gallivanting around? Besides which, I am on nodding terms with the Lord. I just don't particularly care for Him much." He offered her his elbow. "Shall we go to the kitchens and see Mrs. H? I promised I would bring you as soon as I could tear you from the workroom."

"Yes, of course." Sid accepted his arm and he led her out of the room. Pleasure suffused him. Sid was home, and all would be well. She would help him with Jane, with the puppies and with everything. He could rely on her clear-eyed counsel on every particular.

He was becoming as dependent on her as a friend.

"Why are we celebrating my return?" Sid asked as he escorted her down the hall. "You knew I would come back in a week. Why the need to make merry? You know I must start work without delay. I was hoping to begin cutting out one of Jane's walking dresses this evening."

He laughed. Trust Sid to be ready to delve in, her sleeves rolled up to her elbows. "We missed you, Sid. Is that not cause enough for celebration?"

"I missed Grant Park." She spoke with a strange catch in her voice. "Things back in Tansley were not as welcoming as I remembered. Funny, when you said 'welcome home,' I could not agree with you more. This has become home to me."

This was the most she had ever said to him since she came to live there, and her words filled him with fierce joy. "Good. I am glad to hear it. I am happy, too, that you will be coming with us to London." A tiny voice in the back of his mind wondered, *How long can we keep her after London?* That was the problem. After Jane's successful debut, there might not be a logical reason for Sid to live at Grant Park. He must mull the problem over at length. Surely there was a solution.

"Yes. I am, too. I don't know what will happen to me or to my shop afterward," she replied, echoing his concern, "and so I don't see much use for celebrating. But if you insist—"

"I do insist." He pushed open the doors that led to the kitchens. "I know all too well what can happen if we never take the time to have fun. Thus, I take every opportunity. While you work for me, you will, too."

Several times, he had tried to voice his life's philosophy, but this time he seemed to say it best. That he spoke it so well to Sid seemed strangely apt.

# Chapter Fourteen

John popped his head through the door that adjoined his study to her workroom. "Sid, come quickly. I need you."

Sid glanced up from the worktable, fixing him with one of her blue-eyed, annoyed stares. "In a moment, sir. I must finish pinning the tucks on this bodice, or a half hour's work will be for naught."

He laughed, pushing the door open. He strolled into the workroom, his hands shoved in his pockets. "Upon my word, I would never ask you to botch an honest thirty minutes of labor."

Sid made an exasperated murmur and bent closer to her work.

"The thing is, I am looking for the breeding book Davis was speaking of," he continued. "You know, the one that traces the pedigrees of all the creatures here at Grant Park?"

"I believe you mentioned it last night at dinner," she muttered, folding a piece of lavender fabric between her fingers. "What do you need?"

"The truth is, I find it horrifying to spend more than a few moments alone in the library," he responded, forcing his tone to sound easy and light. "So, of course, I require a companion."

Sid shrugged, squinting at her handiwork. "Why on earth would a library terrify you?"

"Memories of the past, I suppose." Her blunt nature kept him from beating about the bush, for it had the habit of forcing the truth from him. "Lots of family history in there."

His direct answer got her attention, for she straightened and put her work aside. "You have no reason to fear anything in there. You are doing excellent work as master. The puppies are all fine and healthy, your sister is going to make a spectacular London debut and your home and servants want for nothing."

Her praise filled him with pride, but there was still a feeling of unease within his soul. "Thank you. I don't think, however, that my ancestors would be quite so full of commendation as you are. I really don't feel up to facing their portraits, staring down at me with disapproval, while I am in the library. Surely you need a respite from your labors, Sid." He offered her his elbow, silently pleading with her to accept. Her bracingly no-nonsense manner would banish any troubling memories of the past.

She nodded, taking his elbow. "Very well." It wasn't a flowery or flirtatious response, but he expected no less from Sid.

He led her down the hallway to the library. Pausing before the doors, he summoned every last ounce of his strength. He had been able to be in this room for short periods of time, while he searched for the book. The hunt always left him gloomy and uneasy. The only way he could finish was to have Sid there. The book must be on the far right shelf, for that was the only place he had not looked.

"Is it locked?" Sid lifted an eyebrow in query.

"No." He pushed through the massive oaken doors, allowing her to pass before him. He waited, on the threshold, for her reaction. Would she feel the same weight of unmet expectations as he did?

"This is a beautiful room," she said, turning her head up to gaze at the portraits. "So all of these people are your family members?"

"Yes. Some more nearly related than others." He sighed.

"You are so fortunate to have portraits to remind yourself of your relatives," she went on, studying each picture in turn. "I don't have anything for my family. What I wouldn't give for one of my father and mother. I was so young when they passed, and I am afraid I cannot recall what they looked like."

He had never considered that particular dilemma. "I'm sorry," he managed.

"Well, I console myself by scratching out little drawings of my sisters and their children," she replied, turning toward him with a smile. "Just for my own amusement, of course. So, where is this book we are seeking?"

"Just a moment." Had he heard aright? "You draw portraits, as well? Is there no end to your accomplishments?"

A pretty flush of color washed over her cheeks.

"I would hardly call it an accomplished skill, but I do enjoy it."

"I want to see this," he demanded. "The next time I go to the barn, I want you to come along and sketch the puppies."

"Yes, sir." She bobbed a small curtsy, and he couldn't stifle the sudden laughter that her impertinent gesture caused.

"Sid, call me sir once more and...well, I suppose I can't think of any other nicknames for you," he admitted. "I am not ordering you as your employer, but asking you as a friend. You have prodigious talent in all things I have seen so far. I look forward to seeing more of your work."

"Thank you." She turned away quickly.

A silence grew between them until she pointed at the picture of Mother. "Who is that? She was lovely."

"Her name was Henrietta Reed, née Ashworth," he replied quietly. "My mother."

She turned, placing a hand on his arm. "You are so fortunate to have something to remember her by. Jane says you were very young when she passed away."

With anyone else, that kind of statement could seem rude or invasive, but Sid was likely searching for common ground. "I was eleven years old. I still remember her well. I certainly don't need a portrait to remind me of her." As soon as he spoke, he wished he'd waited until he'd formed a more jovial response. There was no need to snap at Sid.

"Ah, that's good." If she was affronted, she kept her counsel. "I envy you, I must admit."

He stared at her for a moment. How could his situation provoke any kind of jealousy? "How so?"

"You got eleven years with your mother, and I don't even remember mine," she said. She looked down at her hand, which still rested on his arm, and dropped it as if it were on fire. "I would give anything to have something tangible of them. Alas, I don't suppose I ever will. That's why I sketch what I can of my own family, to keep me company as I grow older."

He really didn't know what to say. Never had he regarded the time he spent with his mother as a blessing, for the aching memory of her death overshadowed any happiness he remembered. He started to say something inane, to pass the moment, but could not. He just stood, regarding his mother beside Sid. His mother was famed throughout the county for her beauty, of course—beauty that she passed on to Jane. What the artist managed to capture was the generous spirit that pervaded her every movement. Funny that such an ethereal characteristic could be rendered in paint.

They stood so for a moment longer, as a slow warmth suffused him.

"It's—it's hard for me to look at Mother, much," he admitted finally. "I am responsible for her death." There, it was out. Now she knew, and Hannah Siddons was incapable of telling a lie, even a white lie that could soften the truth. If she despised him, then he was indeed as miserable a creature as he felt all these years.

"You?" She turned, her skirts fluttering around her

ankles. "How on earth could a boy be responsible for the death of anyone?"

"I was sick, and I made her sick." He closed his eyes at the memory. "Mother never gave a thought to herself, for she was always busy with caring for the other tenants and people on our estate. She worked from dawn until well after dark. Never had any time for fun." The words were carried away from him, like a leaf caught in a swiftly moving stream. "I watched her, day after day, working. She worked so much, Sid. I caught a fever and she got it after nursing me back to health. She was so exhausted, she couldn't fight it off." He stared down at the carpet. "She died within days."

"I'm so sorry," Sid said. She clasped her hand around his and some of her unwavering kindness suffused him. "You know, though, that you had nothing to do with her death."

"But I—" he began.

"You were a child, and you were sick. Your mother cared for you, as any good mother would. Why, would you blame Molly if suddenly she came down with an illness and passed it to Madge?"

She was still holding his hand. He never wanted to let go.

"No, of course not." He couldn't release her and yet he couldn't meet her gaze.

"Well, then, why not offer yourself a bit of the pardon you would give an animal?"

When she said those words, they sounded true. He breathed in deeply. Her compassion was acting as a salve on the raw wound that had tormented him for years.

"Your mother wouldn't want you to feel that way. No mother would." She tightened her hold on his hand. "The Lord wouldn't want you to blame yourself, either. If this is the reason for your schism with Him, then you should know that there should be no alienation, no isolation. He loves all and forgives all. If this is burdening your soul, you should turn to Him in prayer and be healed."

Hannah Siddons would never lie. She was one person, perhaps the only person, who could be absolutely honest at all times. She believed in a God who forgave. No, that would never do. He must not dissemble. She believed in God, not a god, and she remained steadfast in her feeling that no matter what John had done, he would be forgiven. A curious calm stole over him, as though she had made him take a healing draught. "What you say must be true. It's just so hard to believe it, Sid. Rather like when you get a pebble in your shoe. You'll walk around for days feeling the tenderness in the sole of your foot, even when the rock is gone."

"I can understand that. It may take some time, but you'll restore your spiritual health." She gave him a tender smile and let go his hand. "Now, as to the real purpose for our visit. Where is that book?"

Hannah changed the subject because it was necessary. For those few moments, she had grown entirely too fond of John. She needed to focus on an external problem, such as finding the book, in order to maintain her composure. She was offering advice to a man who was hurt, and he had been hurting for some time. She was doing what any decent person would do when confronted with the same display of anguish. He was not seeking her out for any reason other than the simple, driving need to speak to someone, and quickly. She just happened to be that person.

"The only place I haven't searched is over there, in the far right corner," he replied huskily. He pointed over at a tall wooden shelf.

"Very well." She managed to say it in a brisk enough tone, belying her trembling knees. "Fetch a ladder."

He brought over a small flight of oak steps that latched on to the front of the shelf. "How clever," she remarked. Now she could stand up and search without fear of tipping over.

"Yes, the entire library was redone a few years before Mother passed away." He stood, one booted foot on the bottom of the steps. "A master carpenter came in and designed everything so it would fit just so."

"Well, it's lovely." Her heart hammered in her chest. For some reason, having him that close to her was more unnerving than when they held hands just a few minutes before. She must stop this nonsense, for John Reed had made it quite clear he had no interest in her beyond employment. If she didn't keep a close rein on her sensibilities, she'd become as dramatic as Becky, expecting a white knight to fall at her feet every time she left the house. "Here." She handed down a book.

"What's this?" He took the leather-bound volume

and blew on it, sending a cloud of dust up toward the ceiling. "Well, that shows where the maids have been careless."

"I didn't see any writing on the spine, so you must read through it while I continue to peruse the shelves," she ordered. She kicked out gently with the toe of her slipper, pointing toward the nearby table. "Over there, if you please."

"Yes, ma'am," he replied, taking the book over to the oaken table as ordered.

She turned her attention back to the shelf. There were many leather-bound books up here, of varying sizes and states of repair. They were bound distinctly, without the usual gold lettering that graced the other books nearby. They must be unique, perhaps for a specific purpose.

"What is it?" she called. If he could figure out the subject of that book, perhaps they would have a better notion of what the rest contained.

"It's Mother's handwriting." His voice was entirely bereft of its usual joking tone. "It appears to be her journal."

Hannah turned so suddenly that she had to grip the shelf to keep from falling. "Are you certain?"

"I could not be mistaken in this." He looked up at her, his face drawn and pale. "I must confess, I cannot read it just now."

"No, no, of course not," she replied quickly. "Leave it there for now. If that is a handwritten book of your mother's, then we must at least be in the right area of the library. For you see, all these books are bound differently than the rest." She picked another one off

the shelf and leaned her full weight against the wood
frame for support. Thus balanced, she flipped it open.
"This is a ledger book from a long time ago, judging
by the yellowing of the pages."

"So if the breeding book is in here, it's probably
on that shelf." He put his mother's diary aside and
moved swiftly back over to the set of steps. "Hand
them to me. We'll bring each one down. The maids
need to dust up there anyway."

Hannah began passing each volume down to him,
and he placed them on the table. When the shelf was
finally cleared, a mountain of books awaited their in-
spection. As he helped her down, Hannah grew conscious of the vast amount of dust covering her hands
and apron. Well, there was nothing to do about that
now. She would have to clean up later.

John divided the pile of books into two halves, and
they each began reading through the stacks. Ledgers,
account books, different books of lists—the Reed
family certainly kept a clear record of everything that
happened on the estate. This was likely one of the
reasons why everything ran so smoothly, unlike, for
example, her brother-in-law Daniel's estate. Goodwin
Hall had been in complete disarray from the moment
he stepped across the threshold, and it was Susannah
who finally helped him to bring the entire estate back
in order. Yet the book she sought was nowhere in this
vast pile of information.

"Aha!" John crowed, holding a book bound in
green leather aloft. "And here it is."

Curiosity compelled her to rush over to his side.
He flipped open the book, which was wide and flat,

with large, smooth pages. Each page was marked with rectangles connected with lines, and within each rectangle a name had been written. This was a complete record of all the breeding of the stock at Grant Park, for generations past. "How fascinating."

"It is rather." He turned to a page listing the breeding of collie dogs at the Park. "Here is the information we need."

"Why do you need to know all these generations of dogs?" She shrugged. "What difference will it make?"

"I suppose Davis is thinking that we can prove our pedigrees go back for many years, and that we have always had the finest dogs in the county." He closed the book and looked over at her. Why did her heart persist in fluttering every time he looked her way? She was behaving in a ridiculous fashion. "Perhaps that will help establish our position as *the* place to purchase dogs."

"Of course." She nodded. Now that they had found what he sought, there was no need for her to remain in the library with him. "I really should go back to work now."

"I am sorry I kept you from it so long," he replied. Then he seized her hand and kissed it, dust and all. "Thank you."

"Why?" she gasped, resisting the urge to clasp her hands to her chest. It was a chivalrous gesture that any gentleman would make, and certainly nothing special for her.

He placed the breeding book next to his mother's

diary. "I never could have had the courage to do this without you. With your help, I have found the heart and the soul of Grant Park."

## Chapter Fifteen

Some of the poison had eased out of his existence since the hour he and Sid spent in the library. He didn't have the courage to read Mother's journal just yet. No, that would have to come later. Instead, John sat, poring over the breeding book in the comfort of his study while Sid and her assistants worked in the next room. He could just make out the hum of activity as they created Jane's wardrobe, and the sound of it soothed him. It was rather like the roar of the distant surf when he'd stayed in Liverpool one summer with friends. Somehow, too, it was pleasant to know that Sid was right nearby, and available—albeit grudgingly at times—for conversation.

He turned the page. Here was the entry for Bah and Cleo, and there was Madge, listed with several of her siblings, long since sold. He traced the smooth, heavy paper with his finger, drawing the line down from one generation to the next. Beside him, in her basket, Molly snored in her sleep. He glanced over, smiling at her. After a morning gamboling with her brothers and sisters, she was completely worn-out.

In the next room, he overheard Sid talking to one of the maids, and he remembered his promise. Was she making clothes for herself, as well? He closed the book and rose, taking care not to waken Molly as he walked past her basket and into the workroom.

"I say, Sid," he demanded as he strode in, "what about your frocks?"

Sid glanced up, her mouth full of pins. "Hmm?"

"Your frocks. Are any of these girls making dresses for you?" He turned to Amelia and Lucinda. "What are you working on now?"

"I am trimming Miss Jane's riding habit," Lucinda replied with a curtsy.

"I am working on one of her toques." Amelia was already sitting in a chair, so she gave him a respectful nod.

"What on earth is a toque?" Women's clothes were something altogether different. It was a good thing indeed that he had asked Sid to take charge.

"A type of bonnet, sir." Amelia held up her handiwork, which was a velvet bonnet. What made it a toque instead of a bonnet? In plain terms, it was merely a hat.

"So what are you working on, Sid, if these two girls are working on Jane's clothing?" He turned to her.

She straightened and removed the pins from her mouth. "A shot-silk ball gown. The hem must be done very fine or else the silk can rend."

He nodded with approval. "And this you intend to wear when you accompany Jane in London?"

"No." She stood back and tilted her head, giving her work the critical glance he'd come to recognize as an artist would assess her art. "This is for Jane, of course."

"So, when are you making your wardrobe? That is most important, too, Sid. You must think about what you might want." He, too, surveyed the gown. It was very pretty. Too bad Sid wasn't going to have the chance to wear it, for she would look quite fetching in something as elegant as that.

"I really haven't time," Sid protested. "We have so many dresses and hats to make for Jane, and I must have each one done to my approval."

He rocked back on his heels. "So you need more help."

"Why, no, of course not." Sid flushed a becoming shade of pink and looked over at the two maids. "They are working their fingers to the bone. I don't want you to think we are being lazy."

"No, I am quite aware of that. I hear the buzz of activity every day for hours through the doors of my study." He nodded to the two maids to let them know that he wasn't considering their work shoddy. "Jane's wardrobe, in and of itself, is an overwhelming enough task. We must bring in reinforcements if we are to get her work done and allow you the time to make your own clothes. I could bring in a few more servants if that would help. Or, perhaps you would rather have people you've already worked with? We could bring in your helpers from the millinery shop in Tansley."

"There is very little for them to do," Sid admitted with a sigh. "But closing the shop could well mean the end of my business there for good."

"When do you return to Tansley?" He really didn't want her to go, of course, but it was part of their bargain.

"I had hoped to return at the end of this week, provided you approve."

"Leaving at the end of a week? Why? Didn't you go at the beginning last time?" Time had passed so quickly since her last visit. He should let her go, of course, but still it seemed like she had just returned. But she was right. It had been a fortnight. Somehow, having her gone at the end of the week was less tolerable than having her gone during the week. Saturdays and Sundays were so very slow at Grant Park. Her absence would seem interminable.

"I did, but if I go to Tansley before the Sabbath, I can visit with my sisters and enjoy Bible study at Goodwin Hall." She was paying attention to the hem of the ball gown as though the world depended on her complete concentration. "I miss having that."

"Oh, of course." Sid felt none of his conflict when it came to the Lord. After Mother died, he just didn't like the thought of a higher being in control of his life, or of anyone else's. To be perfectly frank, he was mad at God. Jane shared none of his antipathy and, in fact, had grown in her personal devotion over the years, traveling to the church in Crich every few weeks for worship. It made for a lengthy journey, but she always returned full of purpose and more serene in countenance than before she left.

Now his lack of faith was proving to be a sort of wedge between himself and Sid, for she was planning a trip around it, and without her at Grant Park the weekend would simply drag by. He couldn't prevent her from going, though. She asked so little of him as it was.

"While you are in Tansley," he continued, "do you want to bring back your two workers so that they can begin working on your clothing? I would be happy to pay them, of course. We've plenty of room here, as well."

"I hesitate to close my shop completely." Sid put the garment aside and faced him. "Do you mind if we talk about this someplace else? Amelia and Lucinda grow bored with our chatter, I am sure."

The two girls smiled demurely and he gave himself a mental kick. He felt so at ease around Sid that it was difficult to remember any kind of hierarchy existed between them, or with the women she worked with.

"Come, we'll discuss this elsewhere." He offered her his elbow.

Once they were safely in the hallway, Sid spoke up. "I worry that the girls will think I don't like their work if I bring other workers in, and I do not feel comfortable closing the shop," she confided. "Business is terribly slow, but I will lose what little foothold I have if I bring my workers here."

He nodded. Her shop was important to her, and her decisions always seemed to gather around what was best for it, even if what was best for it didn't necessarily improve her own life. "I have an idea. What if you took the items you need with you to Tansley, and then you can have them work on your garments while you are gone? If business is as slow as you say, it might be for the best to keep them busy in some form or fashion."

"I suppose I could." Sid bit her lip in a distracted fashion. "Or I could have them make some of Jane's things while I work on my own. That might be better. I've never had anyone else sew for me. My sisters and I have always made our own clothing."

"Then it's settled. Take whatever you like with you, and that way you'll have time to sew for yourself." He paused before the library. "Shall we return to our respective jobs, then? I am working with Davis this afternoon, and there are a few things I must attend to before I have any fun."

"Work before pleasure?" Sid fixed him with a dazzling smile. "That sounds woefully unlike you, Reed. Weren't you the one who lived only for amusement?"

He blinked a little, blinded by the brightness of her expression. "True, true." He began leading her back to the workroom. "On the other hand, I am beginning to enjoy work as much as play. If my friends in London knew, they would be horrified."

She laughed. Sid had such a sparkling laugh, one that he heard all too rarely from her. "Indeed."

"Yet you are the one who never stops working to enjoy herself," he went on. "That laugh of yours, for example. I think I could count on one hand the number of times I've heard you laugh. But like your dancing, you were born to laugh. Why do you indulge yourself so little?"

"From as long as I can remember, I've had to

work." She said the words slowly, pensively, as though she had never really spoken of it before. "You see, when Father and Mother died, we went to live with our uncle Arthur. He was a wasteful old codger, one who went through our fortune like water. I worked because I had to, in order to survive. I also had to balance my two sisters. Becky was such a hopeless romantic, and Susannah had such a hot temper. So I had to be the one who was practical, for I had to think for three poor young women. There really wasn't much opportunity for dancing, although we used to laugh a lot when we were all together."

"So, essentially, you have had to live for others." Just like she had to change her name to please Susannah. He stopped just short of the workroom door. "You've never had much of a chance to do anything for yourself."

"I don't think I have, though I haven't considered it much before." She withdrew her arm from his and placed her hand on the door latch. "I believe this position has given me more freedom than I have ever enjoyed. Thank you."

"No thanks are necessary," he protested. "It does leave me curious, though. If you could do anything, this afternoon for example, what would you do?"

Her brow furrowed as she concentrated on her reply. "I don't know. I suppose I like to sketch, though I don't often have time to unless it's for work."

"Come with me, then," he offered. Sid had worked so hard that she deserved an afternoon of fun. "When I go visit Davis, you can bring your sketch pad and draw the puppies. That could be fun, don't you think?"

"Yes." She looked up at him. "It could be."

"Then it's settled. I'll fetch you after luncheon." With that, he let himself back into his study, a feeling of happiness settling over him. He was giving her a small gift, in return for her help with the books. It was the very least he could do.

Hannah knelt in the straw, her sketch pad in her lap. The puppies rolled about, yipping and biting at one another while Madge, their mother, looked proudly on. Davis and Reed continued their quiet conversation over in one corner of the barn. It was a jolly pastoral scene, and the sights and smells of the barn relaxed her. She began to sketch with short, sure strokes.

As she worked, her mind drifted. She would have time to make her own gowns, and they would have to be more than serviceable. In fact, if she really was to accompany Jane in society to any degree, she must look as fashionable as any other young lady. Of course, she must remember her place. It would never do to try to outshine Jane, and besides, she wasn't as lovely as Jane even on her best day. All the same, she must try harder to look au courant.

What kind of dresses would she need or even want? There was a fine blue cotton lawn that would go well enough with her complexion. Perhaps she could make it up into a day dress and knit a shawl to go with it in a lighter shade of blue. That would look very fine, and there was still a rough straw bonnet at the shop in Tansley that she could pair with the blue cotton. It would make an excellent walking costume.

She finished sketching Madge and turned her attention back to the pups. She chuckled softly to herself as they barked and tumbled, playing at being fierce, big dogs. It was difficult to even capture their movements, so quickly did they scamper.

Reed, hearing her laughter, nodded to Davis and came over. "What's so funny?"

"These puppies." She pointed her pencil at them. "They are adorable."

"It's difficult to believe that someday they'll be as dignified and composed as their mother," he agreed, kneeling down beside her in the straw. "May I see your work?"

"It's nowhere near finished, but here's the rough idea." She tilted the sketch pad toward him with a slight feeling of unease. Other than Jane seeing her sketch that one time, she really hadn't shown anyone her work and it was a trifle nerve-racking to share.

"You have a real talent," he said, after a moment's silence. "These dogs look lifelike. Have you ever considered doing portraiture?"

"No." She turned the sketch pad back toward her. "To be perfectly honest, I had no aspirations beyond being a milliner." Again, he compelled that admission from her. Her ambitions weren't really any of his business, nor was it her place to reveal them to him. Why wouldn't she learn to keep her mouth shut?

"You know, when we go to London, I could introduce you to some people. Perhaps gain a couple of sittings for you." He ran his gloved thumb meditatively over his bottom lip. "You could do quite well as an artist for the ton."

"I really don't know what to say." She had never considered anything like it, and the possibility was too much to contemplate at the moment. "I don't know that I have that much talent."

"You know, it's puzzling." He sat down, stretching his booted feet out before him. "You have the absolute ability to cut through endless layers of dithering about other subjects, but not about your own talents, your own needs and desires. Why is that? If you can help me face the truth about my mother, why can't you indulge the hope of a life that's different from the one you currently have?"

He had posed an honest question, and one that didn't have the faintest trace of derision. He deserved an honest answer. "I suppose I learned my place early on. The world may be at your feet when you are young, handsome and wealthy—and a man, to boot. But when you are poor, have no connections and happen to be female, the world is very different. I have come to expect that I will end up as an old maid in one of my sisters' homes if I don't carve out a good living for myself." She stopped, suddenly confused. Here she was, unleashing yet another torrent of words—and did she actually call Reed handsome?

His cheeks were flushed a deep brick red, but he said nothing about her comments regarding his person. Instead, he picked up a piece of straw and twirled it around his fingers. Finally, he spoke. "I never thought of it that way, but I understand what you say," he replied, quietly. "The only thing I would tell you is that you should dare to dream a little bigger for yourself, and to seize what opportunities come your way."

"Such as a trip to London?" She made a few more marks on her sketch pad. Outwardly, she must appear calm, even if he had caused a tempest in her emotions.

"Precisely," he responded. Tossing the straw away, he rose. "Shall we?" He extended his hand and drew her to her feet.

They walked back to the manor house in silence, the glamour of the late spring day falling all around them. As they neared the front portico, he stopped. "Promise me you'll make time for yourself, starting with your work in Tansley."

She clutched the sketch pad to her chest and tucked a stray lock of hair behind her ear. "I promise to try."

# Chapter Sixteen

Hannah opened the door to the Siddons Sisters Millinery Shop and breathed in deeply of the familiar smells—dust and fabric. This should feel like home, but it didn't. Being back in Tansley felt temporary, like a perfunctory obligation to take care of on her way to do bigger and better things.

She closed the door and walked inside. Both the girls were already gone for the day, but before they left, they had placed Mrs. Holdcroft's new bonnet out for her approval. She picked it up, looking it over with a critical eye. "It's very good, though Abigail still hasn't learned how to make her stitches nearly invisible," she muttered to herself. Talking aloud was better than the yawning silence of the empty shop. "I wonder if they let Mrs. Holdcroft know it is ready. I'll have to deliver it myself, if she doesn't come in the morning."

She looked around the shop, in the hopes that other orders had come in, or that she would see some evidence of work that had taken place over the fortnight since her last visit, but the shop was painfully empty. Other than her window display and Mrs. Holdcroft's new hat, there was absolutely nothing that pointed to work or industry in the entire shop.

A sinking feeling settled in the pit of her stomach. This was it, then. She'd known it was coming, all along. The store had finally died. She had failed, which was something neither Becky nor Susannah had done. When they left the store, it was still a vibrant and bustling enterprise. Now that it was hers and hers alone, it had faded away. Tears stung the back of her eyes, and she brushed her hand across them with an irritated gesture. Crying would do no good now. It was time to face facts.

She dropped her valise off upstairs. Her workers had remembered to put fresh linens on the bed, as she had requested. However, they had neglected to draw fresh water from the well for her washbasin. She rushed out to get water and then gave herself the luxury of washing her hands and face, still grubby from travel. Then she removed the handkerchief case that Jane had tucked into her valise. If nothing else, she still had Grant Park, and Jane, and even Reed.

Sighing, she made her way downstairs and placed the box back in her display, which still looked bold and valiant despite a few spider webs. Hannah brushed them away, and then she turned and left. Any other time, she would make the effort to clean the entire shop from attic to cellar, but not today. It was simply too defeated-feeling in there. She must leave.

The main road into the village was sparsely populated, with only a few stragglers leaving the shops

on their way to go home. She would go by the bakery and see if Bess, who had been their friend since
they moved to Tansley, would have any scones left.
She would certainly not look at the village shop, and
she would definitely not go in and see what kind of
business the milliner was doing. She'd had enough
heartbreak for today—and besides, the sight of so
much success would certainly wilt what little self-
respect she had left.

Across the village green, a door slammed and a
rustle of activity caught her attention. A slight figure in an enormous hat marched purposefully across
the green, swinging her arms with gusto. She was
muttering to herself furiously. Hannah stopped still,
blinking. The woman beneath the enormous hat was
her archenemy, the Frenchwoman, and judging by
her stride, she was furious.

*"Stupide!"*

Well, that word was rather unmistakable, no matter
what language it was uttered in. Hannah stayed rooted
to the spot, unable to move or look away. Clearly, the
young lady was incensed. When the Frenchwoman
came close enough that Hannah could speak without
shouting, she murmured, "Good evening."

"Hello." The woman snapped the single word out.
"Tell me, miss, are all Englishmen *stupide*?"

Hannah laughed at the impertinent question. She
couldn't help herself. "Many are, I am afraid. But
not all."

The milliner pointed back at the village shop.
"That man thinks I can work all hours and produce

beautiful hats without going home for dinner or seeing my family or sleeping. *Mais non!* I am through."

Hannah's heart leaped in her chest. Was she really quitting her position at the store? "You are so successful, though. How can you bear to walk away?"

"I can leave because I know I can be successful somewhere else," the woman said, putting her nose in the air. "I've done well in other places, and so I shall continue."

She was cheeky, and self-assured, and something in her tone made it clear that this was not the first time she had left a job. Her forthrightness brought out the truth in Hannah. "I must confess, it could do me a power of good to have you gone. You see, your work here has run me out of business. My name is Hannah Siddons, and I own the Siddons Sisters Millinery Shop."

The Frenchwoman gave a curt nod. "*Je suis* Lillian Bellamy. I know your shop. I have seen it often. Did I really close it down?"

Hannah shrugged. "I think you could easily claim the victory. You see, as soon as you moved in, I started losing business. Before you arrived, I was the only milliner in the village. Of course, your creations are so *chic*, I couldn't really compete. I had planned to close the shop, so little business have I now."

"Well, you may open it again with pleasure," Lillian replied. "I will seek employment elsewhere."

Conflicting emotions coursed through her. On the one hand, she had already prepared herself somewhat for the inevitable closing of the shop. On the other hand, did she really want to go back to the way things were? Obligation told her yes, she must continue with the shop. For weeks, though, she had been pulled in another direction; in fact, she had been led there by the Lord. Surely He in His wisdom knew what He was about. *Dare to dream a little bigger for yourself, seize what opportunities come your way,* Reed's voice echoed in her mind.

"Forgive me, Miss Bellamy, but I take it that this is not your first position?" A plan began to take shape in her mind, one that could leave her free to follow the path the Lord was setting for her, and at the same time, give Miss Bellamy some of the freedom she so obviously needed.

"No," Lillian sniffed. "I have had several millinery jobs, none of which turned out well. For every time, the person I worked for thought I was some kind of machine."

"Have you given any thought to owning your own shop?" Excitement thrummed through Hannah. If this worked, it would work so well. "If you have your own shop, then you can dictate what you do and for how long and so forth. You can hire people to help you. At the end of the day, you reap your own profits, too."

Lillian blinked her wide, dark eyes. "I had not considered it, no."

"I think you should, for you obviously have the talent to create business wherever you go." Hannah gave her an encouraging smile. "Have you any money saved?"

The Frenchwoman frowned. "Very little. That man kept most of the profits." She pointed angrily at the village shop. "I take a room above the bakery, and most of what I have, I pay for my own room."

Hannah made a tsking sound and shook her head gently. "That will never do. When my sisters and I started our shop, we had almost nothing, as you do now," she admitted. "We built our shop from the ground up. I imagine with your aptitude, you could do the same."

"True, I think I could." For the first time in their entire conversation, Miss Bellamy was wavering. "I just never thought of it. I am not native to England, and I supposed I must be."

"I don't see why that would make a difference." This was the right thing to do. It was utterly mad, of course, but right. "What I would like to do is give you my shop. The whole thing. Take it and make it yours."

Miss Bellamy gasped, her alabaster skin turning whiter in the dimming afternoon light. *"Qu'est-ce que vous avez dit?"*

Hannah shook her head. "I am so sorry, Miss Bellamy, but the only French words I know are *peau de soie* and *mousseline* and other phrases related to dressmaking and fabric and being fashionable."

"My apologies," Miss Bellamy replied. "I just could not believe what you said. Are you certain? I cannot pay you much at all."

"To be honest, I am not sure the shop is worth all that much," Hannah replied with a rueful chuckle. "But if you agree to take it, I will accept one thing as payment."

"Name it." The Frenchwoman's demeanor turned from shocked surprise to efficient, competent attention.

"I heard from one of my best customers that when our shop came to the village, it changed lives here. All at once, women could get a beautiful hat without ever having to go to London. Suddenly, women who could not afford to make a journey could still have a nice bonnet if they wished. Promise me that if I give you the shop, you will always leave it here. No matter how angry you get, or how many customers offend your sensibilities, never give up on Tansley." She sighed, finding it difficult to go on. "You see, it will actually be easier for me—it will make it seem all right—if I know the shop will always be here, no matter what I do with my own life."

"Not only do I promise, I will sign any paper you give me that will make it official," Miss Bellamy replied. She drew herself up proudly, and it was clear that begging or accepting favors was not something that came easily to her. "Thank you."

"You are welcome," Hannah replied. The weight was off her shoulders, she was as giddy as a schoolgirl. She could barely contain the urge to jump up and down, or toss her bonnet into the air. "I am in Tansley for the next few days, and I will help you get started and moved in. There is a flat above the shop, which will of course be yours. We'll see if we can convince my workers to stay on for you, if you find them adequate to the task. I think that, within a few months, the shop will become a bustling center of stylish activity once more."

Miss Bellamy's sharp features softened, and tears welled in her dark eyes. "You have changed my life."

"Fair's fair," Hannah replied, her heart light as a feather. "You certainly changed mine."

"Are you out of your senses?" Susannah shoved her chair away from the dinner table, her lovely face a mask of disbelief. "You *gave* the shop away? Without consulting me? Without consulting Becky?"

Hannah braced herself. Making this announcement at dinner at Goodwin Hall was surely not the most subtle approach, but it was the most efficient. Everyone was here. Daniel, Susannah, Becky, Paul—everyone who might have an interest or an opinion in the matter was dining in this very room.

"I have tried to consult with both of you many times, but you were both too busy to advise," she replied steadily. "You made it very clear to me that the shop was my sole responsibility. This is the best decision I could have made. The shop will be a raging success under Mademoiselle Bellamy. Her creations are exquisite."

"I am undone," Susannah murmured, passing her hand over her brow. "The shop we worked so hard for—and you just gave it away."

"The last time I was here, Becky pointed out that it could well be that the Lord was turning me down another path, one that was separate from the shop," she recalled. She turned and nodded to her sister, who shook her head furiously, waving her hands. Becky wanted no part in this conversation, and yet she was an equal partner in this debacle, too.

"I don't know that it's such a bad notion," Daniel put in, giving Hannah a wink. "You haven't really had a part in the shop in some time, Susy. Becky will be far too busy soon, as well. Now we know that the shop will remain in Tansley and that the new milliner is talented. I suppose it really did work out for the best."

Susannah gave her husband a sideways glance that would have withered a lesser man, but Daniel just tossed a cheeky smile her way. Hannah looked down at her plate and bit her lip to stifle a sudden burst of laughter.

"I can't say I agree with giving a business away," Paul chimed in. "Couldn't you sell it for some profit?"

"It was practically without value," Hannah replied, looking at him steadily. "I have had one bonnet order for the past two weeks, and Mrs. Holdcroft came in with her son to pick it up today. Miss Bellamy has at least a dozen pending orders at the village shop, which she can now fulfill quickly since my workers are staying on board to assist her. She has the skill and the orders to continue the business. Moreover, the building has been being neglected while I am at Grant Park. She's a Frenchwoman, so speaking natively, she's a born housekeeper."

Paul nodded, considering his teacup. "It sounds like you thought it through. At the end of the day, I have no say in the matter, but if you want my opinion—well-done, Nan."

Actually, she hadn't thought it through. Giving an enormous, life-changing event its due consideration would have put her off completely. Instead, she had surrendered to the Lord, and followed His will. Somehow, she couldn't bring herself to say it aloud.

"You should be here, watching the shop. It would

not have been neglected if you were here to take care of it," Susannah began in the tone of voice that signaled an impending lecture.

"I have another position at Grant Park, one that has been extended to include a journey to London next year," she interrupted. "I cannot possibly care for the shop any longer. I gave it to her on the condition that she continues to run the shop in Tansley. I think it's vital to our community that a stylish hat shop continues to thrive here."

"I agree with Paul," Daniel replied. "Nan, I think you've made the right choice." He smiled at her.

Hannah's heart warmed under her brother-in-law's words. He said them in opposition to his wife, which could cost him dearly once everyone left that night. Daniel was a good fellow, and she'd always appreciated him for all he had done for their family. In fact, he kept her sister busy, which was enough reason to adore him.

"Well, Becky? What say you?" Susannah turned to Becky, who rubbed her middle protectively. Hannah eyed her elder siblings, one after the other, and love suffused her for both of them. They might not see it now, but getting rid of the shop could bring them all close again. For years, it had been a millstone around their necks, a point of contention and an obligation. It was not now what it had started out to be, which was a way for three poor sisters to earn their way in the world. With it gone, she could go back to knowing her sisters as friends rather than business partners.

"If Nan is being called to Grant Park, then I say she must answer the call." Becky smiled slowly at

Hannah. "The shop hasn't been mine for quite some time. I really don't see how I have a say in it."

Susannah shook her head slowly, looking at the assembled party. "I don't know what to say," she said finally. "It has been done, however, and there is nothing more to say."

It was hardly a victory, but it was as close as she was going to get for now. Hannah turned her attention back to her plate and conversation continued on a less rocky path. As her swirling emotions settled, one thing was certain.

She could not wait to tell Reed about her decision. He, above everyone else, would understand.

# Chapter Seventeen

John turned to his sister, who was practicing her violin as they sat in the salon after dinner. "Sid comes home today." It had been a week since she left. Not that he had been keeping up with each day that passed.

"What a relief," she replied, finishing her song with a flourish. "She's a much better conversationalist than you." She scrunched up her face at him, and he laughed.

"True, true. I cannot hope to argue the finer points of what bonnet would flatter your complexion most," he admitted. He put aside the book he had been reading, a fascinating volume about training dogs to herd sheep, and gave his sister his full attention. "Tell me, are you glad she will be accompanying us to London?"

"Of course." Jane laid her violin and bow aside and flexed her fingers. "But, I think, not as glad as you will be." She came and sat beside him, in a velvet chair near the hearth.

"Whatever do you mean by that?" He glanced at her, raising his eyebrows. "I will be happy to have her assistance bringing you to heel, if that's what you are saying."

Jane rolled her large, dark eyes at him. "No, idiot. I know you will enjoy Hannah's company in London because you have developed quite a *tendre* for her."

For a moment, a panicked, suffocating feeling took hold of him. It was predestined that he should marry, because Grant Park needed a mistress and an heir, eventually. He had rather hoped to wait until he had Jane safely married off before he turned to his own matrimonial prospects and selected a woman of proper bearing and breeding. However, he had just grown used to the idea of being master of the house— his own eventual nuptials were too much to consider at present. He schooled his features into bland disinterest. "That is a ridiculous statement. What makes you say that?"

"I can see the way you look at her," Jane replied. "I have also noted that you rely totally on her counsel, and that you trust her as you trust very few people. As soon as I heard she was accompanying us to London, I knew the truth. You cannot bear to let her go."

"Jane, don't be absurd." There was some truth to what Jane said—he did like Sid's company, he relied on her and he had complete confidence in her. But did he love her? Surely not. Sid was not the kind of woman with whom he was used to keeping company. The women he knew in London were a fast set: hard, beautiful and frivolous. Of course, none of them would do as mistress of Grant Park, so he had just assumed that, when the time came, he would find a woman of their class who was no less exquisite, but infinitely quieter and better behaved. "I asked Sid to accompany us because I need her to help me rein you in. Without her assistance, I predict that I will have a terrible time making you attend the requisite balls, reviews and concerts."

"Hmm." Jane tilted her head to one side and fixed him with a mocking glare. "I find it difficult indeed to believe you." She leaned forward, a daring sparkle coming into her eyes. "Why don't you marry her and be done with it, then? Why this ridiculous facade— why must we go to London? I have my heart set on Timothy Holdcroft, and you would do very well to marry Hannah. I say, let's be married to the ones we love now, without dithering about. Come on, John. I never knew you to shy away from something daring before."

For a strange moment his heart leaped at her words, but he shook his head. "No. For one thing, neither Timothy nor Sid are of our class. You know this, as well as I do. If I am to be master here, I must understand this and adhere to what's expected of me—of both of us."

She made a disgusted sound and sagged against her chair. "You are a snob, John."

"No, indeed, I am not." He struggled to put his feelings into words, for he had not properly sorted them out in his head just yet. "You see, you have a vast living at your disposal and could easily fall prey to a fortune hunter. I am not saying Timothy Holdcroft is that type of fellow, but what do we know about him? What do we know of his family? The immense amount of material wealth that is yours could make any man, even a man who professed to be good, turn into a scoundrel."

Jane shook her head, compressing her lips. "It's not true," she choked out.

"It may not be, but it could be, and as your brother it is my duty to protect you," he interjected. This was quickly turning into a slippery slope. He thought he had a foothold, but obviously the entire side of the mountain could come crashing down with him, if he didn't take care. "As for me, well, I must marry someone who could hold a candle to Mother as mistress here. She was good, kind, devoted to the health and well-being of everyone on this place, even to her own detriment." He sighed, pressing her memory to the back of his mind. "She was also cultured and refined, and quite beautiful. I must find someone like her to be my wife. I would disappoint both Mother and Father if I settled for less."

"Hannah Siddons falls short of these expectations in what respect?" Jane was a fairly gentle creature, but when roused to ire, her temper could be alarming, as he well knew. He must tread carefully, for her hardened tone signaled that she was losing all patience with him.

"It's not that Sid falls short. She's just…different, somehow." He'd not thought of her as a prospective mate, because her social status forbade any thought of matrimony. Moreover, he had not considered himself marriageable material until very recently. When one's life is all about chasing pleasure, what time is there for caring about taking a suitable bride?

Jane sighed. "Oh, dear brother, whatever will you do when my time in London draws to a close, and I end up marrying the man of your dreams, and then Sid must go away?"

Her question hit him like a blow to his stomach. He must control himself, for it wasn't his choice to make. The decision was made for him at birth. He must marry a certain type of woman. For years he had thumbed his nose at the conventions of his position, not out of disrespect to his parents, but out of a driving need to have fun. He needed to make it up to Mother, somehow. She died far too young, while serving others. He was, in his own way, making up for what she had missed out on. Now, he had accepted the responsibility of being master of Grant Park. He had to take up the yoke and accept everything that came with it, whether he agreed with the rules and expectations or not. "I don't know," he admitted finally. His head throbbed.

"Well, you had better think it over," she snapped. She rose, picking up her violin. "I personally think that you are being foolish. Whether you realize it or not, you are in love with Hannah Siddons. As to how she feels about you, I don't know. Frankly, I think she can do far better." She flounced out of the room, slamming the door behind her.

The pictures on the wall rattled with the force of her anger. John winced, rubbing his temples.

He had engaged in many fights over the years with his sister, but this one was particularly bruising. He thought he was doing so well. He was taking an interest in Grant Park and making it his own. He was making sure Jane had a proper London debut, right down to a wardrobe that befit a princess. In fact, he had been rather proud of himself, for he no longer felt the burning ire against God that had smoldered within him all those years. Sid's gentle guidance had helped him turn away from anger, and to begin accepting the thought that God hadn't stolen Mother away.

Now he was unsure. Jane was furious and disappointed in him. How could he be doing both right and wrong at the same time?

He needed to be isolated from everyone. Before leaving for the seclusion of the library, he grabbed two books from the table beside him. They were books that he had meant to study when he was in the right frame of mind: the Bible and his mother's diary. As shaken as he felt, and since Sid wasn't here to guide him, he must rely on these books for direction.

He gained the security of his room, and heaving a deep sigh, settled into a chair and opened Mother's journal. The sight of her handwriting hit him like a physical blow. His hands shook as he turned the fragile pages, hardly seeing the words as tears clouded his vision.

One of the last entries snapped him out of his misery. He read, wiping his eyes.

*My poor boy has fallen ill with a fever, and I can hardly bear to see him so low. He is always so full of life. My prayer is that he will make a full recovery and go back to being the mis-*

*chievous little scamp he's always been. He is the dash of pepper that makes everything right. It's wrong to see him feeling so miserable. He should be free to be as lively and loving as always. Whatever shall we do if he becomes a sour and dour old man? That would never do for our Johnny. He should be free.*

Mother wanted him to be free, and she loved his impish behavior, which, at eleven years old, was playful indeed. She wanted to encourage that in him, and probably in Jane, as well. He sat back, closing the book. Mother had not been angry, or upset, or full of blame. This would take a while to fully comprehend, for this changed his entire life.

Hannah smiled as the carriage neared the gates of Grant Park. Freed of the responsibilities and worries of the shop, she could finally enjoy coming home to Grant Park to stay. At least until her time here was done. After that…she could not think beyond the London trip. For the moment, her liberation from the Siddons Sisters Millinery Shop was enjoyable, but it also brought up concerns about her future beyond Jane's debut. Once Jane was suitably wed, there would be no reason for her to hang about. What would she do then? Could she parlay her experience as Jane's seamstress into another position elsewhere?

She sank into the carriage cushions as they rolled through the gates. "I can't think about that right now," she murmured to herself. "The most important thing to remember is that I can't allow my head to be turned." That was, of course, the greatest obstacle she would face once she started helping Jane in London. She could easily get used to the life of a companion, enjoying the ease and luxury that her betters could expect. Then she would be spoiled for the life she could provide for herself.

No, she must put away anything that could cosset her into thinking that she was a fine lady, too, starting with the wardrobe she was expected to provide for herself. She didn't have any workers in Tansley any longer, for Abigail and Mercy had agreed to stay and work for Lillian Bellamy. So she must do her own sewing, and with the scarcity of time she had, she would limit herself to one or two gowns. After all, her current dresses were nice enough for day, though not as fashionable as the dresses she was creating for Jane.

There was the usual welcome-home flurry of activity, from Molly frisking down the back steps to greet her to Mrs. H's outstretched arms and warm hugs. Then she was upstairs in Jane's suite, unpacking her bag for the last time until she tagged along to London.

"So, you gave the shop away? Just like that?" Jane clapped her hands and laughed. "Upon my word, that is delightful."

"The best part of it is, I truly think it was the right decision for everyone involved, no matter what Susannah thinks." Hannah took her sky blue day dress out of her valise and gave it a good shake. "I feel certain that Lillian Bellamy will make that shop thrive, as I never could. I must be meant for something else. I believe that God has set me on this path with you."

Jane smiled. "I like that thought." She paused, plucking at the coverlet on Hannah's bed. "Tell me, did you see the Holdcrofts?"

"Yes, I did. Mrs. Hugh's bonnet was finished, so she came in to pick it up. I introduced her to the new shop owner and made sure to praise Lillian's skills. I am certain she is going to be a lasting customer." Hannah put the blue dress away and withdrew the handkerchief box. "I remembered to bring this home, too. Thank you for letting me borrow it both trips. Somehow, having it displayed out in the store made me feel braver and more certain of myself."

"Of course." Jane took the box with hands that seemed to tremble a bit.

"Jane, are you all right? Are your hands shaking?" Hannah bent close to examine her friend.

"I have a bit of a headache," Jane admitted, rising from her spot on the bed. "I think I will retire. It does us all a power of good to have you back, Hannah. John and I were just talking about how much we missed you this morning."

"Were you?" Hannah squashed the faint hope that rose in her chest. Jane had an exquisite turn of phrase and natural graciousness; what she said was said out of pure politeness and had nothing whatsoever to do with John Reed's feelings.

"Yes. In fact, I encourage you to seek him out and tell him about giving the shop away," she replied. She gathered up the handkerchief box. "Good night."

"Good night, Jane. I hope you feel better."

Hannah finished unpacking her valise, and a gnawing sense of restlessness took over her. Truth be told, she was ready to see John Reed and tell him all about her achievements, but that would certainly not do. He wouldn't really care, and she would be overstepping her boundaries. Perhaps, if she read a book she would calm down. She picked up her candle and made her way downstairs to the library.

A light flickered under the door. The fire must still be lit, even at this late hour.

She pushed open the door and gasped in surprise. John was there, reclining on the settee, asleep. Two books had been opened and draped across his chest. She crept inside quietly, thankful that her slippers made far less noise than her boots.

Hannah selected a couple of novels and was about to leave when John suddenly sat up, sending the books tumbling to the floor. "Sid?" He yawned.

"I am here. I thought it would be all right to borrow a few books to read," she replied, coming around the settee to face him. "I am sorry I awakened you."

"Not at all. I should be awake." He ran his hand through his hair. "How was your trip?"

"Rather amusing," she replied. She told him about Lillian Bellamy, the shop and, of course, her sisters' reactions. "Susannah was the most appalled, even after the matter had been settled," she concluded, with a laugh.

"How does it feel, being rid of all those obligations?" He stooped over to pick up the dropped books.

"To be honest, there are two emotions—genuine

happiness and genuine fear," she replied with a shrug. "I am trying to focus on the happiness."

He laughed. John's laugh was no longer as annoying to her as it used to be, for he laughed as much in professed admiration for her now as he did out of an urge to tease her. "I will never grow tired of your honesty, Sid. Or your bravery, for that matter. You have been courageous in giving up something that no longer served you. I have faced some of my fears, too. I spent the afternoon reading, which in and of itself is unusual for me. I read two things— my mother's diary and the Bible."

"How do you feel?" This was no small victory for a man who had, until very recently, held himself and God responsible for his beloved mother's death.

"I don't know how to feel. You see, my mother did everything out of love, as did our Savior. I spent all these years railing against Him for taking her away as He did. I spent just as much time convincing myself that everything my mother did was out of duty, and I could never measure up. I feel exhausted and buoyed at the same time. As though, for the first time in years, I can see clearly. Does that make sense?" He stacked the books neatly, one atop the other, and looked at her from beneath his eyebrows.

"Yes. It makes perfect sense. I have been struggling with those emotions myself." She cradled her books close to her chest. "I suppose I should go."

"I would not have had the courage to face either of them, my Lord or the memory of my mother, without your help, Sid." He gave her a tired smile, but his eyes glowed warmly. "Thank you for helping me to become a better man."

She nearly lost her hold on the books. How ridiculous. He was merely expressing the kind of feverish gratitude anyone would feel after they stayed up too long, reading through heavy and emotional subjects. "You are welcome," she replied simply, though her voice quavered a trifle. "I really should be off to bed, though."

"Sid, one thing before you leave." He opened the Bible. "Hear these words of wisdom—'Do not be terrified, do not be discouraged, for the Lord will be with you wherever you go.'"

"Ah, the Book of Joshua," she said, smiling. "Then I have these words for you. 'For God hath not given us the spirit of fear; but of power, and of love, and of a sound mind.'" With that, she bobbed a curtsy and left the room in a swirl of skirts.

Somehow, discussing bravery with John was terrifying.

## Chapter Eighteen

Hannah awoke the next morning full of purpose, for every moment of her next year must mean something. She would wring every last bit of joy and hope and determination from every day, preparing herself for the inevitable time when she must part ways with the Reed family.

The thought of leaving Jane was saddening because her companionship was like having Susannah and Becky home again, before everyone got married and went away. It was hard to think of losing Jane. In many ways, Jane had become the sister she never had.

Somehow, it was even more difficult to think of leaving John behind. She had come to rely on him as someone who took her out of herself. At first, his jolly nature and joking ways were merely irritating. He had, though, broken down the wall she'd built around herself. Without him, she would never have given up the shop.

She hurried down to the workroom, eager to begin her day. Amelia and Lucinda were already there, working on an embroidered shawl and pair of gloves. "Has Miss Jane come in this morning?"

Amelia looked up from her work. "No, miss."

"That's odd. I asked her to, as I need to have her try on this ball gown. It's still basted, and I need to make the final seams." She sighed. Jane must still be having breakfast, or else she had started the day by practicing her violin. If that was the case, then she would be gone for quite some time. "Oh, well. I'll work on the riding jacket lapels."

Hannah gathered the brown tweed fabric and sat in a sunny corner. The task of making invisible stitches on rough fabric occupied all of her concentration. When she finished, her neck was stiff and her fingertips sore. She had been stitching for over an hour, with no sign of Jane. If she could take a break from the tweed and work on the ball gown, it would make a nice switch. She stretched her neck, rolling her head over from one side to the other, and straightened. "Lucinda and Amelia, please feel free to take some time away from sewing. Perhaps we should start again in a few hours."

The maids nodded and sent relieved smiles her way.

It was time to hunt down Jane, for there was no finishing the ball gown without her trying it on. Hannah had basted everything together before leaving for Tansley, and what a relief it would be to finally have it done. She scurried up the stairs to Jane's wing, listening for the sounds of Jane practicing her violin. Aside from maids opening and closing doors, all was silent.

She opened the door to Jane's room, but it was

empty, save for a scrap of paper on the bed. That was odd. The maids must have forgotten to throw it away. In solidarity with all working women who sometimes forgot every last detail, Hannah picked it up to dispose of it herself. As she did, the sight of her own name made her pause.

My Dear Hannah—

Hannah sat down, her mouth suddenly dry. What on earth was happening?

By the time you get this note, I will be on my way to matrimonial bliss. Timothy Holdcroft and I are eloping to Gretna Green. I know, as sensible as you are, that you are probably disappointed in me. On the other hand, I think you know how very much I love Timothy, and because of that, I think you will want to see me happy. I tried to go along with John's idea, but another year away from Timothy is intolerable. Your trips to Tansley have kept hope alive for both of us. Please don't be angry with me. John will be, but perhaps you can make him see reason. If anyone can, I think it would be you. With sisterly affection,
Jane

This must be a wretched joke. Was John playing a trick on her? She looked around, desperate for signs that Jane was, in fact, still there. She leaped from the chair and wrenched open the wardrobe door, but only a few pieces remained inside. She whirled around, seeking out Jane's violin, but the entire thing was gone, including the case.

If the violin was gone, then Jane most certainly was, too.

Panic coursed through her, leaving her knees weak. She must go tell John what had happened. Perhaps there was still time to intercept the couple. The Holdcrofts were a good family, and there was nothing of the fortune hunter about Timothy. Even so, an elopement was most unseemly. If only Jane had listened to reason. What silliness, to dissemble over a year. If Jane had upheld her end of the bargain, then Hannah would have worked on John over the course of the year, finally having him agree to the match and everything could have been done properly.

*These romantic women and their impulses. Save me from ever being a fool like this.*

Crumpling up the note in her hand, she raced down the stairs and out of the house. John would be in the barn. He was always out in the barn, working with the dogs whenever there was daylight. Only in the evenings would he come in, and then to read more about training and breeding.

By the time she reached the barn, she was panting with the exertion, her hair untidily windblown from its braided coronet. The grooms gawked at her openly as she hurried through the barn.

"Reed."

He turned around, a smile of welcome on his face. The smile faded when he saw her. "What's happened?"

"Jane. She's run away. Eloped with Timothy Hold-croft." She held out the note to him.

He snatched the scrap of paper, scanning it with eyes that had lost their usual warm light. "What does she mean, you kept hope alive for them? Have you been aiding her in this ridiculous romance?"

"What? No, of course not." She swallowed, struggling to calm herself. "I don't know what she meant by that. Does it matter? Shouldn't we be going after them now? We could try to intercept them before she gets too far."

"That depends entirely on this situation." His jaw muscles tightened. She had not seen him this angry since that one day in his study, when she had spoken to him about Jane's love for Timothy. "I trusted you, when you gave your word. Did you betray me?"

"I did not." Though she was terrified, she forced herself to look him straight in the eyes. "I don't know why Jane said I gave them hope."

"Davis." He shouted the word, and the head groom rushed over. "Did you see my sister leave this morning? Are any of the horses gone?"

"No, sir. All the horses are here, and I haven't seen your sister all day." Davis called to his grooms. "I'll ask all the lads what they've seen."

"Good. If you hear anything, send word to the big house." Reed grabbed Hannah's wrist and pulled her along with him as he left the barn. "Now, let's question her maid."

Hannah had to run to keep up with his long strides. She didn't like this at all. For so long, she had been considering herself, if not Reed's equal, at least his friend. Now, the closeness between them had melted away in the heat of his anger.

He tugged her up the stairs, in full view of any servants passing by, and flung open the door to Jane's room. "Beth," he called. "Get out here at once."

Beth, a pretty, slight girl with a shrinking demeanor, walked hesitantly into the bedroom from the sitting room. "Yes, sir?"

"My sister has eloped. Please don't insult my intelligence by pretending you didn't know." He cast a withering look Hannah's way. "I want to hear every detail of the whole debacle."

Beth burst into tears. "She said you would be angry."

"That word doesn't begin to describe my emotions right now." He let go his hold on Hannah, and she rubbed her wrist. The sudden release was disconcerting, as was his anger. She was no longer a part of his life, certainly not a trusted part of his life.

"It will be better if you tell the truth, Beth," she spoke up. "Please tell us all you know."

"Miss Jane had been planning to elope with Mr. Holdcroft for some time." The maid gasped between sobs. "She conveyed messages to him through Miss Hannah."

"What?" Hannah shook her head incredulously. "I don't know what you are talking about."

"I knew you were involved. Otherwise, why would my sister say that you had given her hope?" He turned on her, his brown eyes sparkling dangerously. "Hannah, I trusted you."

She fought back the ridiculous urge to cry. "Beth,

I had no idea that she transmitted any messages through me. What more can you tell us?"

"I don't know. All I know is, she left first thing this morning. Mr. Holdcroft came to fetch her, and she was gone." Beth sobbed again. "I watched her go."

"You are discharged." Reed spat the words out at Beth. Then he turned to Hannah. "I am going after my sister. With any hope, I can find her before the marriage has taken place."

Beth ran, crying openly, from the room.

Hannah took a deep breath. Panicking and crying would do no good in this situation, as much as she wanted to give vent to both emotions. "I will come with you."

"No, you've done quite enough." He rushed out of the room toward his suite, forcing her to run after him. "Thank you, Miss Siddons. You may consider yourself discharged, as well."

"Wait," she gasped, quick on his heels. "You know how well she has listened to you in the past. At least I could get her to agree to the appearance of going to London. She will pay attention to me. I don't know if she will give you any credence."

He turned around, his brows lowered. "Fine. If you can convince her to return, your position here may be saved. Be outside in less than five minutes."

John made haste to get ready, throwing clothing into a trunk without waiting for his man to help him. He shouted orders to his butler and then begged him, quietly, not to say anything else to the servants. Of course, his temper had gotten the best of him, and surely everyone, even down to the last scullery maid, knew what had occurred.

He ran outside, preparing to yell at Sid for not being ready, but she was already downstairs on the portico. She was dressed in a simple, dark suit and her battered old valise was resting next to her. Had she been crying? Surely not. She had nerves of steel and even though she was in the wrong, she would brazen it out.

"Get in," he ordered curtly. "I'll sit on the box."

He handed her up into the carriage and slammed the door shut. Then he climbed up next to the coachman. Driving was one thing that could soothe his mind now, and he needn't spare the whip. The faster they traveled, the sooner they could overtake Jane and her paramour. "I'll take the first turn," he muttered to Hopkins. "After the end of this stretch, you can take over."

"Very good, sir."

John whipped up the horses and they lurched forward. Grant Park rapidly faded from view as they headed north. As the carriage jolted over the roads, he searched his mind for the moment everything went wrong. Somehow, he wasn't as angry with Jane as he should be. His sister was quiet and shy, but she had a will of iron. He should have seen this coming. She had acquiesced too quickly, had given up on the idea too agreeably. When they had that conversation the other day—was it only yesterday?—he should have known something was brewing in her mind. She was trying to get him to agree to a plan she had already put in motion.

His greatest disappointment was in Sid. How could she have been a party to this? She had asked him openly about the matter, and he had told her his reasons for objecting to the match. She let the matter drop, or gave the appearance of doing so, and then went behind his back. He had trusted in her so implicitly for so long. He had talked to her about things that he had never spoken of to anyone else, and he had grown so used to her. She became a part of his life. He didn't want her to leave it. Now, she had revealed herself as she really was, and he could never trust her again.

He brooded, mulling the matter over and over in his mind. As he rounded the corner, the horses skidded, neighing. Another carriage was in the road, sitting askew. He managed to avoid it, nearly clipping the wreckage as he went past. Then he pulled the horses to a halt and jumped down from the box.

"John!" A familiar voice cried as he neared the ruined carriage. Jane poked her head out of the carriage window. "John?"

He had succeeded in finding his sister, more quickly than he had ever imagined. They must have broken down just a short while after leaving.

"What are you doing here?" he demanded.

Timothy Holdcroft, bent over the axle of one of the wheels, straightened as he approached. "Mr. Reed," he replied, respectfully touching his cap. "I can explain."

"Of course you can explain. The three of you planned this whole matter out and now you got caught," he retorted. "Jane, get down. You are coming home now."

Her expression turned mulish. "I most certainly am not. A broken axle will not deter us, even though it's taken forever to repair."

Behind him, the sound of a carriage door opening alerted him to Hannah's presence. As she drew near, Jane's expression softened. "Hannah?"

"May I join you?" Hannah asked. She placed one hand on the carriage door.

"Yes," Jane replied warily. "You may. My brother can stay out there, on the road."

Hannah vanished inside the carriage with a flurry of skirts. He was left with his coachman and footmen standing behind him, and Timothy Holdcroft standing awkwardly before him. The young man looked at him, regret and appeal warring with his expression. "I didn't mean for this to happen, sir."

"A broken axle happens to the best of us. Hopkins, see what you and the lads can do." He motioned for the coachman to take a look at the axle. "I want to have a conversation with Holdcroft."

"Of course." Timothy walked a few paces away. "You probably want to give me a good thrashing."

"The idea crossed my mind," John admitted. "However, I am trying to live a life that is a bit more along the 'turn the other cheek' way that Christ taught us. What I do want to know is why you chose to wed my sister in such a dastardly fashion."

"Jane insisted that we would not be able to get married in any other way," Timothy admitted, with a sheepish look. "I hated the idea of elopement, but

Jane was most insistent. I didn't want her to think I didn't love her enough to be daring, so I went along with the idea. I wanted to come and explain my case to you, one man to another. In fact, I drove up here with that intention. But Jane intercepted me, and, well, she wanted to run away. So we did, though we didn't get far." The young man looked down at the ground. "I know you think I am a scoundrel, but I assure you my intentions are honorable."

"My sister's fortune means nothing to you?" Why not pare the matter down to the simplest objection, and be done with it?

"I assumed that if we eloped, she would not see a penny of it," Timothy replied. "I am fine with that, and I will provide for her."

That was a direct enough answer, but he had been fooled by simple "honesty" before. "That is true," he replied. "Not one tiny bit of her fortune would come to you."

"I understand."

He glanced back over his shoulder. The coachman and the footman had finished the repair, and the carriage was sitting properly once more. "Come with us back to Grant Park," John replied. "We can do better by all of this if we have a serious discussion at home, and not out here on the road."

Timothy nodded. "Of course."

"In fact, I'll follow you," John continued, stuffing his hands in his pockets. He stifled a sardonic grin. "I would like to make certain that you won't lose your way once more."

## Chapter Nineteen

Hannah sat in the parlor, clenching her trembling hands around a fragile cup of tea. Timothy stood before her, facing the hearth. They were alone, for Reed had gone to see to both carriages, and Jane had fled to the security of her room.

"Miss Siddons, I never meant for this to happen, not in this way," he began, turning pleading eyes her way. "I never gave a thought to anything but Jane's happiness. You must believe me."

Hannah forced herself to meet his gaze. In the depths of his expression, she could discern only regret and sorrow. He was genuinely sorry for what he had done. He loved Jane, and he wanted to be with her. It was as simple as that. "I do believe you, Mr. Holdcroft."

"How do I make her brother understand that I am no fortune hunter? I know what he must think of me. Indeed, I can scarcely blame him." Timothy heaved a gusty sigh. "What a muddle."

"Yes." Hannah paused for a moment, giving the

matter some thought. "Mr. Reed appreciates honesty and straightforward talk, for he has no use for anyone who dithers or tries to evade the truth. This is why an elopement is so repugnant to him. He would have been much more impressed if you had simply come to him, as you intended, and put your case to him."

"I tried—" Timothy began.

"I know, and Jane changed your mind. I know full well how persuasive the Reeds can be, when they want you to do things their way," Hannah replied. After all, she had completely rearranged her life around what John Reed had urged her to do. Without him goading her on, she would be at home in Tansley now. The shop would be in ruins, and she'd end up as an old maid in one of her sisters' homes, but she would not have endured the topsy-turvy ride that characterized life with the Reed family. Life would be quiet, and frustrating, and set in stone.

Life would have been, in short, miserable. Yet here she was, just as wretched as if she had stayed, because John Reed thought she lied to him. She would never betray him, but he would not believe her.

Timothy stood, one hand braced against the mantel. "You know him better than I do. How should I try to redeem myself?"

She shrugged. "I am not certain. At one time, I would have argued your side to him, but he no longer trusts me. He thinks I was a sort of romantic go-between for you and Jane. I wasn't, as least as far as I know, but nothing I say carries any weight with him any longer." She looked at him pointedly. "You will have to do this on your own. Talk to him, be honest with him. He may not agree to anything, but at least you must make the effort. Above all, do not allow yourself to be carried away by anything Jane says again. If you listen to her and defy your own sense of morality, then you are sure to fail."

He nodded. "That is sound enough advice."

She closed her eyes for a moment. There was nothing more for her to do here. Amelia and Lucinda could finish Jane's wardrobe without any further assistance from her, as long as she left a few instructions for them. Whether Jane would be using the gowns for a London debut or for her own trousseau was neither here nor there. It was time for Hannah to leave Grant Park and go home. Her business here was done. It had been done for some time, but she had been cajoled into staying because she felt she could be of help.

No, that was not all. If she was going to be perfectly honest with herself, there was a deeper reason for her staying. She loved John Reed. She could not imagine life without his companionship. Once, she thought of Grant Park as home. Now home meant her sisters. Home meant Tansley.

"Are you leaving today?" she asked. Her heart grew heavy in her chest, but this was the right way. It was, in fact, the only way. If she could leave Grant Park, then she would have a clear mind in which to try to solve all of this mess. Staying here would be no help at all.

"I think I will." He gave her a sheepish look. "I hardly think I will be eloping to Gretna Green tonight. I must also face my mother, and she will be furious."

It was difficult to imagine the aristocratic Mrs. Holdcroft in a screaming fit. Surely, when she grew angry, she was of the icy and precise persuasion. In some ways, that could be more forbidding than an open display of temper. Her heart lurched in pity for Timothy. He was having a rotten time of it, no doubt. "When you leave, I will come with you, if I may. I don't think there's much future for me here. Mr. Reed mentioned that I was discharged, and I doubt he's changed his mind."

"Oh, Miss Siddons." Timothy shook his head slowly. "Our plan ruined your life, too. For that, I am so sorry. You see, when all of this occurred, I never considered that it would affect you at all."

"I know." She gave him a tremulous smile. "I don't blame you. We don't always look before we leap."

"Taking you home to Tansley is the very least I can do," he replied. "I will talk to Mr. Reed and apologize. Then we will make our journey."

The door opened, and Reed strolled in. Hannah forced herself to look him in the eye. He was so very aloof and forbidding, where once he had been warm and teasing. There was nothing in his expression or bearing that spoke of welcome to her. He eyed her coldly and passed by without even a curt nod.

She rose, a little unsteady on her feet. "Gentlemen, if you will excuse me."

"I believe only one of us is a true gentleman," Reed replied, a mocking grin spreading over his handsome face.

Timothy reddened, but accepted the insult without complaint. "I will see you in a little bit, Miss Siddons."

She nodded and curtsied to both men, then quit the room. There was really not much left to do. She was already in traveling attire, and her valise was still packed. The only thing she could think of to occupy herself was to make a list of things to finish for the two maids. She took the stairs two at a time, wanting to be done but at the same time, wanting to stay.

"Hannah." Jane was waiting at the top of the stairs. "What's happening?"

"Mr. Holdcroft is talking to your brother. I don't know anything more." She brushed past Jane and opened the door to her room.

Jane followed her in. "My brother is furious still?"

"I imagine he will be, for some time." Hannah took a sheet of foolscap from the dresser drawer and sat, dipping a quill into some ink.

"What are you doing?" Jane moved over to stand beside her.

"I am making a list of items for Amelia and Lucinda to finish for your wardrobe," Hannah muttered. She began writing.

*Take measurements for ball gown. Have Miss Jane try it on, for it has just been basted together, and a close fit in the bodice is necessary for the proper finish.*

"Why?" Jane peered at the list.

*The lapels for the riding jacket are finished and ready to be attached.*

"I will be leaving soon." A sudden, unreasonable

anger suffused Hannah. Jane had deceived her, too.
Jane had been blinded by love, rendered selfish by her
own desires, but in the process, she had run rough-
shod over all of Hannah's own hopes and dreams.

*Be sure the ruching for the rough straw day bon-
net has been pulled tightly, and use the Valenciennes
lace for trim.*

"Where are you going?" Jane's eyes filled with
tears.

"I am going back to Tansley, where I belong." At
any other time, she would have ended the conversation there, but the stubborn, unreasonable anger
would not abate. "Do you have any idea what you
have done? You told your brother that I helped you
in your romance, when you know full well I did no
such thing."

*The embroidery for the evening shawl must still
be done. Embroider over silk pads for a raised effect.*

"But—" Jane began, her face drained of all color.

"I don't want to hear it." Hannah finished the list
with a flourish, dropping her quill to one side. "Your
brother thinks of me as a liar no matter what I say.
Very well, then. You two can go about your lives,
wrecking into every poor person you meet. I am done.
I will go home to do what I should have done before.
Now I can't go back to the shop, because I gave it
away. So, I must resign myself to being an old maiden
aunt, living in my sisters' homes." She rose, looking
Jane squarely in the eye. "I love you as a sister. But I
am so angry with you right now that I scarcely dare to
speak to you, for fear of saying something truly hate-
ful." She thrust the list at Jane. "Do something use-

ful, for once, and give this to your maids. Not Beth, of course. She's been sacked. Another victim of the Reed selfishness."

Jane accepted the crumpled list, tears streaming down her face. "I never meant for John to be angry with you. I'll talk to him."

"Don't you dare." Hannah rushed past her. "I made a fool of myself, believing that your brother really liked me, that he trusted me, and that he thought of me as more than plain old Nan Siddons. I don't need any more help being humiliated."

Jane followed her out onto the landing. "Hannah, don't go. Please let me mend the damage I've caused. At least let me talk to John, for I think you must be in love with my brother."

"Of course I am," Hannah snapped, trotting down the stairs. "But I am also an idiot."

"All I can hope is to win you over to my side by behaving in an honorable fashion from now on." Timothy Holdcroft gave John an earnest look. "I won't see your sister again without your permission."

"I think, for the moment, that my permission is denied." John sighed. All the anger had drained out of him, and now he needed to think. Yet he couldn't think about this unless he had someone there to mull it over with him. He would normally depend on Sid for help, but if she had aided and abetted this relationship, then he was not about to trust her yet. "Does your family know about this debacle?"

"I am sure my mother has found my letter by now." Timothy cleared his throat. "I must go home to make amends with her, too. Though to be honest, I would rather stay and face your anger, sir."

Despite himself, John gave a short bark of laughter. "You don't think your mother is pleased with you?"

"I know she isn't." Timothy nodded slowly. "You see, my mother still wants us all to behave as we would if our family fortune had not been lost. She would be appalled at anything that could sully the family name, even if our family isn't of the ton any longer. Not that she's a snob," he hastened to add. "It's just that, well, she wants us to never forget where we came from, even if our current circumstances are straightened."

John nodded. "There's something to be said for maintaining a certain standard in a family. For years I rebelled against it myself." Until he found Mother's diary and understood what she meant by duty and loyalty. Everything she did was done out of love, not a sense of obligation. It was a concept that was hard to understand and harder still to apply to his own life, but he was trying. As angry as he was, he was still trying.

"I wouldn't say I've resisted it," Timothy replied with a shrug of his shoulders. "The only time I have gone against it was to marry Jane. I love her, Mr. Reed. I can make her happy. I beg of you to let me try."

"I must consider the matter further." John folded his arms across his chest. He must act out of love, but at the same time, he could not act too rashly. "When I have made a decision, I will let you know."

"Thank you." Timothy held out his hand, and John shook it.

Despite himself, he found himself liking Timothy Holdcroft. He was no Lothario, that much was certain. He cared about his family. He professed to want none of Jane's fortune, and somehow, his words were believable. If he went ahead and gave his consent, though, then he would seem too easily persuaded. So, he must wait just a bit to make sure he wasn't merely charmed by the Holdcroft family, or eager to end an unpleasant scenario in his life. After all, he had always run away from circumstances like this before because they weren't any fun. Now, if he was to prove himself a true master of Grant Park, he must struggle from beginning to end, no matter how unpleasant it was. He would remember Mother's credo as he worked through it, but he must have some time to think over the problem.

A knock sounded on the door, and Sid stepped in. "I am ready when you are, Mr. Holdcroft."

John's heart lurched at the sight of her pale face and packed valise. Was Sid eloping with Timothy now? "What is going on here?"

"I am going home to Tansley, to face my mother," Timothy replied. "Miss Siddons asked to come along so that she may be with her sisters."

"Yes, sir." Sid turned to him with the same brisk, businesslike demeanor she had used in the earliest moments of their acquaintance. "I suppose I am still discharged. In preparation for my departure, I have left behind a list of orders for Lucinda and Amelia. Once they have finished them, Miss Reed's wardrobe should be complete enough, at least until you reach London and can have some work done by a proper seamstress."

This couldn't be happening. She was leaving? She wasn't supposed to go for a year, at least. Yes, he had snapped at her, and yes, he was furious with her, but he did not expect her departure. "I don't know that I am happy with this" was all he could manage.

"I assure you, it's for the best," she replied, giving him a terse smile. Her blue eyes held a bright sparkle that could be anger or tears; it was hard to tell which. "Miss Reed will have an ample wardrobe for her first few weeks in London. I thank you for this opportunity, Mr. Reed. It has certainly been life changing." She turned to Timothy. "Shall we go?"

He gave her a courtly bow. "Yes, if it's your pleasure."

She threaded her arm through Timothy's elbow, and the pair walked out of the parlor.

John followed, jealousy writhing within him as he watched Sid walk arm in arm with Timothy. She could not go. He must have a chance to think the matter through, and he couldn't, not if she was gone. "I am not done with you, Miss Siddons."

She paused, turning to face him. "Is there more, sir?"

"There is, but I shan't say it in mixed company," he replied, nodding at Timothy. For his part, Timothy stood stolidly by her side. The fellow was certainly unperturbed by unpleasant situations, and the way in which he was squiring Sid away from an unhappy state of affairs would have caused admiration at any other time, and under any other circumstances.

"Well, then, perhaps you can put it in a letter," she replied tartly. "I have given you many weeks of hard work and the wardrobe I have created will stand your sister in good stead. I wish her every happiness. And you," she added, her expression softening a trifle.

With that, she nodded to Timothy, and they left the house. His carriage—hired, no doubt—waited outside by the portico. Timothy handed her inside and then climbed onto the box, whipping the horses up.

The carriage traced a semicircle in front of the house. He strained for a glimpse of Sid, but the curtains remained drawn. If she would but turn, he could wave or give some sign that, despite his anger, he still needed her. The curtains did not so much as flutter. With a profound sinking feeling, the realization hit him.

She was not going to look back.

# Chapter Twenty

Hannah looked down at her breakfast, the eggs congealing onto the plate. Her stomach turned.

"Eat, eat, it will do you good," Daniel urged from his end of the table. "I have never seen you looking so peaked, Nan."

She gave her brother-in-law a halfhearted smile and poked at the eggs with her fork. "I am really not so very hungry, Daniel. Is Susannah coming down?"

"She usually has her morning tea in bed, and then she will be down to breakfast later," Daniel replied. He took another bite of ham and eggs. "You came here last night in such a state, Nan. Do you want to talk about it?"

Hannah paused. In some ways, she felt compelled to tell the whole sorry story to Susannah, and withstand all the judgment and questions that would come with it. Her eldest sister had been the head of the family for as long as she could recall, and as such, she should know about the excruciating embarrassment to which Hannah had exposed the family. On the other hand, Daniel was like the elder brother she'd never had. He was kind, and he understood. Moreover, he had a long history of making terrible mistakes that rendered him more sympathetic to the plights of mere mortals than Susannah, who hardly ever made a cake of herself. If she could tell Daniel first, it might help her later when she had to relate the whole sorry tale to her elder sisters.

"I failed," she said simply. She stared down at her plate and the eggs grew blurry as tears filled her eyes. She would not cry now. Crying was reserved for nighttime, when she could bury her head in her pillow and weep soundlessly. She blinked rapidly and bit down on the inside of her cheek. The pain sharpened her focus. "I don't know what went wrong, Daniel. Here is what I can tell you. Yesterday, Timothy Holdcroft went to Grant Park to ask John for Jane's hand in marriage, and instead, they tried to elope. John and I caught them before they got out of the county, for their carriage had broken down. We got Jane home, and Timothy came back to Tansley. I rode home with him yesterday."

"How did you fail?" Daniel helped himself to a slice of toast from the silver toast rack. "It sounds to me like the matter was between Jane and her brother."

"Somehow, and I don't know just how, Timothy and Jane were able to communicate through me every time I came home to Tansley." She sighed. "John thought I was helping their romance along, when really, I had no idea. I promised him that I would help Jane with her London debut, but instead, it looks like

I went behind his back to help his sister. He believes that I lied to him, and he discharged me."

"That's absurd." Daniel slathered butter over the toast. "Are you sure I can't interest you in toast and jam? Here. Try some, it will do you good. Eggs are difficult to eat, even at the best of times." He slid a china plate down to her, with two pieces of toast and jam.

She took a careful bite, unsure if her stomach would stage a revolt. The jam was sweet and soothing, like the kind of food she used to eat as a child in the nursery. She shoved the egg plate away and took another bite of the toast.

"That's a good girl," Daniel said with a smile. "You can't think straight if you are starving yourself. Now, John dismissed you?"

"I suppose so. He threatened to, and I took him at his word. I was sure he was on the verge of it." She took a sip of tea. It was bracingly hot and comforting. "I decided to dismiss myself, first. Besides, Timothy was coming home to Tansley. I figured I might as well save time and energy by riding with him."

Daniel laughed, but somehow, she didn't mind when he laughed at her. "Nan, that is so much like you. Practical and efficient, even when in the depths of despair. But why did you show yourself the door? You should know by now that John has a temper. He explodes like fireworks, but then it all fizzles out. He's a jolly fellow most of the time, and his temper never endures for long. I know that both John and Jane like the work you have done. Why deny yourself the chance to do more?"

"I couldn't bear it if he didn't trust me any longer," she blurted. "I value his opinion of me far too much."

"I see." Daniel gazed at her, his brown eyes softening. "You think highly of him, then."

There was no use hedging. Daniel had guessed at the truth anyway. "I made the awful mistake of falling in love with him. Of course, he can't love me. I am not the kind of woman he is looking for to be mistress of Grant Park. When he started believing me to be a liar, it hurt as badly as if he had cut me with a knife. I couldn't abide the look in his eyes. I couldn't tolerate the feeling that I had failed him. So I left." She took a restorative sip of tea, allowing the golden liquid to wash the bitterness down her throat.

"Oh, Nan." Daniel shook his head. "It's not an awful mistake, and you are precisely the kind of woman that Grant Park needs. Any man would be proud to call you his wife. And if he didn't, he would have to answer to me."

Despite her misery, Hannah chuckled. "You're just saying that, but it's nice to hear."

"You know me well enough to know by now that I don't give pretty speeches." Daniel gave her an affectionate smile. "Of you and Becky, you were always my favorite sister of Susannah's. I've felt a kinship with you from the moment we met. A man knows where he stands with you, and he knows you will always be honest with him. This is such a valuable gift, Nan—I wish you knew how rare it is. John Reed has, until very recently, been around women who compliment and cajole him because of his wealth. They laugh at his jokes, they tolerate his bad habits and they flatter him even when his behavior is inappropriate. They have never dared to disagree with him, or to challenge him. I suspect, though I don't know, that you have had a profound effect on him for the better."

Hannah gasped. This was the kindest thing anyone had said to her, and the most lucid assessment of John that she could ask for. "Thank you."

"I always said the Siddons girls work on a man like a tonic," he replied. "Susannah was just what I needed. Becky has completely changed Paul. I imagine you have done the same for John Reed. When his temper cools and he spends a few hours alone in that vast house of his, he'll come to realize what a horrible mistake he has made and he will come running back to Tansley to fetch you. In fact, I am sure that Susannah will be spending her time making the chapel ready for a wedding, and Becky—despite her present girth—will be hard at work on a wedding gown for you, my dear. I know it's hard not to give in to maudlin feelings of despair, but stay strong." Daniel folded his napkin and placed it to one side of his plate. "If he doesn't, or if he continues to say ridiculous things about my little sister being a liar, then I will have to pay him a call."

Daniel rose from his chair and walked past her on his way out of the dining room. He gave her shoulders a hearty squeeze. Hannah smiled as he left. This was as content as she'd felt in some time. Daniel believed her, and Daniel was no fool. But there was the looming problem of what was to become of her. Lillian Bellamy had the shop—it was no longer hers. She had no place to go, and no prospects. In just a few brief hours, she had gone from a woman full of purpose and sure of her place in the world, to the one thing she had tried to avoid. She was a maiden aunt, a spinster, and she was now dependent on her sisters and their spouses for support.

She left her eggs but finished the tea and toast, for Daniel was right. She did feel somewhat better when she had something to eat. Then she went in search of her sister. Better to tell Susannah the truth and beg to stay with her now rather than later.

Susannah was finishing her tea in bed, a lace nightcap covering her exuberant auburn hair. As Hannah sat on the foot of the bed, Susannah eyed her over her teacup. "Daniel was just here, and he told me everything," she said, before Hannah could open her mouth.

*What a relief.* "Sue, I am sorry."

"Don't apologize," Susannah replied, briskly. "I agree with Daniel. We are affronted that John Reed would consider you a liar. Even in the heat of anger, which Daniel assures me must have bereft John of all reason, no one could consider you a hypocrite. In fact, if he were here, I would take him to task. How dare he?"

"Thank you for believing me," Hannah replied. "But you must think I have no common sense, for I have fallen in love with him despite his many flaws."

Susannah put her teacup aside. "It seems that the Siddons girls are all attracted to men who have their fair share of failings," she admitted. "Daniel and Paul were both men in need of a great deal of work. I suspect John Reed is the same. Daniel feels that John will realize what a donkey he has been and will come and make amends with you. The question is, will you take him back?"

"There's no question of taking back," Hannah replied, plucking at the coverlet. "He was not mine to begin with."

"I suspect he was, though neither of you may have admitted it to yourselves." Susannah set aside her tea tray. "I want you to be content, Nan. If John Reed will make you happy, you have my blessing."

"Thank you for saying that." Both Daniel and Susannah were certain that John would come running back to Tansley, but somehow, she couldn't see him doing that. She had no assurance that he felt anything more for her than a businesslike affection. "In the meantime, may I stay here?"

"Of course. Goodwin Hall is your home." Susannah smiled and rose from bed. She said nothing about Hannah's decision to give away the shop and nothing more about Grant Park. Daniel must have said something to her about it. A surge of gratitude coursed through Hannah. Because of her brother-in-law, the worst conversation of her life had not really been that bad.

John sat, staring at the hearth. The late spring chill was setting in as the sun set, but he would not have a fire. He wanted to be alone, in total darkness. In the past, he would have turned to any kind of dissolute pleasure he could think of to break his depression. He would have at least ordered one drink—or several. But none of that would do, now. He was a changed man, at peace with his past and in accord with his Maker. But for what good was that now? The woman he trusted most in this world, the one who brought him to the Lord, in fact, had deceived him.

His bedroom door opened, and a shaft of light pierced the gloom. "Get out," he ordered.

"I'm no servant, and I won't cower to your ridiculous wishes." Jane closed the door behind her and walked into the room, illuminated by candlelight. Using her taper, she lit all the candles in the room, then busied herself stirring up the fire on his hearth. When it sprang to life, the room was bathed in a mellow, golden glow, which was exactly not what he wanted to see or experience at the moment. He closed his eyes.

"I came in because I have made a terrible muddle of things, and I want to make amends." Jane snapped her fingers. "Open your eyes. I won't talk to you when you look like you're sleeping."

"Fine." He forced himself to look at her as she took her place opposite him. "Tell me." His eyes were full of grit, as though he had sand in them, and his throat was so tight he found it difficult to swallow. This malady had taken hold just after Sid left two days ago.

"You thought Hannah Siddons was involved in my romance with Timothy Holdcroft, but that's simply not true." Jane flushed and dropped her gaze to the floor. "She carried messages to Timothy, but unknowingly."

"What do you mean?" he rasped, rubbing his hand over his stubbled chin. Jane wasn't making sense, or else he was more out of sorts than he suspected.

"I loaned Hannah a handkerchief case, which she

used in her display at the shop. What she didn't know is that the case has a secret part." Jane held out a leather-bound box to him, and he took it. "Open it, and take a look."

He opened the lid, and as he did, spied a small spring just under the ridge. He tapped it with his fingernail and the top of the case opened, revealing a small compartment. "Sid never figured this out?"

"No. Hannah's too circumspect to go around prying into things I loan her. I would stuff a letter in there to Timothy, and he would go to Hannah's shop and retrieve it, and leave one for me. When Hannah returned, she would bring the case to me, and I would find Timothy's message in there for me." She held out two letters. "These are the letters Timothy gave me. As you will see, Hannah had no idea what was happening."

John scanned the foolscap with eyes that still burned.

I will leave this letter in the box in the hopes that Hannah Siddons will bring it to you, albeit unwittingly. I feel bad for taking advantage of her in this way, yet I have no other way to communicate with you, my dear. I hope that, in time, I can present myself to your brother as an honorable suitor. I despise creeping around like a thief.

He folded up the missive and handed it back to her. "Sid never knew." Each word was heavy, as though weighted with a stone.

"She never had an inkling," Jane admitted. "Through this handkerchief box, I was able to convince Timothy to come here and try to win my hand. Only, when the time drew near, I panicked. I begged him to elope with me because I was certain you would never give your consent. Of course, the whole plan was foiled and Timothy is back in Tansley, so I didn't get what I wanted anyway." She tucked the letters back in the box. "I am sorry because I hid all of this from you. I used Hannah, and because I was so callous and only thought of what I wanted, I ruined her life and yours, too."

John sat, brooding as he stared into the fire. He had accused Sid of lying, when he should have known that she would never go behind his back. In everything, she had always been painfully honest with him. He snapped and lost his temper and because of his actions, she was gone. He had been a complete buffoon, and she left with her spine straight and never looked back.

She was too good for him by half.

In fact, Timothy Holdcroft and Hannah Siddons were far better people than the residents of Grant Park. Timothy had tried to be aboveboard and honorable, and only when Jane insisted did he waver from that path. He was a good man, a simple and direct man, with nothing of the fortune hunter about him. Hannah Siddons was as straight as an arrow, exquisite and desirable.

He was as smitten with Hannah Siddons as Jane was with Timothy Holdcroft. Mother had wanted nothing more for her children than to act, as she did, out of love. She had wanted them to be free and happy. She would, above anyone else, want them both to make this situation right.

"Fancy a trip to Tansley?" he asked.

Jane gasped. "Do you mean it?"

"Yes." He hunched forward in his chair. "We don't deserve them, Jane. They are both far superior to us. But we can't live without either of them. Should we try to convince them that we are worth it?"

Jane nodded, tears sparkling in her eyes. "Yes. A thousand times yes. I know how much Hannah means to you."

He smiled for the first time in days. "I think you will make a good enough farmer's wife, provided you will put your violin away when it's time to milk the cows."

Jane slapped his arm, half laughing, half crying. "All talk of a London Season is over, then? I have your consent?"

"You do, as well as my apologies for acting like a stubborn, snobby fool." He leaned back in his chair. "Do I have your consent to marry Sid, provided she will even allow me in the front door of Goodwin Hall?"

Jane smiled. "I think she is essential to your well-being, John. Because of her influence, you have become an infinitely better man. I couldn't pick a better woman to be my sister."

"I couldn't agree more. It's settled." He rose, full of purpose and determination for the first time in days. "We'll leave just after dawn."

## Chapter Twenty-One

Hₒw bad could her worst nightmare be? Hannah gathered her skirts beneath her and knelt before her nephew. Charlie smiled and clapped his hands. "Are you ready for a story, then?" This was her new role, that of a maiden aunt, so she should start practicing without delay. "Auntie Nan would love to tell you one. Let's read about Jonah and the whale."

She gathered her nephew into her lap and opened a large, beautifully illustrated children's book. As she read, she nuzzled her chin against Charlie's hair. Little ones smelled so good. There was just something so sweet about him, as his grubby hands reached for the pages, ready to crumple them in his tiny, powerful fists. There was nothing at all alarming about being a spinster. This was lovely. The only run was that none of this would be hers alone. At the end of the day, Charlie would go back to his mother and she would be alone. That was the nightmarish part—never being more than a temporary comfort to anyone, and knowing that she would be by herself for most of her life.

What would it be like to have a child of her own? The sudden yearning to know made her feel slightly dizzy. She would never know, and this wondering was futile. Obviously, God intended for her to live her life being of service to others at Goodwin Hall, and there wasn't much more that she could ask for. There were far worse positions to be in.

She pushed the longing to the back of her mind. Now was the time to enjoy Charlie, and not brood over what could never be.

As she read, the door to the nursery opened, but she did not pause in her reading. The maids were in and out all day, and likely one of them came in to change the linens in Charlie's crib.

Charlie stopped paying attention to the story and instead began cooing, raising his arms up in the air. Mystified by his sudden change in focus, she glanced up.

John Reed stood before her, and he held Molly in his arms. As she lifted her eyes to his, he placed Molly on the floor. The puppy frisked about Charlie, who laughed with genuine delight and screeched as she had never heard him screech before. Molly, far from being cowed by this awesome display of toddler affection, licked Charlie's face. Hannah placed the book on the table nearby and regarded John warily. Why had he come back?

"He doesn't seem to be afraid of dogs," John said, smiling at Charlie. "That's a mercy."

"Indeed." She was grasping after dignity, but it was hard to remain frostily polite with a child and a puppy playing together in her lap. Their effusiveness rather lightened the mood. Why was he here? She must put some businesslike distance between them in order to think properly. "Perhaps it would be best if we went outside."

John scooped Molly up and Hannah found Charlie's jacket. She hoisted the toddler onto her hip and led the way downstairs and out into the front garden. She placed Charlie on a warm patch of grass and watched as John set Molly nearby. In a matter of seconds, the collie pup found the little boy and they grew absorbed in a game whereby Charlie threw fistfuls of grass into the air, to Molly's great delight.

Hannah turned to John. "Is anything the matter with Jane's wardrobe? I left instructions for the girls to use as they finished."

"No, her wardrobe is perfect. The rest of my life is a muddle, though." John grabbed her shoulders, holding her tightly enough that she could not move away without wriggling free. "Sid, everything's all to pieces without you, especially me. I don't deserve you. I never have. I was an idiot to think you had deceived me. Jane told me the whole tale, that she had you carrying notes to and from Tansley but that you had no knowledge of what you were doing."

"What?" Nothing he said made any sense, and his touch on her shoulders was mightily disconcerting.

"The handkerchief box had a hidden compartment," he explained tersely. "She used it to pass messages to Holdcroft."

"Oh." Mixed emotions welled within her—anger at being used, humiliation at being tricked and sudden relief that he knew she had not been knowingly involved. "I see."

"I don't expect you to want me," he continued, his dark eyes flashing. "I'm no prize. I am a better person with you than without you. Because of you, I came to understand the truth about both of my parents. I am now at peace with God. I can't offer you anything beyond what you already know about me. But if you promise to be mine, Hannah Siddons, I will spend the rest of my days trying to make you happy. Will you marry me?"

Hannah swallowed. Had she heard correctly? After all, there had been a misunderstood proposal once before in their past. "I am not sure I understand."

"How could I be plainer, Sid?" He laughed, holding her closer. "Normally you are so astute."

"I'm not trying to be thick," she protested, stepping away from the safety of his arms. She must have some distance between them to clear her mind. "Once before, my family thought you had proposed to me and it was all a terrible mistake, and I don't like to be humiliated for the same thing twice, if I can help it."

"I'm sorry." His face fell, and he looked at her from under his brows. "I was acting stupidly then. I am in earnest now. I don't know what to say, Hannah. I am not a man who makes pretty speeches easily. In fact, it is hard for me to stay solemn about anything for very long."

"True," she blurted. Honestly, would she ever learn to control her caustic comments?

If John minded her sarcasm, he didn't show it. "I don't know why I wasn't smart enough to propose to you that night, because I knew then, when we were dancing together, that we were a perfect match. I have, since then, come to feel in every respect that you are the only woman in the world for me."

She looked at him, and elation warred with anger within her. Why was she angry? She really couldn't say. All her life, she had been Nan—unlikeable, not pretty, boring and practical. She had accepted her role in her family and in the world. She didn't like it, but she had grown used to being the girl who nobody wanted. Now, here he was, changing all that she had grown used to and it was difficult to suppress the sudden strange thread of irritation that came with her whole world changing.

"I never expected to hear you say these words," she admitted slowly. "I don't know what to say. I thought everything was one way. Every time you come into my life, you turn it upside down."

"In a good way?" he pressed, looking more abashed than she had ever seen him.

"Yes, you've changed me for the better." She smiled, despite her roiling emotions. "I'm just not accustomed to these changes. I don't know what to say."

"I think I know what you mean, because I had started fulfilling my own circumscribed idea of who I was, too." He folded his arms across his chest. "When you were at Grant Park, you started allowing yourself to become Hannah. Now, you're back in Tansley, and you're Nan." He stepped back and gave her one long assessing look, from the crown of her head to the tips of her slippers. "The question before you isn't really about whether or not you want to marry me. It's about what you want. You can bob along and allow other people to tell you what to do, or you can decide for yourself. The choice is before you."

John Reed was challenging her, just as he had done several times before. When he did, and she rose to the dare, good things happened. With his help and encouragement, she had broken away from the rigid mold that had defined her all these years. She would have never done so without John.

"It's difficult for me to believe that you love me." She turned away, watching Charlie and Molly play together. Somehow, she couldn't bring herself to look John in the eyes when she confessed to the depths of her feelings for him. "I have loved you, most unwillingly, for some time now."

John chuckled, taking her hands in his. "Only you could say it that way, Sid, and yet it gives me some hope. So, we return to my initial question. Will you marry me?"

Hannah hesitated one moment more. If she said no, and went back to all that she had known and had grown comfortable with, she would never see him again. In all likelihood, he would walk out of her life and never return. In her mind's eye, she saw him turn his back and walk slowly away, and pangs of fear and regret shot through her. No, she didn't understand why he loved her, or how. She could only trust that God was leading her on a new path, one that would allow her to grow in faith and love with a man who had driven her nigh to distraction for several months.

She lifted her gaze to his. He was staring down at

her with such intensity that it made her knees a little weak. "Hannah?" he murmured.

"Yes, Reed. I want to marry you, and I will."

A rush of exultation swept through John. He seized Sid and spun her around, laughing. "Darling Sid," he cried, and then he kissed her with all the pent-up fervor of a man who had been given a second chance at life. Sid returned the embrace fully, not the least bit shy or timid about his passionate display.

He finally broke away, not because he wanted to, but to give them both a chance to take a deep breath. Sid gazed up at him with a swoony look in her large blue eyes that drove him nigh to distraction. "There are things I need to do now," he began, giving himself a brisk mental shake to focus his thoughts. "I need to ask Daniel for your hand, to start."

"Yes, of course." Sid straightened and set herself away from him. She patted her coil of braids with her hand. "Do I look all right?"

"You look lovely, as always." He reached out and touched her cheek. He could do that now. He no longer had to restrain himself, to distract himself, or otherwise busy himself when all he wanted to do was hold Sid. "Which reminds me, whatever happened with your own plan to make your own clothes?"

She smiled and shook her head. "I had no plan. For one thing, I didn't want to think too highly of myself, or to think I was better than I am." She cooed over at the little boy and Molly, who were still playing games together.

He groaned. "That's probably the last thing in the world you would ever do, Sid."

She rolled her eyes and moved on. "Moreover, I felt that my own wardrobe was sufficient. After all, I wanted all the attention to go to Jane. If I dressed myself up like a doll, then I could give the appearance that I was trying to compete for male attention."

He stifled a grin. Sid was always so formal, so proper. She didn't seem to be able to bring herself to say simple things like, "I could have been competition for Jane." She wouldn't allow herself to even come near to portraying herself as desirable. Over time, he would see to it that she would come to know and respect that she was the most attractive woman he had ever met.

"Well, that's neither here nor there, for Jane is no longer making her London debut." He patted his hands together and Molly came running. The little boy, startled at losing a playmate, began to cry.

Sid ran over and scooped him up, cuddling him close. He snuggled into to her, resting his head on her shoulder. Sid had a natural knack with children, just as she did with almost anything else. The sight of her holding the little boy was utterly delightful. The mistress of Grant Park was standing before him. She would help him create a family, and she would be beside him on every journey from now on. The certainty of it, after weeks of insecurity, both humbled and enchanted him.

"Why isn't she? Did she finally convince you otherwise?" Sid began to walk down the garden path, giving the little one a rhythmic pat on the back as they strolled.

"You could say that, yes." He followed, with Molly close on his heels. "The truth is, Jane came to Tansley with me. I must convince Timothy Holdcroft to ask for my sister's hand in marriage."

She spun around to face him, yet her movements were so contained that her nephew never stirred. "She is going to marry Timothy?"

"If I can persuade him, even after the way I treated him at Grant Park, then yes." He stooped down and grasped a stick from the garden path. With a quick flick of his wrist, he sent it flying for Molly to catch.

"I don't think you treated him poorly, or at least offended him to the point that he won't marry Jane," she said, sending him a radiant smile. "None of us were behaving very well that day, anyway. I think it's marvelous. Timothy is a good fellow, and his family is aristocratic stock. Besides, he makes Jane happy. So, Jane's London clothes will be used as her trousseau. Well, I should have created more practical day dresses. Some of those gowns will get ruined after just one day of farm life."

As they rounded the corner of the garden path, Jane came running from the house. She waved at them both, and as she drew near, she smiled. "Is the proposal done, then? Has Hannah accepted?"

John fought back an unreasonable wave of annoyance with his little sister. "And if she hadn't, wouldn't you feel awful right now? Suppose I hadn't asked her yet?"

"Oh, I could tell by your posture that you two were

close," Jane rushed on, oblivious to his irritation. She waved one hand at him, and then gave her full attention to Sid. "Hannah, darling, I owe you a thousand apologies. I should never have used you to further my communications with Timothy. I know it was wrong. I was thinking only of myself, and I didn't give any thought to the fact that I was deceiving you."

"You were in love," Sid remarked. "It can blind us all."

"You forgive me?"

"Of course I do." Sid shifted the child, who had now fallen asleep, and embraced Jane with her free hand. "Not only do I forgive you, but I love you as I do my own sisters."

"And now we will be sisters in truth." Jane returned the embrace. "Who is this little one? He's adorable, isn't he?"

"My nephew, Charlie. I should put him inside, in his crib." Sid directed her steps toward the house. "I suppose that seeing Timothy will be a large part of this afternoon?"

John whistled, and Molly came running. "Yes, and as my betrothed and as future mistress of Grant Park, I should very much like for you to come along, if you will." John flicked a glance at Jane, who smiled back at him. "I have to humble myself quite a bit, and I need you to prop me up."

"I shall come with you gladly," Sid replied, mounting the steps.

"While you put Charlie in bed, I shall put Molly in the barn and then go see Daniel, if I may." A little nervous trickle worked its way down his spine.

Daniel knew of his dissolute past and had, in fact, indulged in it himself once or twice. As a reformed man, would he like John enough for his sister? Well, there was nothing to do but brazen it out.

Sid had taught him to be brave, that much was certain.

# Chapter Twenty-Two

After Charlie had been safely deposited in his room with a nursemaid, Hannah followed John and Jane downstairs to Daniel's study. Even though John held her close to him as they walked, trepidation still seized her. If only she could marry John and be done, without the clamor of a ceremony. While she was skilled at helping others prepare for the big events in their lives, she had no liking for formal procedures, such as a wedding.

Her heart leaped as John knocked on Daniel's study door. "Enter," Daniel called.

John ushered Jane and Hannah through the doors, closing them tightly after the trio walked in.

"John! Upon my word, man, it does me good to see you again." Daniel walked around his desk and clasped John's hand in his. "Miss Jane? Nan? This is quite a delegation, I must say. What's amiss?"

"Nothing at all. In fact, on the contrary, all is well with the world." John sent Hannah a gaze that caused her cheeks to warm unexpectedly. "May the ladies sit down?"

"Of course, of course. We don't stand on ceremony here at Goodwin Hall, John. You know that." Daniel beckoned the two women over to a pair of chairs by the hearth.

The windows had been opened and the lace curtains fluttered with the late spring breeze. Hannah closed her eyes and raised her chin toward the gentle puffs of air, allowing it to cool her face. *Oh, do hurry and be done with it,* she thought, trying to maintain a semblance of composure. If he delayed much longer, she would have to leap from her chair and announce the news herself, just to end the tension.

"Daniel, I have come to ask you for Hannah's hand in marriage, as you are the head of their family." John came to stand beside her, resting his hands protectively on her shoulders.

"Hannah?" Daniel looked at them quizzically. "Who is Hannah?"

"I am." She raised her hand, weakly. "I don't suppose you ever knew Nan was my nickname."

Daniel laughed. "No, I had no inkling of it. But it makes sense, after all, Rebecca is known as Becky." Daniel looked over at John. "As far as I am concerned, my good man, you may have Nan's hand in marriage. However, my consent has no real weight. We all know that the true head of their family is Susannah. Shall I fetch her?"

"No, don't." Hannah rose, patting John's hand. "I'll go and see her myself, if I may." She cast a tremulous smile at her beloved and then fled the room. In all likelihood, Susannah was up in her suite, readying herself to go out and see the tenants, as she always did in the afternoons.

She burst through Susannah's door, not bothering to knock.

"I want to marry John," she blurted.

Susannah, who was having her abundant auburn hair dressed by a maid, looked up in startled surprise in the mirror. "I say, this is interesting news. Very well. Does he know?"

The maid went on calmly placing hairpins in Susannah's coiffure.

"Yes." Hannah twisted her hands together to still their trembling. "He asked me."

"Thank you, Tess. I can manage from here." Susannah put her hand up to her head as the maid bobbed a curtsy and left. Then Susannah half turned from the dressing table. "Help me, Nan?" she queried.

"Of course." Hannah had dressed both of her sisters' hair for years, before they married and left home. It would be a good distraction for her hands. She took hold of one lock of hair and began twisting it and pinning it into place. The familiarity of being with her sister in such a comfortable fashion put her mind at ease. All would be well.

"John Reed is a good man, and Grant Park is quite grand, from what I hear," Susannah murmured as Hannah worked on her locks. "It sounds an excellent match to me. If you love him, that is."

"I do. I fought against my affection for him for a while, because, well, I'm just Nan," she replied, reaching for another hairpin. "I wasn't sure if a man like John Reed could love me."

"What nonsense. Of course he could, and he does." Susannah snapped open a glove box and began selecting a pair as Hannah finished her job. "You were born to be mistress of a fine home like Grant Park. My worry is whether or not you love him, and not the other way around."

"I assumed I would become a maiden aunt, taking care of Charlie and any other children you have," Hannah admitted, standing back to look at her handiwork. "I never thought marriage would be for me."

Susannah's gray-green eyes softened, and she shook her head. "Nan, I know that you took the position of the practical and prosaic one in our family, and as such, perhaps you felt relegated to a certain role. In truth, you have all the makings of a lady as fine as Mrs. Reed herself. Your organizational skills will help keep Grant Park running smoothly. Your honesty will keep everyone around you in check. Moreover, you have lovely eyes and a lithe figure. Your artistic talents show you to be refined, and you dress well. John Reed recognizes this. I applaud his good sense."

This shower of praise was completely uncharacteristic for Susannah, who usually tempered any kind remark with some caustic comment so that her sisters would not become overly proud. Hannah waited, poised for the inevitable "But…" Yet nothing came. Susannah rose, tugged on her gloves, and gave Hannah a swift peck on the cheek. "You have my blessing, if you desire it."

"I do," Hannah blurted, tears springing to her eyes.

"I just don't know what to say. I never expected any of this. I thought you would be angry."

"I was upset when you gave the shop away, it's true," Susannah admitted. She opened her wardrobe and selected a wool shawl, draping it around her shoulders. "I was furious, in fact. I talked to Daniel about it—the poor man, I gave him quite an earful—but then I realized, I was forcing you to hang on to a relic of our past. I was so proud of that little place, and when it was no longer mine, and then it was gone, I didn't know what to do. Then I realized, I have Daniel and I have Charlie. I have the tenants and the servants. I have you and I have Becky. My life is different now, and it is full and happy. There's no need to cling to the past. The shop served us well, and now it will help Lillian Bellamy."

"Not just the shop. I just thought—well, I don't know what to think." To her horror, the tears began streaming down her cheeks. She had never cried before Susannah in her entire life, but she could not check the sudden flood. "I had grown so used to the idea that I would be a spinster, that I was this unlikeable person. I can't believe all this is for me."

"Oh, Nan." Susannah folded her into a warm, orange blossom scented embrace. "Go on. Get married. Have children. You deserve all of this, and more."

At that, Hannah began to sob in earnest, as Sue held her tightly. As the flood ebbed, Susannah handed her a linen handkerchief. "Are you going to be all right?"

"Yes. Thank you." Hannah sniffed, searching for

a dry spot on the scrap of fabric. "I don't know what came over me."

"Nerves," Susannah pronounced decisively. "It happens to the best of us when romance is in the offing. Now, as to the wedding. Shall we have it here, in the chapel?"

"Yes. That would be lovely." She blew her nose. "I am sorry about all of this. I suppose I've made you late to work with the tenants."

"Not at all." Susannah drew herself up and smiled. "This was more important. You are important, Nan. Never forget that. Now, before I leave, I want to speak to your betrothed. I suppose he is downstairs, talking to Daniel?"

"Yes." Hannah threaded her arm through her sister's as they left the room. "He asked Daniel for my hand."

"I do hope Daniel gave his consent," Susannah said with a laugh.

"Daniel gave his consent but admitted that it meant little. He then referred John to you as the true head of our family." Hannah bunched her skirts in one hand as they descended the stairs.

Susannah nodded. "Quite right. Daniel is a wise man. It seems he grows wiser every day."

As they rounded the corner of the hallway, Hannah caught sight of John through the open door of Daniel's study. He was speaking politely to Daniel, but his posture was tense. He must be as nervous as she. She broke free of her sister and bustled over to his side. "She gave her consent." Hannah gave him an encouraging smile. "We may set a wedding date."

There was a general melee of embraces and kisses and congratulations as Hannah, John, Jane, Susannah and Daniel gathered together. As she received and returned the warm wishes happily, she still struggled against the feeling of disbelief. How could all this be? Why would it happen to someone like her?

After being released from Susannah's hold, John turned to her. "I imagine the wedding is already being planned," he said with a wink.

"Only down to the location," she replied. "That's as far as we've gotten."

"I hate to speak out of turn," Jane spoke up. "But now that we've secured your happiness, brother, could we attempt to heal my fractured relationship?"

John nodded. "Yes. You've been very patient for an enamored little sister. Come." He beckoned first to Jane, and then to Hannah. "You too, Sid. I trust you to help me handle this in such a manner that I don't appear to be a complete idiot."

Hannah laughed and accepted the elbow he offered her. "By all means."

As she left the Hall on the arm of her future husband, accompanying him to set things right with the man his sister loved, a feeling of peace cloaked her. She was loved by her own family, and loved and needed by another. It was too much to fathom after years of feeling useless and unwanted, and it would take a long time to fully comprehend. She glanced at her future husband's handsome profile as the carriage turned out of the Park and on the well-traveled road to the Holdcrofts' farm. She had the rest of her life to consider the matter fully.

* * *

Now was the time to ask forgiveness, and yet it did not seem an insurmountable task. In times past, he would have ignored this issue altogether—or any other unpleasant issue, for that matter—and taken himself off to London for a month to indulge himself in a raucous whirlwind of delight. Now, he faced the problem squarely. He had been wrong to deny Jane her true love, and wrong to assume anything about Timothy Holdcroft's character. The elopement seemed as distasteful to Timothy as it was to John. However, having fallen in love himself, John could see how a man might act out of desperation, if it meant winning his heart's desire.

He paced the parlor floor, the boards squeaking in protest as he moved. Mrs. Holdcroft's maid, likely the only one the family employed, had bade him to wait in the small room until she could fetch Timothy from the fields. Hannah and Jane waited for him out in the carriage. There were some things a man needed to start alone, and in this case, it was essential that he meet his future brother-in-law in a fashion befitting the head of his family. The tension emanating from the carriage was palpable. At any moment, Jane was likely to burst in and throw herself headlong at Timothy.

The parlor door opened and Holdcroft walked in. His attire made it obvious that he had been working outdoors, and that John's visit had interrupted vital, life-giving work. It would be best to come straight to the point.

"Holdcroft, I was wrong to come between you and

my sister. I apologize. Moreover, if you still wish to marry her, I give you my blessing."

Holdcroft took a step backward, shaking his head. "I cannot believe this. I must have gotten too hot while I was working. Surely you are a figment of my imagination."

"No, indeed." John slapped Holdcroft on the back. "You see? All real."

Holdcroft massaged his shoulder where John had struck him. "You do feel real." He paused, eyeing John carefully. "Why this sudden change of heart? Has Jane's reputation been ruined? I am willing to tell everyone I know that nothing happened between us during the elopement. I don't want you to force a marriage for all the wrong reasons."

John smiled, relief flowing through him. He had been fairly certain that Holdcroft was a good choice, but his reaction now proved beyond all doubt that he had Jane's happiness in mind. That was what mattered most. This fellow would spend the rest of his days living for Jane. "I suddenly discovered for myself what is best in a marriage," he admitted. "Money, status, one's place in society—none of that matters without love. I believe you love my sister. Therefore, I can no longer object to the match."

Holdcroft closed his eyes for a moment. "Thank you," he said, simply. Then after a moment's pause, he continued. "I believe Hannah Siddons must have changed your mind."

John stared at him. "How—how do you know?"

"I don't know. I suppose I just noticed something about her, and about your interactions together,"

Holdcroft replied. "When she and I left Grant Park for Tansley, we were as miserable as two human beings could be. The kind of sadness I perceived in Miss Siddons matched my own. It was not the kind of desolation she should feel upon leaving a stable position in a fine household. She was sick at heart, and that could only mean that like me, her heart had been broken. I assumed her affection for you had been rebuffed."

"Not precisely," John hedged. "I would say that it merely took me a moment longer than it should have to realize what a treasure I had in Hannah Siddons. I realized shortly after she left that she was the only woman in the world for me. We are going to be married, too, so I daresay we both should be dancing at each other's wedding."

"A double wedding." Jane smiled from the doorway.

Behind her, Hannah stood, her expression shifting from happiness to uncertainty. Likely Jane had decided it was time to come in and Hannah had followed, unsure of whether or not they would be interrupting. He smiled. Even now, his future wife was still trying to guide and shape Jane.

Before another word could be uttered by anyone, Holdcroft rushed over to Jane and seized her in an embrace. John averted his eyes. He was happy about the match, but didn't precisely care to see an outward display of affection between the pair.

Hannah stepped around the couple and drew close to his side. He wrapped one arm around her shoulders and pulled her closer still. "A double wedding?" he murmured under his breath.

Sid nodded, looking up at him with an expression in her eyes that caused his breath to catch in his chest. Would he always feel this astonished by Hannah's beauty? Likely so. At any rate, he had the rest of his life to find out.

"I'm afraid it's all been planned out," Hannah admitted as a mischievous expression crossed her face. "How else was I supposed to keep Jane in the carriage as long as I did? Wedding preparations were the only thing that gave you two any time to work out your differences."

"Oh, really? Well, I thank you, then." John laughed. Out of the corner of his eye, he saw Timothy and Jane break apart, still standing close, but no longer locked in an embrace. "Tell us all the details, then," he went on, raising his voice.

"Oh, the ceremony will be at Goodwin Hall, in the chapel," Hannah began.

"I shall wear my new pink ball gown," Jane put in.

"I will try to convince Lillian Bellamy to make something for me," Hannah added.

"There will be roses," Jane continued with a happy sigh. "I shall play my violin."

"My nephew can be part of the ceremony," Hannah added. "Molly, too, of course."

Timothy chuckled, glancing over at John. "It sounds like our lives have been arranged for us. Or at least, the beginning ceremony for our new lives."

John nodded, taking Hannah by the hand. "As long as I am invited, that's all that matters."

He was starting his life anew with the best partner a man could dream of.

# Chapter Twenty-Three

The ceremony was supposed to start in just a short while. John checked his pocket watch and took a deep, steadying breath. The picture of a nervous groom before the wedding was just too much of a formula. He couldn't very well continue acting like a character in a play. If Hannah trusted and loved him enough to marry him, then all would be well. He mustn't be so obviously jumpy, for everything was progressing as planned.

For one thing, he had already had his time saying goodbye to Jane. She would live in Tansley, for her soon-to-be husband's farm was already showing signs of prospering. In fact, all her gowns had been packed away at Grant Park and only a select few work dresses had been prepared for her journey. Jane was taking the role of farmer's wife seriously and wanted nothing that would seem too grand for her new life. He was actually proud of Jane, putting aside all the frivolous aspects of her existence to pursue what she really loved. She loved Timothy Holdcroft and was prepared to live simply along with him.

So, there was nothing to worry about as far as his sister was concerned. She was marrying a good man who would take care of her. Beside him, Timothy Holdcroft started muttering.

"What's that?" John turned to behold his future brother-in-law looking very pale indeed.

"Can't help it," Timothy gasped. "Nerves, old fellow."

John clapped him soundly on the back, just as he had done on the day of all the proposals. "Proposal Day" had just the right ring to it. Surely it was one for the annals of Grant Park. "I feel the same way, but we must bolster our confidence with the knowledge that we are marrying two of the loveliest young women in Derbyshire."

"Oh, I am quite aware of that," Timothy rejoined. "I am just utterly humbled by the fact that someone as beautiful and fine as Jane can love a poor farmer like myself. I also cannot believe that you consented to the match. My cup runneth over, you see."

John nodded. The same shocked disbelief surged through him often over the past few weeks. As the banns were read at St. Mary's in Crich, he had expected Sid to come to her senses and cry off, but she had not. The separation between them, necessary now that she was his betrothed, was difficult to bear. She was too far from him, staying with her sister at Goodwin Hall until the ceremony, and without her by his side he'd felt unbalanced. Soon, she would right him again. After the wedding, they would go home to Grant Park, which needed its mistress. He needed Sid.

Reverend Kirk, the kindly pastor of St. Mary's, approached, his hand outstretched. "Mr. Reed, Mr. Holdcroft, so good to see both of you on this fine day."

John accepted the handshake gladly. Reverend Kirk had been a friend to the Siddons family for years, and Daniel and Paul both found him to be a solid, thoughtful member of the clergy. "Thank you, Reverend."

Reverend Kirk smiled and then turned his attention to Timothy Holdcroft, chatting about local Tansley Village news. John sidled away, eager for a distraction. Not that he didn't like Reverend Kirk or Timothy, but perhaps, if he wandered around just a bit, he could catch a glimpse of Sid. The more he strained to see past the crowds of people in the small family chapel, the more people poured in. How on earth would they fit everyone under this roof? Already, villagers stood with their backs pressed against the stone walls. Soon, the congregation would spill out onto the lawn.

"It's no use, old man. Susannah has her bundled out of sight." Daniel laughed, coming close. "She is a stickler for etiquette. You won't get a glimpse of your beloved until she is walking down the aisle."

"I should have known." John straightened his cravat and tried to give the appearance of being calm. "It's just been too long, you know. I miss her."

"I know. I felt the same way on my wedding day, and we were even in the same village." Daniel waved to a villager passing by. "It's good that you two were good friends before falling in love. Susannah and I were, too. I longed for her companionship as much as I longed for romance. Once we were married, my life became complete."

"Exactly so." John nodded. "I have not felt like myself. I've tried to stay busy, working with the dogs and, of course, overseeing things on the estate, but I need her by my side."

"Well, just a few more minutes and you'll be done. You two can go home to Grant Park and raise dogs and have children and continue making Grant Park the finest home in Derbyshire." He smiled, shaking his head. "Our Nan. I can hardly believe it. I still think of her as I did the first day they came to Tansley. All my thoughts were focused on Susannah, of course, but I remember Nan looking like a wise little urchin. She doesn't miss much, that girl."

"Nay, she's as sharp as a knife," John responded. Daniel still thought of her as a little sister. He still called her Nan. He never knew, never even suspected, the talented, driven, sensitive young woman that Hannah had become.

It was good that they were going away to live at Grant Park. Sometimes, you had to go away to find yourself. He had fled to London for years for that same reason. Coming home, he had learned just how precious his family and his life truly were. Sid had helped him to discover the truth. He owed her nothing less, and would spend the rest of his life making her happy.

A hush descended over the crowd and the local

musicians, recruited to make a quartet, began tuning their instruments. "This is your cue," Daniel announced. He nudged John back to the altar with a none-too-gentle shove.

As Hannah drifted in, flanked by her sisters, and followed by Jane, his nervousness dissipated. This was right. She was here, and all would be well.

In the years to come, she might remember the ceremony, but all Hannah was conscious of was John's presence beside her. How she hated these kinds of formal gatherings! If only they could be married quietly at Grant Park, with her in one of her old work dresses. She glanced down and smoothed her skirt with her gloved hand. She did look remarkably fine, thanks to Lillian Bellamy's handiwork. In fact, her wedding gown was far prettier than Susannah's or Becky's had been, in her own private opinion. In truth, though, she was fairly straining to run away to Grant Park. She had missed John and their home dreadfully.

Then, all at once, John was kissing her and the ceremony had ended. There was laughter and tears and joyful celebrating, and yet she wanted desperately to be done. The wedding breakfast came and went in a blur. Becky, her high-waisted gown hardly concealing her far-advanced pregnancy, burst into tears, quite overcome with the emotion of the day. Susannah ordered people about.

It was a blessed relief when she was able to slip away and change into her traveling costume. She folded her dress and placed it inside her trunk, ready to go home. As she did, the corner of a piece of paper caught her eye. What on earth? She withdrew it, and unfolded the crumpled foolscap.

It was the picture she had drawn of John with Molly tucked inside his coat, when Jane had spied her work and when she herself was in love with John, though she didn't know it.

She gasped. This was the perfect present for John. She threw her Spencer jacket on and rushed downstairs, the drawing still clutched in her hand.

John was standing at the foot of the landing, talking with Paul and Becky. He smiled as she approached.

"I have your wedding present," she said with a smile, waving the paper. "Come, I'll show you."

John followed her into the library, where she placed the foolscap on one of the nearby tables. "Here. This is for you." Her heart hammered in her chest. Why was she so nervous? She was becoming as sensitive as Becky. John already knew she liked to draw. Moreover, she really didn't have anything of value to give him. This was the best she could do.

"Darling Sid, how marvelous." He swept her into his arms. "You have quite the gift, you know. Anyone who can make me look that handsome deserves accolades."

She swatted his arm. "You are handsome, as you very well know. I just captured the truth. I drew this one day when I was supposed to be working on Jane's dresses. It was all quite unconscious. She saw it, though, and I was so embarrassed. I stuffed it into my drawer, and one of the maids must have found it when she packed my trunk to send here to Goodwin Hall."

"Why are you embarrassed by it?" He squinted, giving it a critical assessment. "It's a fantastic drawing. You are a fantastic artist, my dear."

"I was mortified because I was falling in love with you, and had gotten caught mooning over you like a silly schoolgirl." Her cheeks still burned at the memory, and yet here she was, married to the very man she had developed a *tendre* for.

He tucked the drawing into his jacket pocket and then embraced her tightly. "I don't have a special gift for you, Sid. I mean, the house is yours, and Mother's jewels. All of that sort of thing. But none of that seems right for you. I want to give you something that's as unique as you are. A necklace, a ring, all fine, but not very Sid-like." He nuzzled his lips in her hair. "What do you want, my darling? I'll give you whatever you wish."

All at once, an idea came upon her. She chuckled. "Do you really want to give me whatever I want?"

"Of course. Tell me." He drew away from her a little, gazing down into her eyes. "What present do you wish? I'll bring it from the ends of the earth."

"My freedom." She smiled, dreamily. How lovely it would be.

John shook his head, his face draining of all color. "I don't understand. Do you mean…? Are you saying…? Sid, we're just married."

"Not my freedom from you," she replied quickly. She was making a muddle of this, and it could prove to be rather disastrous if she did not take care. "My freedom from Tansley. Come, let's elope."

John smiled, his brows drawing together. "Still not sure I follow what you are saying, Sid, but feeling infinite relief that you aren't immediately seeking an annulment. So, are you asking for an elopement after the wedding?"

"Well, yes." She sighed. "I hate all this ceremony, and I miss Grant Park. I want to be away from all of this. I know there's supposed to be the rest of the wedding breakfast, and all sorts of social obligations, and then, of course, Susannah has organized an informal dance for later. A wedding is a chance for festivities, and we are doing the lot of them today. I just feel like—getting away from this. I missed you and I want to go home." Admitting this out loud seemed the height of unladylike behavior, but John did prize her directness.

"Sid, I feel the same way. Are you packed?" John smiled down at her, his eyes taking on that intensity that signified he was ready to do something mischievous. "We can leave now. The horses are ready and it will take me but a moment to hitch the carriage up."

"Yes. Let's go." She grabbed his hand and whirled out of the room, but people pressed in on all sides. Mrs. Holdcroft cast a regal smile in their direction, one eyebrow lifted delicately. Hannah nodded and smiled. Then she wound her way through the crowd, still holding John's hand. She couldn't move the trunk by herself, as it was far too heavy. Yet the only way they could make it up to her room unseen would involve taking the back staircase, the one the servants used. Somehow, that didn't seem right, either. Her urgency would not be satisfied until they were long gone from Tansley.

She pressed forward, moving him through the throngs of well-wishers and to the doorway leading to the barn at the rear of the house. Once outside, she breathed deeply. "Is it all right if I leave my trunk here? I know going back to get it will just slow us down, and Susannah might see us."

"Yes. Let's leave it." John looked down at her. "Do you want to say goodbye to your sisters? Shall we leave a note?"

"Let's have one of the grooms relay the message once we've left." They were so close. "But if you need to say goodbye to Jane—"

"No, I said goodbye to her earlier. I knew she would be busy with the social whirl, and I wanted to say how much I love her when everything was quiet and calm." He gave her that look of challenge, daring her in the way he had done so many times before. "This is your gift, then? An elopement?"

"Yes. I wish I could have demanded one earlier," she replied tartly. "But that didn't seem to go so well for other members of your family."

He chuckled and grabbed her hand. "Then let's go." He pulled her, running, across the lawn and down to the barn.

She helped him hitch the horses up and then climbed onto the seat beside him. A groom wandered in, no doubt thinking that he had been remiss in his duties. A gentleman should never have to hitch his own horses.

"Ah," John said, beckoning the young lad over. "We are leaving the festivities early. Would you give us about a half hour's start, then inform the butler? The bride and groom are eloping, you see."

The groom pushed back the brim of his hat, scratching his head. "Come, now? Not sure I understand, sir."

"In about a half hour, people may start asking about John Reed and his new bride, Hannah. All we ask is that you tell the butler we've gone home to Grant Park. We'll send for Mrs. Reed's trunk later." John reached into his waistcoat pocket and pulled out a gold coin, flipping it to the groom. "We appreciate your help."

The groom nodded, grinning. "Glad to be of service, sir."

Hannah watched the lad leave. "Do you really think he'll give us a half hour?" Her heart hammered in her chest as though they really were eloping. "What if he goes back and tells the butler right now?"

"We'll have to make haste, then. Brace yourself," he recommended. "I'm not going to spare the whip."

Dutifully, she caught hold of the railing beside her as he urged the horses into a full gallop. The wind caught at her bonnet and she clamped it down with one hand, unable to keep from smiling. She was going home now. She was free.

As they rounded the corner of the village, a small group of children were playing in the road. The wind caught her bonnet again, but this time, she did not hold on to it. The beautiful confection, crafted by Lillian Bellamy, sailed through the air, landing at the little girls' feet like a bouquet. One of them snatched it up, jumping up and down, while the other girls clamored for their fair chance at it.

She smiled and waved, turning to watch them until the carriage sped far enough away that she could no longer distinguish their faces. Then she settled back beside her husband, rejoicing in his daring, his closeness and his strength. She may have given him a small trinket in that picture, but in truth, he gave her so much more. Because of him, she was no longer Nan, that wretched, plain, unhappy girl who had reconciled herself to a small life because that's what others expected for her.

His kindness, his boldness and yes, his brokenness had opened an entirely new world to her. With him, she had dared to try more, to be more and to let go of things that would have terrified her to relinquish just a few months before. She was grateful to him, and she loved him.

She could not wait to begin this new adventure together, as one flesh—that dear old phrase oft repeated in the Bible.

She was her beloved's, and he was hers.

# Epilogue

*Six months after the elopement*

Hannah stood beside Becky and Susannah, their arms interlinked. The autumn breeze ruffling their skirts had an icy edge to it. Winter would be upon them soon. Soon, they would need to bring more hay into the barn, fresh straw for the horses, and the pumps would have to be wrapped to keep from freezing. She must remind John of this when she returned to Grant Park.

"Well, girls, say goodbye to the Siddons Sisters Millinery Shop," Susannah pronounced, breaking into Hannah's domestic reverie. "Lillian Bellamy has a new sign ordered. The shop is really and truly hers now."

Hannah gazed across the meadow at the small building that had been both her home and her torment for many years. The sign proclaiming Siddons Sisters Millinery Shop had grown so faded, it was difficult indeed to distinguish the writing. It still leaned against the front wall, never having been hung up properly in all the time they had owned the shop.

"What will become of the sign?" Becky asked. The cool breeze blew her dress closely against her figure. Hannah shook her head in wonder. Already her beautiful elder sister had slimmed down to her normal, slight frame. Not a pound lingered from her pregnancy.

"Daniel said he would have one of the men come down and remove it." Susannah tucked a stray auburn lock back into her bonnet. "We will keep it in the barn, I think. I can't bear to burn it. If I destroy the sign, it's like it never happened."

"But it did," Hannah interjected. How ridiculous to think that all their shared history could be obliterated by the destruction of a single wooden plaque. "Don't you both remember what it was like when we first arrived in Tansley?"

"We had just stepped off the mail coach," Susannah began, a pensive look crossing her pretty face. "The solicitor said he'd left a key, but, of course, we couldn't find it."

"Just as Sue was about to break into the shop, Daniel happened along and picked the lock," Becky continued. "Paul was with him. Who knew, on that day, that those two men would change our lives?"

"Through Paul, of course, we met John Reed." Hannah hated to have her own husband, who had wrought the most profound changes of all, left out of this narration.

"Yes, I met John for the first time when Paul took me to London with Juliet," Becky replied, tugging

Hannah closer. "I thought him an awful dandy and a bad influence on my beloved. Of course, he was, and yet it was he who helped Paul understand just how much we had fallen in love."

"But this story isn't just about the men in our lives," Susannah interjected, turning to them both with that leashed intensity that signified how very moved she was. "Through the shop, we each gained our independence. I'll never forget the first time we made a sale, and it was to a genteel client—The Honorable Elizabeth Glaspell. How proud I was that day! We left Uncle Arthur's house so downtrodden, so broken and absolutely penniless. We built this little shop up from the ground. We must never forget that."

Hannah nodded. The shop hadn't been her salvation in the same way it had helped Susannah. It had been a burden and an obligation, a sort of well-worn path she had to follow to secure a future she didn't actually want. Yet, without it, she could not have understood, perhaps, what she wanted and what she was fighting against. In that way, she could appreciate the impact it had on her life.

Becky squeezed her hand, and Hannah looked at her sister. Her violet eyes held an understanding light. Becky hadn't found the shop as vital as Susannah had, either. She, too, could comprehend the mixed emotions flooding through Hannah.

As they stood on the ridge, watching, the shop buzzed with activity. Customers came and went, some with packages, some empty-handed. Occasionally, she could discern Lillian Bellamy's imperious French accent raised in excitement or anger. She stifled a smile. Yes, this shop was certainly not the Siddons sisters' any longer. It didn't even sound or look the same.

"I hate to leave, but it's time for me to go home and nurse Sam." Becky squeezed Hannah's hand once more and released her. "This is the longest I've been away from him since he was born, and I can't bear it any longer."

Susannah nodded. "I should go see what mischief Charlie's been up to."

"And I am ready to return home," Hannah replied. "I have so much to do to get the Park ready for the winter." She paused, struggling for the right way to end this scene. After all, this was likely to be the last time the three sisters would stand together, looking over their shared early lives. Susannah had been right to bring them all together, to witness and testify to the end of this phase of their lives. "Sue, thank you for having the courage to stand up to Uncle Arthur all those years ago. Without your bravery, we would not have found our places in life."

"Hear, hear," Becky chimed in. "Nan is right. We are grateful to you, Susy."

Susannah turned to look at them both, tears welling in her gray-green eyes. "Thank you for coming along with me," she replied, in the humblest tone of voice Hannah had ever heard her use. "I could not have done it without you two."

Hannah smiled, fighting back the tears stinging her own eyes. This was no time for sadness. Rather, this was a time of purpose and strength. She turned, following her sisters as they struck back across the moor, returning to their own homes and their own lives. The carriage was waiting for her at Goodwin Hall, and in just a short while, she would be back with John again. With difficulty, she restrained herself from breaking into a run. Already she had gained some disapproval from her eldest sister by running away from her own wedding festivities. She could not ruin the delicate balance of this bittersweet day by running once more, as hard as it was to slow herself down to a decorous pace. She would see John soon enough. She must be patient.

She was not sure what the future held, but as long as it held John and he was by her side, she could not wait to see what the Lord had in store for them. Or for all of them, for that matter.

\* \* \* \* \*

Dear Readers,

It was difficult indeed to write Nan's—or, rather, Hannah's—story, because she was never really intended to have a story line of her own. Originally, I was going to write about Susannah and Becky alone, but it seemed coldhearted to keep the third Siddons sister from her own happily-ever-after. Thus, I had the rather daunting task of fleshing out her story and her character, and I hope I did her justice.

This book was also difficult to write because it is the last one I am writing, at least for the near future, about Tansley Village. Tansley is a real place in Derbyshire and I picked it off a map one day when I was writing my very first book, *Captain of Her Heart*. Since that book, every story I've done has featured Tansley either as the main setting or as the background for the rest of the story, as characters depart for other places in England.

My next series will also be about three sisters, but they will be a continent and a few generations apart from Tansley and the Siddons sisters. The Westmore girls are born and raised in New York at the turn of the last century, and must make the adjustment to life on a Texas ranch after their father passes away. I hope you will enjoy their stories, as well.

As always, you can read more about my upcoming books at www.lilygeorge.com, follow me on Twitter as @lilygeorge2, catch me on Facebook as lilygeorgeauthor, or shoot me an email at lilygeorgeauthor@gmail.com. Thank you for reading!

Blessings,

*Lily George*